OF TERAVINEA

THE CROWN

D. Maria Trimble

ISBN-10:0985575344
ISBN-13:978-0-9855753-4-2

To those who persevere in the face of misfortune,
and continue to fight the good fight.

Contents

Chapter One 1
Chapter Two 6
Chapter Three 10
Chapter Four 13
Chapter Five 16
Chapter Six 20
Chapter Seven 23
Chapter Eight 26
Chapter Nine 31
Chapter Ten 39
Chapter Eleven 44
Chapter Twelve 48
Chapter Thirteen 53
Chapter Fourteen 57
Chapter Fifteen 63
Chapter Sixteen 73
Chapter Seventeen 77
Chapter Eighteen 82
Chapter Nineteen 87
Chapter Twenty 90
Chapter Twenty-one 93
Chapter Twenty-two 100
Chapter Twenty-three 106
Chapter Twenty-four 111
Chapter Twenty-five 115
Chapter Twenty-six 120
Chapter Twenty-seven 125
Chapter Twenty-eight 134
Chapter Twenty-nine 138
Chapter Thirty 148
Chapter Thirty-one 151
Chapter Thirty-two 154
Chapter Thirty-three 157
Chapter Thirty-four 164
Chapter Thirty-five 169
Chapter Thirty-six 173
Chapter Thirty-seven 176
Chapter Thirty-eight 179
Chapter Thirty-nine 182
Chapter Forty 188
Chapter Forty-one 193
Chapter Forty-two 199
Chapter Forty-three 208
Chapter Forty-four 212
Chapter Forty-five 224
Chapter Forty-six 229
Chapter Forty-seven 236
Chapter Forty-eight 243
Chapter Forty-nine 246
Chapter Fifty 254
Chapter Fifty-one 258
Chapter Fifty-two 262
Chapter Fifty-three 268
Chapter Fifty-four 271
Chapter Fifty-five 244
Chapter Fifty-six 278
Chapter Fifty-seven 284
Chapter Fifty-eight 291
Chapter Fifty-nine 297
Chapter Sixty 301
Chapter Sixty-one 310
Chapter Sixty-two 319
Chapter Sixty-three 324
Epilogue 327
Character Name Meanings 332

To Orchila
N
W
E
S
Kep
KINGDOM
OF
SERISLAN
Serislan Castle
Castle Beag
Trivingar
Arevale
Outpost
Arevale
Tramoren
Nunn
City
of
Teravinea
Castle Outpost
Castle Teravinea
KINGDOM
OF
TERAVINEA
Anbon
Nicobar
Nicobar
Outpost
Krose
Outpost
Glinfoil
Dorsal
Dorsal
Outpost

To the Valley of Dragons
Amáne is lured.
A quest for knowledge,
A betrayal endured.

The Chosen One captured
A sacrifice to please
The Ancient Dragon, Senolis,
His wrath to appease.

On frothy current
The kingdom's hope may drown.
The death of our hero
Means the loss of the crown.

Broken with failure
Amáne paid a high price.
Will she take from Senolis
His prophetic advice?

~ Ballad of Amáne and the Valley of Dragons

Chapter One

The flames of Anbon licked the night sky. Noticeable, even at the distance from which Eshshah and I soared. I couldn't help but feel I was to blame for the suffering of its citizens. Because of me they lost their village to Galtero's army.

King Galtero swore he would seek out and destroy every dragon rider in Teravinea. The reason? Because I had humiliated him. His revenge against me focused on the people of Teravinea. He began with Anbon — the township I claimed as my home when I entered the castle as a male candidate for the Hatching Ceremony several weeks ago. My acceptance as a candidate disgraced Galtero. First, because I am not a male. Secondly, because I escaped his wicked games in an arena of death.

Fueling his anger, as if my escape was not enough, I was also responsible for the loss of his two 'pets.' One creature destroyed by the other — the other, the Black Lizard, Charna Yash-churka. He who linked with me when his venomous bite nearly took off my foot in the dungeons of the castle. *It seemed a lifetime ago.* Charna Yash-churka sided against Galtero and saved my life in the arena.

Perhaps the greatest incentive for Galtero to destroy the dragon riders was his fear of the One from the Prophecy ... me. According to the prediction, through Eshshah and me the rightful heir would regain the throne. It rang of truth to me, and I accepted my duty. So far it appeared the prophecy had unfolded as foretold.

Galtero's evil reign seemed about to collapse. Even still, we were not naive enough to think that prophecies were written in stone. He would do everything within his power to prevent it. Any number of events could change the outcome. Our success was not assured.

Fortune remained on our side — no one had discovered the dragon egg missing from the Hatching Grounds. Eshshah and I delivered it to the Healer. No sooner had I removed it from the satchel than the egg began to hum and vibrate. Sovann, the golden dragon broke from his shell and found his Chosen One — Ansel Drekinn, my best friend, my love, and heir to the throne.

Ansel and Sovann's training, under the Healer and Gallen, came to an end. We said our good byes and they headed back to Trivingar. Less than an hour later, the communication disc buzzed. It was Bern with urgent news. Anbon was under siege.

"We've been able to hold the town gates," reported Bern. "Our soldiers are putting up a brave fight. But against Galtero's army, I don't believe we can hold much longer. If it doesn't look like we can stave them off soon, I'm going to call a retreat. We'll pull back and take cover in the mountains — the women and children are already evacuating. We know the terrain well. Galtero's army doesn't stand a chance against us there."

When the Healer signed off, she turned to me, "Amáne, I have no choice but to send you and Eshshah to extract Bern. The timing is unfortunate. I would have sent the four of you, but Ansel and Sovann have been gone too long to catch up to them. They won't arrive in Trivingar for another three hours, and that would be too late."

"We'll leave straightaway, Healer," I replied as I rushed to make ready.

I secured my breastplate and threw a dark tunic over my head. I pulled on my dragonscale boots, strapped on my sword and grabbed my riding cloak. Leaving my weapons and gear in the kitchen, I helped the Healer gather sacks of herbs and medicines for the refugees.

Gallen saddled Eshshah with the double saddle. We loaded the sacks and additional supplies on the second seat, then Gallen gave me a leg up.

With my thumb and forefinger forming an 'o,' and my remaining three fingers straight, I put my hand to my heart and gave the dragon salute to the Healer and Gallen. Eshshah and I spiraled into the night sky. It all happened so quickly, I never had the chance to consider our next quest had begun.

My mind drew back to the present. Smoke filled the air from the besieged town. We circled high above to assess the situation. My heart went out to the townspeople as they filed up the mountain path, fleeing their homes. From our vantage point I caught a movement below. A small battle ensued in the town square. A lone fighter held off several attackers as the last of the citizens escaped.

"That's Bern, Amáne," Eshshah informed me.

"Of course — he would be one of the last out," I said.

Bern's instincts as a dragon rider would clash with the thought of retreat. But he knew full well that he had to assure his own escape. No dragon rider could allow himself to be captured. It would mean disaster. All would give our lives to safeguard our secrets and our progress to gain the throne. But dying for our cause was not the issue. If Galtero had any more sorcerers at his disposal, one of his evil minions could be capable of extracting our plans. Ansel would be exposed as a dragon rider, the locations of the other riders would be revealed as well. Bern had no choice but to flee.

We spiraled down toward the town square. I shook my head in amazement at Bern's skills as he engaged a group of Galtero's men. He clearly had the advantage as he pushed back his opponents, even though they outnumbered him.

Distracted by a movement, I turned my attention down a dark alleyway behind Bern. A large group of soldiers lurked in the shadows making their way toward the scrimmage and their comrades.

Eshshah banked in their direction and went into a dive. I took in a deep breath and leaned back in the saddle as we plummeted toward the alley. A few of the soldiers looked up in time to see a large fierce dragon falling from the sky. Their faces froze in fear. Some turned in an effort to escape, but found themselves tangled with their fellow soldiers in the narrow alley.

We knew what needed to be done. With remorse for the loss of lives, Eshshah inhaled and connected with her upper stomach that held her combustible gasses. Her exhale mixed the gasses with her venom, that acted as a catalyst. She belched out a massive flame and stopped the soldiers where they stood — leaving nothing but ashes.

Eshshah pulled up just before we collided with the buildings and dipped toward where Bern fought. We only needed to land behind him. One look at Eshshah and the soldiers beat a hasty retreat.

Nocking an arrow on my bow, I let it fly. One escaping soldier went down. I continued to release my arrows until the last man fell. We couldn't have news of Eshshah's presence in Anbon passed on to the enemy.

"Get on!" I urged. Bern ran and leaped on to Eshshah's foreleg. We locked wrists and he swung himself up behind me. He had to sit on top of the sacks piled in his seat. Eshshah pushed off smoothly and took flight as Bern grabbed on to the leather straps that held down the supplies.

We circled the town, and saw none of its citizens remained. Bern was literally the last to leave.

"I had to go back for the communication device," he explained as he patted the large satchel hanging from his shoulder. "Galtero's men had breached the gate before I could get out. Thank you Eshshah and Amáne. You got here quickly. Eshshah, your speed is remarkable."

I was pleased with the compliment to my dragon. Eshshah hummed her approval.

Chapter Two

The moon lit brightly on the scene below us. Men, women and children of Anbon, along with their livestock, made their way up the mountain to safety. A distance behind them we spotted a small contingent of Galtero's army as they attempted to overtake the group that brought up the rear. Eshshah dealt with them. I wished them to their ancestors, along with all of the people who had perished in the battle ... from both sides.

We arrived at the encampment in a small valley. There were several cave openings in the sides of the mountains.

"We've been stockpiling provisions and weapons for just such an event. It was only a matter of time before Galtero would turn on us," Bern said.

Tents had been set up. Workers bustled about to get the camp ready for the main body of the refugees now trudging up the mountain road. A groan escaped from my lips as I caught sight of the occupied blankets and cots overflowing from out of one of the caves — the wounded. There were several children included among them with their mothers in tears by their sides. A lump rose in my throat.

Eshshah backstroked her powerful wings as she touched

down in a nearby clearing. Bern swung his leg over and slid off. I removed my helmet and dismounted after him.

One of Bern's captains rushed up to him, one eye on Eshshah, as he gave Bern the dragon salute.

"Sir, if you'll follow me, I'll show you to your command tent."

He turned to Eshshah and me and gave us a crisp salute.

"Permission to speak to your dragon," he said to me.

"Of course."

"Greetings mighty dragon. Your strength matches your beauty."

Eshshah nodded her acknowledgment.

"Amáne, you're in charge here," Bern said. "Assign people to help you unload and deliver the supplies to their proper destinations. I believe our medic will be happy to see what the Healer has sent him."

"In charge? Me? But —"

"Look behind you," he said. An amused look on his face. "I'm sure you have no shortage of willing helpers. Take charge."

He wheeled around and strode off with his captain.

I turned and found a rather large group of mostly young men, staring at Eshshah and me, eagerly awaiting my word. I blushed as I noted the looks on some of their faces — they openly gawked at me. Had they never seen a girl in male clothing?

I swallowed my embarrassment and did as Bern asked. "You," I pointed to the one who ogled me the hardest. A tall young man who looked like he never combed his shaggy hair. "We'll need a cart."

"Yes, sir," he said as he winked at me. I narrowed my eyes at him, but it didn't appear to affect him. He turned and left to do my bidding.

I climbed back up on Eshshah and undid the lashes that secured the provisions. I removed the smaller bags and satchels that held the herbs and medicines. The boys and girls lined up and caught the items as I tossed them down. They took off in the direction of the hospital cave.

The obnoxious, boy, I learned his name was Darqin, came back with a cart and donkey. I tossed him the larger sacks, which he caught easily, and loaded in the cart.

"You want to go with me to unload these things, Sir Amáne?"

The title he used didn't bother me, but his mocking tone grated on my nerves. I didn't deserve the disrespect and should have reprimanded him. I took into account he had just witnessed the destruction of his town. He may have lost a family member, and I didn't know his story. So, I gave him the benefit of the doubt, holding myself from an angry response.

Keeping my voice even, I answered, "I have other things to attend to. I'm sure you're capable."

After I removed the saddle from Eshshah, I headed to the cave where Anbon's healer ministered to the wounded. I grappled with my emotions as I came into the reality of the results of war. The smell of blood and death, the sounds resonating around me. Some lay moaning softly while others cried out in agony. Children wailed as their mothers tried to comfort them without aggravating their pain.

A few weeks ago Eshshah finally convinced me that Gallen had been right when he said I had healing powers of my own. I thought they were only present with Eshshah's help. But after placing my hands and healing a young girl's ankle in a slave ship when I was abducted, and my own wrist in Galtero's arena of death, I began to accept the fact that, indeed, I shared some of Eshshah's healing abilities.

"Eshshah, please. I need you here."

She made her way to where I waited on the other side of the

camp. People cleared a path for her large bulk as they saluted her and gazed at her in admiration. Young girls and boys, who should have been asleep at this hour, followed a safe distance behind.

Eshshah had never been exposed to anyone other than dragon riders, except for Kail and his brothers. She stood fascinated by the people staring at her, and was particularly attracted to the young. They had the least fear of her. She enjoyed their persistent curiosity. Some even scampered closer and touched her tail as she trod by.

Together we visited the injured. I placed my hands on their wounds, or above them and poured out my healing power. My palms heated with the effort. Eshshah placed her nose on them and breathed her healing breath. We treated as many as we could — of those that were not at their ancestor's door. My hands burned as we went from cot to cot. I hid my blisters and my exhaustion as we did our best to help. Eshshah could not fit in the cave, so the more seriously wounded were carried out to her. We could at least relieve them of some of their suffering.

Finally, Eshshah entreated, "Amáne, you cannot help heal anyone else. You're spent. You'll make yourself sick. I can take care of the last of them. Please, you must rest."

My head reeled. I'd been stumbling for the last several minutes and had no strength left to argue with her. She treated my hands, then turned her attention to the rest of the wounded.

Bern found me just before daybreak. Without protest, I allowed him to lead me to the corner of another cave. I fell onto the pallet he'd prepared for me, pulled the quilt over my head and let sleep take me.

Chapter Three

I awoke to the sound of the Healer's voice. It took me a moment to remember where I was. I turned over in my quilts and focused on Bern. He faced the communication device he'd hung on the cave wall as he reported to the Healer.

"Anbon has been defeated. The majority of the town escaped, and we're now holed up in the mountains. We don't expect any further attacks, but if Galtero's army draws near, Anbon's defenders could overpower them here."

I dragged myself to my feet, joined Bern at the disc and greeted the Healer.

"Amáne, thank you," the Healer said. "The people of Anbon, I'm sure, appreciate what you and Eshshah have done for them."

"We did what we could, Healer. But, it's no consolation for the loss of their homes." I let out a distressed sigh. "I owed them at least that much."

"Amáne, the attack was inevitable. It was not your fault." She gave me a measured look. "I suggest you be careful when using your healing powers in the future. We don't yet know the nature or the limit of your gift. It may be possible that you can spend yourself irreparably if you don't stop to rest when you need it."

I nodded in acknowledgment as I shot a sidelong glance at Bern. No doubt he'd been the one to tell the Healer and caused her to worry about me.

"I've spoken with Ansel," the Healer continued.

My heart beat fast at just the mention of his name.

"He was upset that he left when he did and that you and Eshshah had to go on your own. I didn't think when I told him that it would have the effect that it did. It would be doing him a favor, Amáne, if you would contact him — let him know you're all right."

"Yes Healer. I'll speak with him straightaway."

I paced as Bern continued his discussion with the Healer. At last he signed off and released the brass knob below the glass disc of the device. I immediately put my hand on it. "Gyan," and then, "Ansel," I said. The disc shimmered and the engaging face of my love appeared. I caught my breath at his smile of relief.

"Amáne! Poor timing on my part to leave when I did. I'm sorry."

"No need to be sorry, Ansel. How could we have known?"

His eyebrows knit as he brought his face closer to the disc. "Are you all right? You look worn out."

"Thanks for pointing that out," I said flatly.

"She's tried to heal the entire township of Anbon," Bern said.

I glared at him for sharing that. "There goes my privacy again. Must my every move be made known to everyone?"

Ansel stifled a laugh. "Bern, this rider hasn't gotten used to the fact that there's very little that's private in a dragon rider's life."

I rolled my eyes. "How was your journey, Ansel? You must be happy to be home at last. I'm sure Lali and your staff have missed you. You were gone for quite a while."

"They missed me and were very happy to have me home. But

I'm lonely already." He threw me such a wistful look, my knees almost gave out.

"I miss you, too," I said shyly as Bern decided to stand beside me and listen to everything I said to Ansel. *I'm just going to have to get used to it, I guess.*

"We'll leave at nightfall for Dorsal. And, you know, it's just a few weeks until the Healer and Gallen pledge their troth, so we'll see each other soon, right?" I said.

"Of course. I wouldn't miss it." A longing reflected in his eyes that I couldn't fail to notice.

"Give my love to Sovann ... and Eshshah sends hers too." I felt Eshshah's heart pound as she gave me her message to pass on.

We kissed the air to each other and signed off.

CHAPTER FOUR

I felt a pressing need to be with Eshshah. As I exited the cave, I found myself nearly overrun by the children of the camp. They crowded around me, giving me their various versions of the dragon salute as they pleaded with me, "Lady Amáne, Dragon Rider, please may we meet your dragon?"

I looked at the sea of little faces, bright eyes shining, and my heart melted. I could not have denied their request, even if I'd wanted. Smiling at them, I nodded, "Of course you may."

Feeling like a mother hen, I turned and led the way to my dragon who waited nearby. There were more children around Eshshah when we reached her. They stayed their distance, obeying their mothers who reprimanded any that got close.

"It's fine." I assured the cautious mothers. "She won't hurt them."

It was as if flood gates opened. The young ones rushed up close to Eshshah and put their hands toward her to touch her foreleg or her tail — still too nervous to get near her fangs.

"Thank you, Amáne." Eshshah said. "I thought you would never get here. These poor little ones have been keeping their distance for longer than I would have thought them capable. I decided it would be better that you tell their mothers it was safe. I wasn't sure I would be believed if I communicated it to them."

"I'm sorry, Eshshah, I overslept." I walked to her large head, grabbed her fangs and placed a kiss on her nose. A collective gasp went up from the mothers and cheers from the kids. Many raised their chubby little arms for me to pick them up so they could imitate my show of affection to Eshshah.

"Amáne, I've never felt this innocence. They're so small for such strong feelings. Do all humans start this small and guiltless?"

"Yes, Eshshah. They start even smaller and more helpless. See that tiny baby in his mother's arms?"

"Then what happens to turn such beauty into the ugliness that is Galtero?"

"I don't know, Eshshah. I really don't."

"Hey, Sir Amáne. You can't find better company than a bunch of snot-nosed brats? Don't you want a more worthy escort?" Darqin shot me a smug glance along with a half-hearted dragon salute as he eyed the little ones with disdain. He didn't even acknowledge Eshshah.

I barely managed to hide my outrage. "Darqin, I would appreciate it if you would show some respect to my dragon. I also ask that you cease using that title for me. And, to answer your question, the company I'm keeping is by far more pleasant than any other I can think of."

Darqin shrugged and laughed off my anger, which only made me more so.

"My apologies." He gave half a nod to Eshshah. "Eshshah, greetings to ya," he said with not enough courtesy to suit me.

He turned to me, "I would think you'd welcome my attention. There can't be many men who would vie for a dragon-riding, sword-carrying female, who dresses like a boy." His eyes grazed by body. "Maybe you'll change your mind and join me later."

Eshshah let out a low rumble that only I could hear. "If these children were not here, I would give him reason to take back his insult and give you a proper apology."

"I would gladly let you, Eshshah. Unfortunately, that's not possible right now."

I glared daggers at Darqin. He flinched and looked away quickly, which gave me a small degree of satisfaction. "I won't change my mind," I said.

"Well, I'm sure, with time, you'll wise up." He sauntered away.

I let out a long exhale, trying to bring myself back to the peace and joy I'd felt before, with these innocent little ones.

"That's Okay, Lady Amáne," piped up a little boy of about seven. "You don't have to listen to Darqin. He's always mean. My mum says he was borned mean, and his father was mean and his grandfather was mean."

I looked at the boy and smiled. My anger dissolved.

Chapter Five

It had been a few days since Bern, Eshshah and I landed in the Healer's courtyard to salutes from the Healer, Gallen and Dorjan. I couldn't help but allow a small amount of pride when I thought about how Eshshah and I had now completed our third quest since our linking — all successful.

The Healer, Gallen, Bern, Dorjan and I sat around the Healer's table at our evening meal. Their discussion steered toward people they'd known throughout their long lives. None of the names sounded familiar to me. I quickly lost interest. I picked at my food and listened halfheartedly, trying to find an opportunity to excuse myself from their company.

"Did anyone meet Leyna, rider of Sitara, before they left for the Valley of Dragons?" Bern asked.

I stopped playing with my food. My ears perked up.

"No, she left shortly before I linked with Unule," Dorjan said. He was the oldest of the three.

"I wish she would have left more information on that place. If we could persuade the Ancient Ones to come to our aid, it would mean sure victory — riding dragons into battle once again." Bern's gaze focused far away.

"Bern, maybe that last tankard of ale has done its job," Gallen said.

Dorjan laughed and added, "There's been no proof that anyone has found that place. It's still just legend, or at the least, ancient history."

"No, it's not," Bern said. "Leyna searched for it and I believe they found it. There's a little-known saga written by a poet close to her just after they left Teravinea."

Bern inhaled and hummed a tune to himself, trying to recall the song. He nodded. In a deep and beautiful voice he began the ballad — a haunting tune about two dragon riders of long ago. I sat riveted, no longer bored, as the song unfolded.

Leyna, rider of Sitara, fell in love with Hajari, rider of Dinesh. The two dragons, Sitara and Dinesh, were mates. Leyna and Hijari's love was unprecedented. Alas, Hajari met his ancestors too soon. His dragon, Dinesh, distraught, exiled himself to find the Valley of Dragons. He couldn't end his life because of his mate, yet could not survive any longer in Teravinea without his rider.

Leyna and Sitara remained for a short time, persevering in their duties to the king. Sitara could take her mate's absence no longer. Leyna scoured the kingdom for any information on the whereabouts of the Valley of Dragons.

King Rikkar, Ansel's grandfather, gave them a pardon, excusing them from their duty. They left in search of this legendary place and were never heard from again.

Bern finished the ballad. I was moved by their story.

"Sitara or Dinesh were not of the Royal Dragon line, so neither were bound to King Rikkar," Bern said. "I personally believe Leyna found the Valley of Dragons."

"Where do you think she found it?" I asked.

My enthusiasm drew attention. The Healer raised her brows. Dorjan narrowed his eyes at me. I shifted my expression to what I hoped showed mild curiosity.

"I heard she flew down here to the Dorsal Outpost to research, but I can't be sure if she actually found anything there," Bern replied.

My pulse quickened as I absorbed this news. I kept my expression neutral.

Gallen, inappropriate as usual, said, "I don't know about the Valley of Dragons, but I am familiar with some ballads about Leyna and Hajari's love. I wouldn't sing them in mixed company, though. What that must have been like — a couple in love, linked to dragons who were mates." He looked pointedly at me, as the heat rose in my cheeks.

The next second, his face contracted as he winced. Guessing that the Healer had kicked him under the table, I shot him a 'you-asked-for-it' smirk.

"I believe there's more to it than just legend," the Healer said. "I remember seeing a manuscript at the Dorsal Outpost when Torin still flew."

I saw a brief flash of pain in her eyes. My heart went out to her when I thought of the loss of her dragon. He had perished saving Ansel's life. Torin had sacrificed himself by flying in front of the Healer and the infant prince when an explosion destroyed the royal living quarters of Castle Teravinea. Ansel's parents, King Emeric and Queen Fiala, lost their lives in that explosion.

"Yes, Bern, it would certainly make a difference if we could ride dragons into battle again. But right now, it's only a dream for us." The Healer sighed.

To my dismay the conversation came to a close. It had gotten late. Everyone suddenly found themselves tired, except for me. I couldn't stop thinking about the possibility of other dragons somewhere. It would surely mean victory for us if someone could find them.

I joined Eshshah in our chambers, but couldn't sleep.

"Eshshah, do you know anything about the Valley of Dragons?"

"My ancient memories do recall a valley where our ancestors began. But, what are you thinking, Amáne? Do you think the Council will ask us to search for the Valley? Are you hoping for that to be our next quest?"

"I'm not quite sure what I'm thinking yet, Eshshah. It doesn't sound like a mission which all the riders would support. Not to mention, Ansel. But what if it was possible to find the Ancient Ones? And what if they could be persuaded to help us win the throne? Would that not be worth the effort?"

"Hmm," she rumbled. "It depends on what kind of effort you're implying."

"Don't worry, I won't do anything foolish. I'm certain you would be the first to put me straight."

CHAPTER SIX

Sweat burned my eyes as Dorjan and I exchanged blows. He worked with me in a preliminary preparation for my training as swordmaster. My official instructor would be Avano. Until he was available, Dorjan had stepped in. My lungs burned. I had serious doubts that I was actually ready for Avano, but I didn't voice my insecurity.

"Good hit, Amáne. Remember to attack, then get out of measure straightaway ."

"Amáne, take a break," called Gallen from the kitchen garden. "Avano needs you to contact him."

"Avano?" I wasn't accustomed to receiving contact from any of the dragon riders. They usually only spoke with Ansel or the Healer. Ansel was the only one who asked for me on the communication disc.

Dorjan and I thanked each other as I rushed to the laver outside the kitchen to wash up. Maybe Avano wanted to arrange our training. It was an honor of which I didn't feel worthy, but looked forward to with excitement.

I took the stairs quickly up to the Healer's library. Placing my hand on the brass knob of the communication device, I said "Gyan," then, "Arun." Avano's former name when he rode Cira.

Avano's handsome face shimmered in the glass disc before coming into clear focus.

"Greetings, Avano." We saluted each other. "Gallen said you needed me to contact you."

"Yes, I have somebody here who wants a word with you."

"What? Someone wants to speak with me?"

Avano mouthed something to a person out of my line of sight. His eyes twinkled as he gave me a wink then stepped aside.

"Father!" I screamed. My father's face filled the disc. "What are you doing ... what ... why?" I sputtered.

The blue eyes of Duer crinkled on the edges as he laughed at my reaction.

He saluted me proudly. I nodded in response.

"Amáne, I'm so happy to see you again. Yes, you are as beautiful as I remember you at our last meeting. The spitting image of Catriona. I'm thankful you received her looks and not mine."

I laughed. "I'm afraid I have quite a bit of you in me. The reason I recognized you under the castle is because it was a familiar face staring back at me every time I gazed in a looking glass."

"I haven't stopped thinking about you, my daughter. I have only a moment. I'm on king's business. Since I was passing through, I thought I'd take my chances and see if Avano could conjure you up. I heard about this amazing contraption, and wanted to see it for myself. Avano was gracious enough to oblige. I'm only several paces in front of the king's spies. I think they may have their suspicions about me, but I had to take the chance to see you again."

"Oh, no! Why don't you just quit Galtero's court? Come down to Dorsal and stay here. The Healer has plenty of room. We can rebuild the cottage and live there. There's so much we need to talk about."

"I wish I could, my beauty. For now I'm more valuable to your cause if I stay in Galtero's circle for as long as I can. I do have much to tell you. But we'll have to wait until Galtero is overthrown. When that wondrous day arrives, I promise I'll talk until you can't take it any longer. You'll know everything and more that you've ever wanted to know — about your mother, your relatives and your ancestors. And you can fill me in on everything I've missed out on. Deal?"

"Deal." I smiled at the familiar interchange. I, too, used that word in the same way.

"If you come again to the City of Teravinea," Duer said, "please let Avano or Bern know and they can try to contact me. I long to see you."

"And I, you."

"I must be going. I've tarried too long. Take care, my sweet Amáne. Your father loves you."

"I love you, too."

Avano signed off just before the tears began to roll down my cheeks.

Chapter Seven

Several weeks passed since Anbon fell. I'd been so busy planning the Healer and Gallen's celebration of their vows, I hardly had time to wonder about the Valley of Dragons. With the heaviness of war looming, the Healer and Gallen didn't feel right having a large celebration to pledge their troth. That, and the fact that they had known each other for so long, they wanted only a simple gathering. All of the dragon riders would be attending and only a few of the people of Dorsal. Tomorrow was the big day.

Gallen and the Healer had behaved like young adolescents for the last week. Sometimes I felt like their mother. It was fantastic. It made a nice break from the seriousness that had surrounded us lately. Just for a bit, we could escape the concern of war.

"Well, that's the last one, Amáne," Fiona said as she placed the vase of dahlias on the cloth-draped table.

Fiona and I had become close friends since that fateful night when the sorcerer and his thugs terrorized Dorsal. Her father lost his life while protecting her.

I surveyed our surroundings. It exploded with color from the tied table cloths to the vases of flowers sporting every hue I'd ever seen.

"Fiona, what would I have done without you? Look how

beautiful you've made this courtyard. It looks like a garden at an exotic palace."

"It wasn't just me. You've worked right beside me the entire day."

"I know, but I don't have your talent with color and cloth. I couldn't have come anywhere near to how you've transformed this place. Thank you so much for your help." Fiona smiled and put her arm around my shoulders as we admired our handiwork.

"Well, I think your lantern idea was brilliant. I can't wait to see how they look after dark," Fiona said.

Paper lanterns hung from ropes stretched across the courtyard. I had used some of Sitara's scales, so that at just the right moment, I'll whisper *Sitara* and they'll light up the courtyard with their soft glow.

"We'll test them tonight." I said.

Fiona turned to me with a serious look. "Amáne, I want to thank you for allowing me your secret. I'm so proud of you. A dragon rider. Although, it comes as no surprise that you were chosen. You were always more interested in the cutler's booth than the silk and ribbons at the mercer's, or in battle stories over romances.

"But more than that, you've lifted a veil that hung between Kail and me. He refused to share anything with me about the time he spent here. And he's been silent about an incident that happened the night my father met his ancestors. He tried to hide it, but I saw his injuries and the stricken look in his eyes. We've never kept anything from each other. Now I know that it had to do with what you're doing here — your mission to unseat Galtero."

"Kail is an honorable man, Fiona, sworn to secrecy. I'm sorry that made it difficult for you."

"I understand, now." She turned to me and her face lit up.

"When is your Lord Ansel arriving?"

A thrill went up my spine. "He'll be here after dark."

Ansel and Sovann already left Trivingar manor to fly the long route over the ocean so they could travel in daylight without being spotted. They should be at the Dorsal Outpost by now waiting for nightfall. I could hardly contain myself.

"Amáne, that will be in no time at all. You need to get cleaned up and into a nice gown before he gets here. You don't want to keep him waiting."

"I plan on getting cleaned up, but I'm not putting on a gown. Some clean tights and a tunic will do fine."

Fiona looked aghast. "Tights and a tunic? How long has it been since you've seen him?"

I hadn't told her about the communication disc and that Ansel and I talked every few days. "He left here several weeks ago."

She turned me forcefully and pushed me inside toward the bathing room. "He will not see you in a tunic and tights tonight. I won't allow it. I brought a few gowns over because I wasn't sure what I wanted to wear tomorrow. I'll choose one for you to wear tonight."

Fiona paused, shot me a sidelong glance and shook her head. "Honestly, Amáne ..."

CHAPTER EIGHT

"Amáne, have you drowned in there? It's nearly dark." Fiona called.

I'd lost track of time. I jumped out of the bath, wrapped a towel around me and ran down the hall to my chambers. Fiona held up a blue gown and insisted helping me into it.

I gave a reluctant shrug. Eshshah curled up to observe the process.

"Ow, I thought we were the same size," I complained as she tightened the dress around me.

"We are. This is the latest fashion. It's supposed to be tight."

"I'm not going to be able to breathe. If I faint before I get to him, you'll not hear the end of it."

Fiona laughed but kept pulling at the laces until she had it to her liking.

"Now for your hair."

"Fiona, this is not a ball. I don't need my hair done. It's fine."

"Just sit down and I'll put a couple of quick braids in it."

I huffed loudly, but sat as she requested.

"Sovann's here." Eshshah's heart beat faster as she rushed out of our chambers. Her excitement matched mine.

"Ansel's here. Never mind my hair."

"Sit still. I'm not done. He can wait a bit for you."

"I thought you told me I shouldn't keep him waiting."

"It depends on the circumstances. In this case, it'll be good for him."

"Ugh, I'll never understand."

Fiona's musical laugh filled the room. I just rolled my eyes.

"Mistress Amáne!" A familiar voice broke in. "It seems like such a long time since I've seen you, and look how beautiful you are."

"Lali!"

Eulalia charged into my chambers and threw her arms around me. Fiona maneuvered out of her way and at the same time managed to keep a hold of my braid.

With hardly a breath between sentences, Lali kept up her banter. "You're more striking than when we last met, although you left rather abruptly then, it breaks my heart when I recall the disturbing circumstances, but we won't even think about that time, all is well, now, and Lord Ansel has shown the best of moods. He's been beside himself, anticipating his trip here.

"I have to tell you, flying here was the most exciting thing I have ever done in all my life, if someone would have told me when I was a young girl that I would get to ride on a dragon, I would have thought them mad and told them so directly — not given them one more second of my time. Truthfully, though, that's a long time to sit in a saddle. The pain in my —"

"Lali, you don't know how good it is to see you. It's a fantastic surprise," I said.

She turned to Fiona. "Who is this? Someone who knows how

to bring out your feminine side? How did she ever get you into anything other than tunic and tights?" She nodded with approval at Fiona.

I made the introductions. Lali took up Fiona in a big hug, talking the entire time about how she had to fight me to get me into the ball gown for Ansel's birthday. Not entirely the truth, but I did give her a difficult time.

At last both Fiona and Lali agreed that I could be excused to find Ansel. I hurried out of my chambers.

"Don't run, Amáne. Walk like a lady," Fiona called as I rushed down the hall.

I found Ansel in the kitchen speaking with Bern. My heart leapt to my throat. My breath caught when I saw him. I had to stop and concentrate on taking small steps, lest I fall on my face.

Both men turned as I entered. My attention riveted on Ansel.

I blushed at his reaction — his eyes went wide and his face lit up. *Maybe wearing a gown isn't so bad after all.*

"At the risk of feeling your dagger at my throat," Ansel said, "I'm going to say out loud that you look dazzling." His hands reached out for mine. A warmth spread through me as I took them.

"I'll spare you tonight, since it's the eve of a special occasion — and besides, my dagger is in my chambers." I laughed, then paused to survey the handsome man in front of me. "And I'll have to say out loud that you look striking."

He pulled me to him. In our customary greeting, he took my face in his hands, kissed my forehead and both cheeks, and without hesitation, my lips. The kitchen receded. My world consisted only of Ansel's warmth and his spicy, musky scent as I pressed in closer.

Suddenly, I remembered Bern. Drawn immediately back into the kitchen, Ansel and I parted. I tore my eyes from his. My face went red as I looked at Bern in apology.

"This is certainly a time of love." He smiled, relieving me of my embarrassment.

Ansel took my hand as we walked through the decorated courtyard to where Eshshah and Sovann exchanged affectionate gestures.

"Sovann, your golden beauty knows no bounds. I'm so pleased to see you." I took his fangs and brought my forehead to his nose.

"Amáne, it is my pleasure to be back here again."

Ansel greeted Eshshah, then we bid them farewell as they took flight to hunt. We stood hand in hand beaming with pride as our dragons disappeared into the night.

Ansel turned to me, eyes smoldering. I couldn't resist him as the raw emotions of Sovann and Eshshah washed over us. We locked in an embrace and kissed like never before. We couldn't get close enough. My head spun. His arms tightened around me. My fingers clutched his shirt.

"Ahem, you two!" Fiona called from the courtyard, "Maybe that's acceptable behavior for two dragon riders, I don't know, but in civilized society, it's quite disrespectful — especially since my love is not here to take note of your lessons."

Ansel and I pulled apart, breathless. My eyes went wide. When I saw Fiona was not offended at all, the three of us laughed.

"Fiona, forgive us," I said. " We'll make an effort to restrain ourselves — at least until Kail can be here with you."

"Lord Ansel," Fiona approached us and curtsied as she offered him her hand. "It's so nice to see you again."

Ansel gave her a low courtly bow, took her hand and kissed it. She blushed as she curtsied again.

"What do you think of our decorations?" Fiona asked Ansel

as we headed back to the courtyard.

"You've made a garden paradise."

I whispered "Sitara," to light the lanterns. We gasped our delight as the soft glow transformed the courtyard.

Chapter Nine

The morning of the celebration dawned beautifully. Ansel and Gallen left early for Dorjan's. They were to remain there until it was time for the ceremony to begin. Ansel would do the honors of presiding over the vows.

Lali helped Fiona and me with the finishing touches around the house. We scrutinized our handiwork to make sure we didn't miss anything. The food, prepared by a group of women from Dorsal, would be arriving soon. All we had left to do was to get the Healer ready and then ourselves. I was so nervous, I could hardly stand it. This was almost as nerve-wracking as embarking upon a new quest.

The three of us assisted the Healer don a beautiful gown she commissioned in Serislan. It was of silver silk. Slashed sleeves revealed gold inner sleeves. Jewels outlined the low neckline. We placed a silver and gold circlet crown over her intricately-braided hair. Hanging from the crown were spoon-shaped bangles, symbols of love. They signified a happy union. Lali added the finishing touches — a small amount of rouge for her cheeks and red for her lips. When we were done, the glow on the Healer's face made her seem as though she was young again. I never saw her look so beautiful — this was her day.

Lali turned her attentions to Fiona and me. Fiona wore a stunning dark blue gown that set off her blonde hair. It hugged her body, accentuating her very feminine curves.

They assisted me into a light gray gown decorated with the same silver silk the Healer wore. Shiny silver embroidery ran across the bodice. I didn't remember it being as tight at my fitting as the two of them insisted it should be.

Kail arrived with Fiona's twin sisters, Rio and Mila. Fiona rushed to join him. Kail's eyes lit up when he saw her. His delight put a smile on my face. They made a fine couple.

At last came the moment for the ceremony to begin. Musicians took up their instruments, lute, dulcimer and flutes, and struck up our traditional march. Twenty-three dragon riders entered the courtyard. They lined up in two lines, turned on their heels and faced each other. The Healer and I watched from the kitchen. It was my part to walk the Healer to the arch where Ansel would hear their vows. The wooden archway before which they would pledge their troth symbolized the joining of bride and groom. After the pledge, they would walk together through the archway to signify they had begun their new lives together.

Gallen, accompanied by Ansel, appeared at the street entrance of the courtyard. Both the Healer and I gasped at the same time. They looked amazing. My gaze went from one to the other. I forgot to breathe when my eyes fell upon Ansel. He beamed with happiness for his aunt and Gallen. Gallen and Ansel walked between the riders who saluted them as they passed.

The groom wore a white ornately-embroidered shirt.

The balloon sleeves decorated with symbols and designs. His dragonscale breastplate all but glowed over a royal blue calf-length tunic. Black polished knee-high boots over white tights completed his wedding attire. His sword hung in a jewel-bedecked scabbard. Ansel was dressed less showy, but just as striking as Gallen.

As the two reached the archway, Gallen and Ansel stopped, faced each other and saluted. They took each other in a warm embrace. Gallen stepped back as Ansel continued to the other side of the archway. He turned and faced the guests.

This was my cue. The music changed, the signal for the bride to start her walk. Standing to the Healer's right, I tied a silver silk rope to her right wrist, then clasped my left hand over it, and wrapped the rope around both our wrists. We left the kitchen and proceeded through the riders in the same path Gallen and Ansel had taken. The riders saluted us.

My eyes locked with Ansel's as we moved forward. I managed to take slow even breaths. My heart thudded in my chest as I noted the longing in his eyes. A lump formed in my throat. I glanced at the Healer. Her expression brought me back to the ceremony. The way she looked at Gallen made my heart burst with happiness for her.

We reached the front where Gallen waited. I unwrapped my hand and left the rope to dangle from the Healer's. Stepping back and to my left, I stood as witness as the Healer and Gallen closed the space. I could feel Ansel's eyes on me. Our eyes met once again before he directed his attention to the bride and groom.

The ceremony itself was short. The Healer and Gallen exchanged words of troth, fidelity and love to each other. Then Ansel stepped forward. Taking the silk rope tied to the Healer's wrist, he wrapped it around Gallen's, tying them securely to each other. Ansel requested everyone's blessing upon the couple. He invited the two to step through the arch. Then asking them to turn around to face the guests, he introduced them as husband and wife. The Healer and Gallen kissed a long and meaningful kiss. I blushed as the riders clapped, whistled and shouted encouragements.

The couple, still tied together, moved back through the dragon riders' line-up and seated themselves at a small head table covered with flowers. The guests found their tables and the feast began.

Food poured out of the kitchen. Nothing extravagant, just traditional Dorsal fare, but the flavors and aromas matched those of a royal ball. Wine and ale flowed freely. It was a brief moment where we could put aside the woes of the kingdom to honor this remarkable couple that had given so much to Teravinea.

We were all well sated when Bern lifted his drink in a toast to the bride and groom. Then he began to hit the side of his cup with his dagger. The action was picked up by Avano and soon we were all beating our cups or tankards.

"Tell us the tale! Tell us the tale!" we shouted.

During a Teravinea ceremony of vows, by tradition, the newly-joined couple is encouraged to recount the tale of their meeting and their story that led up to this day.

Gallen began, "Our story has taken an unprecedented amount of time to finally reach this point. But I will start the tale and hope you'll all not age noticeably while we tell it. We'll try to keep it brief.

"I was known as Kaelem, and my lovely bride was known as Nara. She was fifteen and I, seventeen — young healer's apprentices, living at the Castle Teravinea and studying under King Rikkar's healer. Nara was always his favorite." He looked at her and they smiled at each other from a distant era.

"We were best friends and helped each other with learning the concoctions and measurements of our craft. She never forgot a formula, reciting it without effort when the old healer tested us. It took me a little longer, but she always gave me hints that he never noticed and I was able to pass his tests.

"Our friendship became stronger and I often wished we'd lived a common life, where I could negotiate a betrothal for her hand. But, neither of us had parents still living and she was satisfied with us remaining friends. In fact, she insisted upon it."

At that, the Healer met my eyes. I realized what she meant so long ago when she told me I reminded her of herself when she was young.

The Healer took up the story, "I loved him as my companion, but being serious about my studies and the healing arts, I didn't think I could do both — to give him my all, and pour myself into my profession. I was stubborn, but wrong."

Gallen continued, " I believe it was to placate me, but we agreed when she turned twenty, if no one had swept either us away, we would consider taking vows. Well, her twentieth birthday approached quickly. Besides wishing to earn Nara's attentions, my dream in life was to become a dragon rider. I thought if I could be a rider by her birthday, then maybe she would bend to my wishes and she would want to keep our childish promise. After much coaxing I finally talked the old healer into signing me up as a candidate."

"I was so proud of him," the Healer said. "In those days the privilege of attending the Hatching Ceremony as a spectator was by lottery, after the king had chosen his guests. Many people wanted to attend, so they had to try to make it fair. Having already been to numerous hatchings, as I lived and worked in the castle, I didn't plan on trying to get in that year. That is until I found that Kaelem was a candidate. Letting nothing deter me, I convinced the guards that as the king's healer's apprentice I needed to be in the arena. Of course my real reason was to support Kaelem. Well, as many of you know, it was I who was called by Torin that day. I fell into a trance and was drawn to his egg, it could not be prevented. I heard that King Rikkar was aghast when he saw me climb over the railings and head toward my dragon's egg."

"So, she linked with Torin," Gallen said, "and that nullified our vow ... he was the one who swept her away. I found myself quite envious of her being chosen — I was passed over that year. She tried to comfort me and keep up our relationship, but she became only half available to me. I understand the bond, now, but not then.

"Finally, the following year a rare thing happened. I'd been accepted again as a dragon rider candidate. During that Hatching Ceremony, Gyan chose me. Now we had our dragons in common. Nara and I became close again. We were truly in love, but Nara insisted because of our double duties as riders and healers, we couldn't jeopardize our commitments to our king and our dragons.

"With our obligations, we didn't make time for each other," Gallen continued. "I knew Nara looked upon her duties seriously. She didn't need the additional pressure that I caused her. I made an effort to accept that fact — I backed away. When I met a lady who showed an interest in me, I accepted her attentions. I made the choice to marry her since I couldn't have Nara. Nara actually gave her approval and was happy for us."

"Only for your happiness," the Healer said in a small voice. "Inside I was dying."

Gallen turned his head toward her. His eyebrows knit, a shadow drew across his face. He looked at his hand, still tied to hers, then took a deep breath before continuing his narrative. "My wife was only with me for fifteen years when her ancestors called her. After her death, Nara and I resumed our friendship, but marriage was not in her herb jar.

"King Emeric sent Gyan and me across the sea to participate at an exhibition in another kingdom as a show of our solidarity with them."

Gallen's speech slowed, his voice lowered, almost as if he talked to himself. "I never put a breast shield on Gyan whenever we did an exhibition flight. It was not a mission of war, but one of peace — it was a festival. But that day offered no peace. The enemy showed their face with weapons I hadn't seen before. They catapulted fire balls that exploded on contact. They aimed one at Gyan —"

My eyes filled with tears. I took Ansel's hand and squeezed it hard. The Healer put her hand on top of Gallen's.

She cleared her throat and said in a thick voice, "I heard the news of his loss. Torin and I received permission to go find him and bring him back. We searched far. I feared he took his own life.

"I later learned he hunted those who killed Gyan. One by one, he brought them down. Years passed. There was always a piece of me missing. I regretted being so headstrong. I hated how I pushed him away. But he was gone."

"Then it was Nara's turn for her greatest tragedy," Gallen spoke. "She lost her family and her Torin. I heard the news when I returned to Teravinea. I was told Nara had also met her end in that incident. No one knew she and Lord Ansel had survived. I rejoined the other riders and we vowed to revenge the great losses we suffered — King Emeric, Queen Fiala, the newborn prince, Torin and Nara. Two years later Nara contacted Avano. He told her I had returned."

The Healer continued, “I asked Gallen to meet me in Dorsal. That was where Torin predicted we would find the next dragon and rider — a female rider.” She looked at me with pride, then went on, “We fell in love all over again, and after much procrastination, here we are in front of our close friends to pledge our troth.”

A tragic story that at last ended in happiness. I wiped away my tears and started clapping, which was taken up by the other guests. We toasted the couple countless times. The rest of the night was a blur of music, and dancing.

Chapter Ten

The communication device buzzed in the Healer's library. I was at the laver outside the kitchen washing off the dirt and grime from my morning practice. It continued to drone impatiently. When it seemed like no one would be answering the device, I sprinted to catch it. I put my hand on the knob and Ansel's face shimmered into view.

My heart accelerated. He smiled and said, "I was just ready to give up."

"I'm sorry, I guess the Healer and Gallen aren't around."

"It was your face I wanted to see, anyway."

I blushed then remembered my manners. I saluted him and said, "Eshshah and I send our greetings to Sovann."

Ansel returned the greeting.

"To what do I owe this pleasure? I heard you already contacted the Healer this morning while I was out," I said.

"I need yours and Eshshah's assistance and wanted to ask you personally."

"Our assistance? Do you have a quest for us?" I brightened.

He laughed. "Not in your grand sense of the word. But I

have secured an audience with King Tynan that I want you to attend with me."

"An audience? You want me to take part in a meeting with the King of Serislan?"

"Yes, exactly. I'm about to reveal my identity to King Tynan and petition his backing. We could use his strength when we face Galtero. I've requested to meet with him."

"And how would Eshshah and I be of any help with that? I know I need the experience, but right now I know nothing of diplomatic affairs, especially an audience with a king." My chest tightened at the thought of facing King Tynan.

"You'll be fine. I know your powers of persuasion." He gave me a knowing look. "Besides the use of your talents, a show of another dragon from Teravinea would be to our advantage."

"You wouldn't rather have the Healer or Braonán? Eshshah and I would be happy to transport them. Truthfully, of what use would I be to you? What if I hampered your chances of any aid from him?"

Ansel's eyes danced, "So, you're declining a direct order, dragon rider? Do you want to be charged with insubordination?"

"Hmm. I see you're throwing your rank around." I feigned disdain. "No, I would never want to be charged with insubordination. Very well then, as you wish, Your Grace. When do you want me?"

His eyebrows raised. With a devious smile he said, "Always!"

I rolled my eyes. "Let me rephrase my last question. When is the council with King Tynan?"

Still smiling, he answered, "In less than two days time. I'm sorry for the short notice, but can you and Eshshah fly here tonight? I miss you. We can spend some time together and go over what we'll discuss with the king. You'll have to excuse me for a few hours tomorrow afternoon, as I have some business to attend. I'll be free by the evening meal. The next morning we'll fly to Serislan Castle."

I brightened at the thought of a long flight for Eshshah and me. "I assume you've already discussed this with the Healer and I'm the last to know?"

"Well, you're probably not the last to know ..."

Feigning annoyance, I shook my head. "Regardless, Eshshah and I would be honored to accompany you and Sovann to an audience with King Tynan."

I released the knob on the communication device. My panic at the thought of a meeting with the king subsided as I realized the advantage just presented. The opportunity arose a little sooner than I'd anticipated, but already a plan began to formulate.

"Amáne? What are you thinking?"

"Eshshah, this is our chance to do more research on Leyna and the Valley of Dragons. I've read everything that the Dorsal Outpost had to offer. I believe there are some manuscripts at the Arevale Outpost that Leyna used. And she may have left some written information. It's our excuse to go there and find what we need to get to the Valley." My excitement increased as I left the library and headed out to the courtyard where Eshshah lay in the sun.

She turned her gaze on me. "I get the feeling you don't plan to propose your intentions to Lord Ansel, the Healer and the Council."

"You know as well as I that Ansel would oppose such a plan. It wouldn't even get to Council. He'd quash it before I could finish my plea. I'd need more information before I involve him."

"And you know as well as I that you cannot leave on some wild quest just because you think we can find the Valley of Dragons, Amáne."

I remained silent as the ideas churned in my head. *This could work.*

"Amáne?"

"Okay, Eshshah, how about this? Bern believes Leyna found a way to get to the Ancient Ones. The Healer finds truth in it. I'm thoroughly convinced she found the Valley. Our purpose would just be a short flight to Orchila. That's the village where Leyna went to find out how to get to the Valley of Dragons. It would be a small discovery journey. We won't take long. We'll find someone who can give us the location, or even a map, and return with some proven information. We can then propose a more concrete and well-researched plan to the Healer, who can convince Ansel. He and Sovann can go back with us. Ansel can petition the Ancient ones for their backing. Just like we're doing with King Tynan."

"I don't know. Even the short flight to Orchila doesn't sound like a trip the Healer would deem necessary. Can't you just ask her for her input?"

"I think you're making more of this than you need to. We'll be in Serislan at King Tynan's castle. At that point we'll be only a few hours from Orchila. We won't be missed. And just think of the advantage for our cause. Dragons, Eshshah. That would turn the events in our favor. Galtero wouldn't stand a chance against a fighting wing of dragons."

Eshshah eyed me sideways.

"Eshshah, it's one short day of asking questions. I'm simply seeking information to support our proposal. That's it. Nothing more."

"Amáne, you know I'd follow you to the Other Side if you asked. I just want you to think this through, to make sure you don't do anything unbecoming of your position."

I grabbed her fangs and placed a big kiss on her nose. "Eshshah, I love you."

She hummed her pleasure.

Chapter Eleven

Darkness finally arrived as the Healer, Bern, Gallen and I finished our evening meal. It was decided that since Eshshah and I were heading north, we would go by way of Anbon to the mountain camp and drop Bern off. He would continue his work in training recruits for our army.

While we ate, the three of them briefed me on the protocol and etiquette of a royal audience. Just talking about an encounter with the monarch of Serislan and the accompanying aristocracy left me fighting for breath. I'm not cut out for this kind of thing. What was Ansel thinking?

At least this time I'll have suitable gowns to wear. Fiona stepped up as my champion in that field. She'd created several gowns for me, and made me vow I would never wear one of my old Dorsal skirts anywhere near a manor or castle … ever.

Gallen saddled Eshshah with the double saddle. He was rubbing her between her eyes as I made my way to the courtyard. She hummed with contentment. I smiled.

After hugs and farewells and a good deal of salutes, Gallen gave me a leg up. I locked wrists with Bern and he swung up behind me. We buckled in as Eshshah pushed off. Spiraling upward, I watched Gallen and the Healer grow smaller below us.

The flight was thoroughly enjoyable, even though we flew at the frigid height Eshshah loved. I'd wrapped a silk scarf around my face and had on plenty of layers as well as my riding cloak to guarantee my warmth. For once, I was actually comfortable in the freezing temperature.

In the distance, I spotted the destroyed town of Anbon. It sat like a scar upon the hill, charred buildings its only inhabitants. A sadness crept upon me. This could have been Dorsal. I couldn't imagine how Bern felt.

We arrived at the small valley where Anbon's encampment lay. It was dark and quiet, unlike the first time we landed there — the night Anbon fell.

Bern and I unloaded the items the Healer had sent. I grabbed the last small bag of herbs and headed to the hospital cave.

"Well if it isn't Sir Amáne," came a familiar voice. "Did you miss me so much you had to come back to see me?"

"Hello Darqin." I managed to keep an even voice.

He turned to Eshshah with a weak salute and said, "Hey dragon."

I clenched my fists. "Her name is Eshshah," I said slowly. "I've asked you before to show more respect. And, I've also asked you not to call me Sir."

He looked at Eshshah and said with little sincerity, "Greetings Eshshah. May your fire never burn out." He gave her a crisp salute, that in my opinion bordered on mocking.

Eshshah nodded back only out of politeness. A small rumble in her chest vibrated in my ears. I don't think Darqin heard.

"Eshshah, I'm sorry," I said.

"It's not your worry, Amáne. I feel sorry for someone so confused that he seems to feel satisfied only if he's insulting someone."

I headed toward the medical supplies to deliver my package, hoping Darqin would go the other way, but he kept pace at my side.

"So, Sir ... I mean Amáne, are you going to stay a while? I could use some female company. I can overlook the fact that you dress like a boy." His eyes swept over me.

I suppressed my urge to smack him across the face. Eshshah rumbled again and this time he heard her.

"Whoa, call off your dragon. I was just saying you might be interested in spending a little time with me."

"Thank you anyway, Darqin. I'm not interested. Besides, I'm not staying."

A flash of anger showed in his eyes.

"What's the rush to get back to your little tip of the kingdom, Dorsal, right?"

"Yes, I'm from Dorsal."

"So, does Dorsal have their contingent of recruits training for the army?"

"Yes."

"And I assume you're part of it?"

"Yes."

"You don't have to be so short with me. Like you're better than me. I'm just trying to have a friendly conversation with you."

"I'm sorry, Darqin. I don't mean to be rude. I just have somewhere else I need to be. If you'll excuse me, maybe I'll be back here sometime in the future and I'll have the time to talk."

"Or, maybe I'll just come to Dorsal. We can talk there. That is if you're not too busy, or too important."

With that, he spun around and stalked off. The thought of him in Dorsal irritated me. But he was just talking nonsense. I shook it off and brought my thoughts around to being with Ansel in less than three hours.

Bern and I said our farewells. I wrapped myself back up in my scarf and riding cloak and hoisted myself into the saddle. We saluted and Eshshah took to the air.

Chapter Twelve

As we approached the Arevale Outpost my heart beat fast. My excitement was double-purposed. Not only would I have the opportunity to research Leyna's findings, but more than that, I would be seeing Ansel. I hadn't seen him since the ceremony several weeks ago. *What would our separation be like without the advantage of the communication disc*? I needed to thank Gallen for that invention.

From a distance, I could see the open door of the entry cavern, its light shields glowing. Eshshah's heart beat as wildly as mine. A small campfire burned in the open field near the outpost, lit more than likely by Braonán. I spotted someone else with him, probably Avano. They would accompany Ansel and me to Trivingar Manor.

We landed smoothly in the outpost entry hall. Eshshah and Sovann touched noses as I unbuckled my saddle belt.

Ansel rushed up and swept me into his arms before my feet touched the stone floor. "What is all this wrapping? Is it to keep me from your lips?"

I laughed as he tried to find the end of the silk scarf. Just as much in a hurry as he, I pulled off my helmet and released myself from my wrappings. I stood on my toes as he kissed my forehead and cheeks more quickly than usual, so he could at last occupy my lips.

Before my knees gave way, we drew back and gazed into each other's eyes. Our lips joined once more.

I threw a thought at Eshshah, "Block me out before this cavern heats up more than it already has."

She rumbled her deep laugh. "Then you can do likewise. I'm not so sure your passionate greeting is my fault."

Ansel and I parted and we both laughed. Evidently he had a similar discussion with Sovann. Heat rose up and filled my cheeks. I leaned my forehead into Ansel's chest as he held me. Both of us waiting for our hearts to slow their beat.

"If we stay here much longer," Ansel said, "Avano will be throwing insults and taunts at us from the field. Believe me, he can be crude when he wants to."

We reluctantly released each other and I turned my attentions toward Eshshah. After removing her saddle, we flew bareback to the field. We were greeted and saluted by Braonán and Avano. I jumped off Eshshah as Braonán gave me another sharp salute and then a quick hug. Avano picked me up and swung me in circles. By the time he let me go, my head spun.

"I was trying to figure out how we were going to get to the entry cavern before it was too late," teased Avano. "What would the Healer say if we failed in our duties as chaperones?"

I punched his shoulder, hard, then put my arm in his as I let him lead me to our horses.

After a quarter-of-an-hour ride, we arrived at Trivingar Manor. Warm light poured out of the large open doors and onto the front courtyard. We dismounted. Ansel ushered me into the entrance hall. A young boy, no more than six years old, rushed up to take my bags.

"Ah, young Kaeson, what are you doing up at this hour?" Ansel asked.

After a quick bow to Ansel and another to me he answered, "Mother said I could wait for your return my Lord. I wanted to meet Mistress Amáne." He looked up at me with wide, yet sleepy eyes.

"Mistress Amáne, allow me to introduce Kaeson, son of my head chef. Kaeson meet Mistress Amáne," Ansel said with a formal air.

"I'm very pleased to meet you, Kaeson." I tipped my head.

Without taking his eyes off of me, he said, "I've never seen a lady in trousers, but you're pretty anyway."

I couldn't help but smile at such innocence. Ansel cleared his throat, "Yes, well, Kaeson, perhaps you should learn to keep certain observations to yourself, and mind your manners before a lady. Sometimes it's better not to voice such opinions."

The boy's face went red. He bowed deeply toward me. "I'm sorry, my lady. I meant no disrespect. I like your trousers. You look like the dragon riders in the paintings around here. I'm going to be a rider when I grow up."

My eyebrows raised, "I'm sure you will, Kaeson. You are exactly what a dragon would look for in a Chosen One."

He brightened — a wide smile came to his face. He took my bags, but struggled a bit. They were nearly as large as he. I gave Ansel a look — a silent plea to offer the boy his help. Ansel just smiled at me. With a small shake of his head, he let Kaeson bear the load.

We made our way down the corridor. My stomach twisted as

we approached the guest wing I had occupied on my last stay. To my surprise we passed it.

"We've set you up in the private wing. I didn't want you in the guest wing in case it brought you unpleasant memories." His green eyes turned to me.

"How do you do that?"

"Do what?"

"Anticipate my every need, my feelings? You're amazing, Ansel."

"You're forgetting how much a part of me you are." He put his arm around me and pulled me closer. I wrapped my arm around his waist and tried to match his long stride.

We came to a door in a beautiful part of the manor I hadn't seen in my previous visit. A thick carpet ran the length of the hallway.

"Lali is waiting inside to attend to you. I know you're probably tired, but if you have it in you, once you get settled in, I'd like for you to meet me in my private dining room. We can have a late snack before you retire." His eyes pleaded. *How could I resist?*

"I am tired, but I'm sure sleep won't find me any time soon. Of course I'll meet you there."

Satisfied, he kissed my forehead and then brushed my lips with his. Kaeson uttered a small groan. I looked over and saw the boy's face go red. Reluctantly, I separated from Ansel, turned and let myself into my chambers.

I surveyed my beautiful accommodations. A frieze painted with shields and symbols of King Tynan and Serislan's famed silk trade surrounded the room near the ceiling. The walls were blue with painted fleur de lis. A small tapestry at the other end of the large chamber caught my eye. I approached and examined it closely. It was a scene of a beautiful red dragon on a beach. Its rider stood before it and held its fangs while she kissed the dragon's nose. My eyes went wide. I gasped. *That's Eshshah and me.*

I stood admiring the beautiful work of art. A door opened to my right and Eulalia stepped out.

"Mistress Amáne!" she cried, "I didn't hear you come in. I was preparing your bath." She rushed to me and nearly crushed me in her embrace. "Do you like the tapestry? Lord Ansel had it commissioned for you, it was just barely completed for your arrival, he drove the poor artists relentlessly to assure it was done on time, quite pleased he was with their skills. He wanted a full report from me on your reaction, I am sorry to have to tell him, I missed your first glance, but I can see you're stunned by it, no need to tear up, but I do understand your emotion, it's truly a fine work, exemplary of the artists here in Serislan. Come let's get you to your bath, will you be joining Lord Ansel afterwards?"

"Yes, I told him I'd meet him in his dining room."

"Very well then, you won't be needing your boy clothing tonight. I'll choose a gown for you."

I rolled my eyes as she pushed me into the bathing room.

With a deep sigh, I sank into the delightfully-hot tub and let my travel-weary body relax.

CHAPTER THIRTEEN

After my bath, Lali helped me into a blue gown from Fiona's creations. I wanted to make sure to tell Fiona that Ansel was quite pleased with it. His eyes lit up the moment I entered the dining hall.

We enjoyed the fare the staff laid out for us — fresh fruit and cheeses in a fabulous display.

Avano joined us later. Although they had nothing to worry about, I think the Healer held him strictly to his chaperone duties.

I could barely keep my eyes open when they escorted me to my chambers hours later. As soon as I closed the door behind me, I dropped into my bed and let sleep take me. However, it was short-lived. My mind filled with confusion and guilt about my plans to make it to Orchila. *Is it the right thing to do? Would Ansel or the Healer be angry with me? How can I guarantee our success?* No answers came to mind. I had to figure out a way to leave Ansel after we had our audience with King Tynan. Hiding anything from him would be difficult. I wish I didn't feel it necessary to keep my plans from him.

The following day, Ansel and I spent most of the early

afternoon riding the grounds while he briefed me on royal etiquette. I was nervous about the audience, but doubly so with my additional intentions. Thankfully, my anxiety about the Valley of Dragons was hidden behind the mission Ansel had arranged. I caught him casting curious glances more than once.

"I'm sorry if asking you to accompany me is putting you through unnecessary stress, Amáne. Maybe I should have put more thought into it before coercing you into this trip."

Ugh, he's blaming himself, when most of my anxiety is of my own doing.

"Ansel, don't worry. It's a necessary part of my training. It will give me an occasion to practice and improve my negotiation skills."

"I'm not sure your negotiation skills need improving. You're already a master of persuasion."

I hoped he didn't catch the strain in my laugh.

Ansel had meetings with the local silk merchants in the afternoon and offered to arrange a diversion for me until he would return early evening. I assured him that was not necessary, as I planned on visiting Eshshah at the outpost. Internally, I sighed my relief when he complied, but only after shooting me a sidelong glance. *Is that suspicion in his eye or simply my guilt?*

The afternoon passed quickly as I pored through all the books in the library regarding Orchila. I danced for joy when I came across what I'd hoped to find. A manuscript in which Leyna had given the location where we could find information about the Valley of Dragons. Her writing filled the margins of the book. I couldn't discuss it with Eshshah at that moment for fear Sovann would become curious.

That evening Ansel and I ate again in his private dining room. My mood was light but distracted as I still reeled over my good fortune of finding Leyna's notes. I'd committed her directions to my memory and would inform Eshshah when I thought it was safe.

I made an effort to listen to Ansel's further discussions regarding Serislan and King Tynan. Information that may prove to my advantage should King Tynan wish to address me. My heart constricted when I caught Ansel's frown. I tried my best to hide my restlessness, but my guess was he knew he didn't have my full attention. Asserting the fact I was overly tired, which was the truth, I excused myself from his company earlier than I cared to. I couldn't take the chance he would ask me what was on my mind.

The night brought turmoil to my dreams — visions of trees flashing past as water raged around me, swirling in a dark vortex. I fought for air as it pulled me under. My hand thrust out of the water, reaching up to the sky. I pleaded with an old gray dragon that flew above. A dark, painted face floated before me, then lunged. I screamed as I bolted up in bed. Hurried footsteps and a knock at the door brought me fully awake.

"Mistress Amáne," a male voice called. I recognized the voice of one of the manor guards. "Are you all right in there?"

"Yes. Yes, I'm fine, thank you." I called through the door. "I must have been dreaming. I'm sorry to have alarmed you."

I fell back into my bedding and sighed as I heard his footsteps retreat.

The night passed agonizingly slow as nightmares continued to invade my rest. Fortunately, I managed to stifle any more outbursts.

Morning found me not very well rested. I gazed into the looking glass and frowned at the redness in my eyes. I splashed water on my face, donned my riding gear and rushed down to the dining room to join Ansel for a bite to eat before we were to leave for King Tynan's castle.

Ansel peered at me over his cup of tea, his eyes troubled.

"Amáne, although I think it's a necessary learning experience for you, I'll release you from your duty of accompanying me to the audience. I heard you had a rough night. I'm truly sorry."

I swallowed hard. Of course word would have gotten back to him. "No, Ansel, it's just my usual dreams. You know that nightmares have always plagued me. Please. I want to go with you. Besides, you probably wouldn't be able to persuade King Tynan by yourself. You'll need my help," I teased, trying to ease his mind.

Should I just give in now and let him know my real reason for my anxiety? No, he wouldn't understand. He was not there when Bern spoke so convincingly of Leyna and her quest. Neither did he hear the Healer's affirmation of the Valley of Dragons. I'll tell him when the time is right. Not now.

Our eyes locked. My heart ached as I noted his unease. I raised myself from my chair across from him and moved to his side of the table. He put his cup down with a smile and a raised an eyebrow. I ran my hands through his long dark hair. My fingers laced behind his neck as I brought my face close and pressed my lips against his. He pulled me to his lap and held me in a tight embrace.

We parted. I smiled as I gazed into his smoldering eyes. The concern that had tightened around them now softened.

CHAPTER FOURTEEN

There's nothing like the thrill of soaring above the fields and forests — watching it speed by below us. The elongated shadows shrank as the sun rose. Our flight was under three hours. This would be the first time the four of us had flown in daylight and landed in a populated area. It was time for people to know that dragons and their riders did exist. We decided to start with the people of Serislan. It was a long way from Castle Teravinea and there was no danger that King Galtero would find out any time soon.

No longer tense — flying eased my nerves and gave me a sense of calm — I began to formulate a plan. Our long flight gave me the opportunity to converse with Eshshah. I revealed my strategy that we would leave Serislan Castle after the audience with the king and head for Orchila.

I felt her reluctance.

"Amáne, as I said, I would follow you anywhere, or in this case bear you anywhere. I'm relieved you planned only a day trip for information, and that you will confide in the Healer and Lord Ansel when we return to Dorsal."

"We'll be in and out of there in less than a day. I promise.

Then I'll share my findings."

The castle appeared ahead and grew in size as we approached. It was a breathtaking sight. Like Castle Teravinea, Serislan Castle was built on the cliffs overlooking the eastern sea. But that was where the similarity ended. The stonework on this fortress showed architectural embellishments and ornamentation that contrasted with the comparatively austere castle of my homeland. The shadows and light danced off the turrets and cone-shaped roofs. King Tynan's wealth echoed from its walls. The silk trade was certainly lucrative.

Ansel's messenger to King Tynan several weeks prior had informed him that dragons would be flying above his kingdom. He had been a close ally of Ansel's father, King Emeric, and was therefore familiar with visits from the king and other dignitaries arriving on dragons. He didn't yet know that it was King Emeric's son flying in, but only that a lord of one of his manors somehow managed a ride on a dragon.

The king recognized this great honor of hosting dragons and their riders. It was apparent that he had declared this a festival day. I noted the colorful flags blowing from the battlements and tents set up in the castle grounds. A large empty field spread before us, obviously prepared for us to land. It had been roped off to keep the people clear of the field. Cheers could be heard as we spiraled downward. Ansel and I locked eyes as our excitement echoed that of the crowd.

"This is how my memories recall the arrival of dragon and rider. As it should be." Eshshah said.

We dismounted as attendants stepped up to us, one eye on us, but a nervous one on Eshshah and Sovann. They saluted us and our dragons. After asking permission, they bestowed extravagant compliments upon Eshshah and Sovann, who acknowledged them with pleased rumbling. The attendants took a hesitant step backwards. I translated that our dragons were pleased with their greetings. The sound of my voice seemed to have taken them by surprise. I guessed they had just figured out I was a female. I kept my amusement to myself. Ansel conducted himself in a most formal manner which I tried my best to emulate.

The king of Serislan, surrounded by his guards, came forward from where he had sat to watch our approach and landing. The people bowed as he passed.

A herald approached, and after a quick word with the attendants, he stepped back. In a formal voice he announced, "King Tynan of Serislan may I present Lord Ansel of Trivingar Manor, rider of Sovann, and Amáne of Teravinea, rider of Eshshah."

The king gave a sharp dragon salute as Ansel bowed and I executed a deep curtsy. When I straightened, I noticed quite a few raised eyebrows. I managed to not roll my eyes, but decided I should at least remove my helmet and let my hair fall. Hopefully, it would avoid any more doubts as to my gender. My error — the removal of my helmet had the opposite effect. It initiated more murmurs throughout the crowd.

The king laughed and eased my embarrassment. "Well, Rider Amáne, I believe my people were unaware that females may be chosen as dragon riders. Although, if I remember my Teravinean studies, you are but the third female rider. Am I correct?"

With another curtsy, "Yes, Your Highness. You are well-versed in our history."

After a nod from Ansel for permission to address our dragons, he said, "Mighty Sovann and beautiful Eshshah, the honor of having your presence at my castle brings back the past when your magnificent kind and your riders were frequent guests of mine. May that time return in full before my life is over. If you care to take a meal, the field to your north is stocked with sheep and cattle at your choosing."

Ansel responded, "Your Highness, our dragons are very pleased with your generous compliment. They hope your desire will become reality. They also thank you for your offer of a meal, but they are not hungry as they just ate before we left Trivingar."

He nodded in acknowledgment, then said, "So, you've doubly surprised me, Lord Ansel. First, you take over my least productive sericulture enterprise at Trivingar Manor, and you work it into the most lucrative silk operation in the land; and then you arrive at my castle as a dragon rider. What other surprises do you have in store for me?"

You have no idea, I thought.

"Thank you, I appreciate your praise, your Highness," was the extent of Ansel's response.

Brilliant how he skirted around that question without even a pause.

With a motion, King Tynan summoned for the horses to be brought. He waited patiently while Ansel and I removed our dragons' saddles. Attendants took them to store in a nearby tent.

The king mounted his horse. I watched Ansel wait until the king was settled before he hoisted himself up. I followed his lead and mounted after Ansel. We were led in a procession through the fairgrounds and to the royal palace. Eshshah and Sovann stayed behind, content to be the center of attention in the field.

Ansel and I were ushered to guest apartments while the king went another direction. He graciously entreated us to get freshened up from our journey, and he will meet us in his council chamber in two hours time. I noted we were followed by two guards. My guess was they were to protect us as well as keep their eye on us.

I found ladies-maids in my chambers ready to do my bidding. Still not accustomed to such a life, I pressed my lips together as they fussed about me. In no time, I found myself soaked, scrubbed, dressed and coiffed.

After perusing the contents of my bags, the ladies decided which gown I was to wear. They slipped on a white long sleeved chemise, then proceeded to lace me into a deep blue silk velvet gown. The sleeves laced tightly up to my elbow and then fell wide and loose up to my shoulders. My hair was braided and pinned up. Satisfied, they had me turn around for them to give me a final inspection. I obliged halfheartedly.

My sword hung in its scabbard on the back of a chair. I wished I could have slipped it on over all the trappings of my gown. That wouldn't be possible. However, my duty remained — Ansel's safety was my responsibility. I ignored the horrified looks of my ladies-in-waiting as I grabbed my dagger and placed it in a special sheath that Fiona had sewn into my gown. They couldn't stifle their cries as I pulled my smaller knives out of my pack and secured them in various places in my loose sleeves and under my skirts. Gown or no gown, I would be armed. Even a small knife could make a difference, I mused, as I thought back to the dagger I used against the sorcerer in the arena of death.

As prepared as I could be, I slipped into the hallway to await Ansel. I found him waiting for me, instead. He leaned against the wall opposite my room. The dark blue color he wore took my breath away. How uncanny, we both wore similar colors. His eyes couldn't mask his pleasure as he discretely took in my appearance. If only we weren't surrounded by attendants and guards, I would have had my arms around his neck immediately. I struggled to recover a cool façade.

To help me back into my role, Ansel addressed me rather formally. “Rider Amáne, that blue gown becomes you. May I say you look well-refreshed.”

“As do you, Lord Ansel,” I managed to choke out.

Chapter Fifteen

The great doors of the council chamber were opened for us. We entered a large room with thick carpeting. Tapestries hung on the walls depicting detailed scenes of Serislan. A massive round table spread before us. The king sat on an ornate high-back chair, his men-at-arms standing at attention behind him. Two advisors sat on either side. To his right, sat two young men. One just a boy, maybe eleven or twelve, the other probably a bit older than I. They had to be brothers or closely related by the similarity in their looks. I stopped and took in a breath. They looked vaguely familiar, but since there was no chance I'd ever met them, I shook off my curiosity.

Ansel bowed, I curtsied deeply as the king gestured for us to take the two chairs across from him. I arranged the extravagant fabric of my gown around me. It was nearly impossible to find a comfortable position. This was more confining than the gown Lali sealed me into for Ansel's eighteenth birthday ball. I didn't know how the aristocratic ladies could get used to such attire. Next time Fiona would have to design a gown in which I could breathe.

My eyes were drawn back to the young men. They both stared

at me with mouths agape. I wondered if maybe the ladies-maids had put something unusual in my hair, or if my gown had failed in some way. I didn't want to draw any attention to myself by checking my clothing, or putting my hand to my hair, so I directed my eyes to a spot on the table in front of me. The heat rose in my face.

In desperate need of Ansel's touch, my foot inched its way to his foot under the table. I wrapped my ankle around his. He shifted in his seat and crossed his other boot over my ankle, but didn't look in my direction. His gesture gave me comfort.

"Welcome once again, Lord Ansel and Rider Amáne," the king began. "I've asked for my nephews to join us. Ryant," he indicated the older boy, "and Ewan," he nodded toward the younger. "It's time they sit in on castle business. The queen and I are not able to produce an heir. Ryant, my sister's eldest, will accede to the throne after me."

The two young men continued to eye me as they gave us the dragon salute.

King Tynan turned to Ansel, "You were vague in your request to speak with me, but I believe it has to do with ..."

Before he could finish his sentence, the younger boy whispered loudly to his brother. The king cleared his throat at the interruption, and scowled at Ewan. Unaffected by his uncle's stern look, the boy left his seat and whispered into the king's ear. They weren't aware of dragon riders' extraordinary hearing.

Without meaning to eavesdrop, I heard, "That's her." The monarch looked at me and then back at Ewan, his eyebrows nearly touching.

"The one on the ship," the boy added.

King Tynan's eyes widened and he turned to me once again. By that time, the heat had risen in my face, I wanted to fan myself, but froze. My heart beat dangerously loud. *What is he talking about?*

Disregarding the conversation he began with Ansel, the king fixed his eyes upon me. I swallowed hard as I tried to meet his gaze. *Have I done something to offend them*?

"Rider Amáne," the king addressed me.

I tried to rise quickly to respond, but my foot was entangled in Ansel's. I lost my balance and knocked my chair over backwards. It fell with a heavy thud on the carpet. I just managed to grab the table as Ansel gripped my arm, preventing me from following my chair to the ground. Ewan giggled. I tried to catch my breath.

"Are you certain about that, boy?" Tynan asked.

Still scowling, the king continued to focus on me as attendants righted my chair. My knuckles turned white from clutching the table.

"What do you know of the slave trade, Rider Amáne?"

"Excuse me, your Excellency?"

"The slave trade. What can you tell me about it?"

"Well, I know that ..." My voice quavered. Then, like a Valaira, it hit me. I turned to the nephews. My mind reeled. I had to concentrate to stay on my feet. "I've met you two," my voice but a whisper. "You were on the slave ship."

The younger boy nodded as his eyes widened. Mine stung. I heard Ansel take a breath, but he didn't interrupt. The nightmare came back — the morning I was abducted from Ansel's manor and put on a ship to be sold as a slave. I had removed that terror to a dark corner of my mind, as I'm sure we all had. But now, here it was, opened up again, with two of my fellow captives sitting before me. I lowered myself back onto my chair. Ansel locked ankles with me again.

Seeing our reactions, the king took control of the situation. "Look now, it's over and done with. This was months ago. Good has come of it. This is not the time to dwell on the evils of the past. With this rider's remarkable skills, you were all saved. That is what we can look to." He threw an approving look at me. I wanted to shrink from the attention.

His business-like assessment at first sparked the heat of anger in me. But then I realized he must have suffered greatly himself. Both of his nephews, heirs to his throne, had been abducted. My anger quelled.

Ryant's gaze was piercing. If I could have crawled under the table, I would have.

"Rider Amáne," Ewan spoke up. "I've written a ballad about you."

"About me?"

"You were brilliant. You were like the wind as you flew out of that cage we were in and gave them all what they deserved — the way you took down all four guards single-handed."

"It wasn't single handed," I said quietly. "I had Eshshah and Gallen, and everyone back at Trivingar manor." I didn't dare look at Ansel. "It was only because of them ..."

"Uncle," Ryant broke in without taking his eyes from me, "may I have a word with you in private?"

King Tynan shot an annoyed look toward Ryant.

"Please excuse us," The monarch said. "You may wait behind that door." He motioned to a door at our right.

I fought every urge to hang on to Ansel's arm as we exited the room.

We found ourselves in a hallway with a few chairs lining the walls. I dropped into one, disappointed that again, we were in the presence of guards. I wouldn't be able to confide in Ansel to get his take on this situation. Ansel chose to remain standing. Our eyes locked and he gave me an encouraging look with a slight shrug of his shoulders. He didn't seem bothered that we still hadn't gotten to the main purpose of this meeting.

Low tones seeped through from the other side of the thick door. I couldn't make out what they said. Moments later, we were summoned back into the council chambers. We took our seats across from King Tynan. My gaze was drawn to Ryant. Again, he didn't take his eyes off of me. My throat caught as I saw his triumphant smile.

The king cleared his throat. "Rider Amáne, who represents you in our country?"

I rose to my feet to address him, this time without mishap. "Excuse me, your Excellency?" *Ugh, I have to think of another response. He's going to think that's all I know how to say.*

"In our country, a young lady travels with attendants or chaperones — someone to speak for them. I assume you did not enter Serislan alone?"

"I came only with Eshshah, my dragon, your Majesty."

Surprise shown on his face. "With whom would I negotiate a betrothal contract for your hand? Your guardian in Dorsal, then?"

"Excuse me ... I mean I beg your pardon, King Tynan. You are asking for my hand in marriage?" I stammered. *What kind of a country is this?*

The king burst out laughing. "No, not me. My queen would throw me from our bed chambers if I even thought such a thing. I would like to offer a contract to your guardian on behalf of my nephew here, Ryant. It seems he is quite stricken with you. It would be a most beneficial arrangement."

My mouth dropped open. The air sucked out of my lungs.

Misunderstanding my shocked silence, he said, "Have you been promised to someone, then?"

My gown became even more confining. I found it hard to breathe. Heat rose up my neck and into my face. *How do I respond to his question*? The heat began to turn to anger. In a controlled voice, I said, "My Lord, the answer to your question is no. I am not *promised* to anyone. With all due respect, your Excellency, I don't have —"

"Amáne!" Ansel leaped to his feet.

I jerked my head in his direction. Whatever seething retort I may have entertained disappeared at the look in his eyes. *Is he just as shocked as I?* Fortunately, I remembered my place and pressed my lips together.

Ansel addressed the king. "Your Majesty, please excuse this rider's manners. She has come a long way and I'm sure she's had quite a shock in meeting up with your nephews. Allow me to answer your questions. Amáne is my responsibility while she is in Serislan. I've promised her guardian I would represent her."

He turned to me, "Rider Amáne, you may be excused while I discuss this matter with King Tynan." He motioned me back toward the door to the hallway from which we had just come.

My best option was to acquiesce. In the not-too-distant past, to have been excused in such a manner would have set my tongue on fire. Instead, I inhaled, turned to the king and said, "My apologies, King Tynan." I curtsied to him, to his nephews and to Ansel.

I exited the chamber once again — my teeth clamped securely. Apparently women played a different role in Serislan than I was used to in Teravinea. Ansel caught on to that before I had.

Back in the hallway where Ansel and I waited only moments ago, I slumped into the same chair as before and stared at the carpet. *What am I doing here*? So far my presence had done nothing for Ansel, but confuse matters more. How long had we been here and still the king had no idea who sat across from him?

Again, I couldn't hear anything understandable coming from the other room.

The door opened and I was motioned back into the council chamber. I took my place in the chair next to Ansel. He was seated again, and kept his eyes forward.

I found the atmosphere around the table noticeably different — uncomfortable. I glanced at Ryant, who did not meet my gaze. Ewan's eyes were lowered, but he had a hint of a smile on his face.

As if the previous conversation regarding my hand in marriage had never come up, the king cleared his throat, and said, "So, young Lord Ansel. Let us at last address the reason for your visit. As I started to say earlier, I can only guess it is about your successful management of my silk operation at Trivingar Manor. You've taken a failing silk farm and made it more prosperous than any other I have in all of Serislan. I suppose you would like to plead for a larger percentage of the profits? Name your percentage and I will be happy to negotiate."

How could the air have changed so quickly? Why did everyone avoid eye contact with me? I knew better than to ask. My stomach tightened, wondering if I would be taking a betrothal contract back to the Healer. The way Ryant avoided me made me think probably not. But the way Ewan behaved gave me doubts. It became obvious that I would not know the outcome of the conversation until I could get it out of Ansel.

Ansel stood. His manner majestic. "King Tynan, my Lord, I thank you, again, for your praise. I am truly honored. In other circumstances that would be a desirable discussion to have with you, but that's not the purpose of our visit. I'm here to properly introduce myself. You were well-acquainted with my father, whom I'm told, held a great admiration for you."

King Tynan's eyebrows raised. Both nephews as well as the king's advisors took notice.

"My father was King Emeric of the Royal House of Drekinn. I am the true heir to the throne of Teravinea."

A silence fell upon the room as the magnitude of Ansel's announcement sunk in.

King Tynan broke the silence. "But the royal family was said to have perished in the explosion and fire. King Emeric, his beautiful Queen Fiala and their infant son, I never learned his name."

"Ansel. They named me Ansel. My Aunt Nara, rider of the late Torin rescued me before the nursery exploded. That was when Torin met his death. Word that I had lived was kept secret by the dragon riders. Nara also lived and became known only as the Healer. It was necessary that Galtero thought us dead."

"You do bare a likeness to King Emeric, but how can I be sure?" asked Tynan.

Ansel pulled a gold chain from beneath his tunic on which hung his father's signet ring. "You may recognize the insignia that my father used to impress upon the wax seals. If you doubt, then I believe within your archives you can find an imprint to match."

An attendant took the ring and brought it to the other side of the table for King Tynan to examine. He spent but a moment looking at it, then handed it back to the attendant.

"Prince Ansel, I loved your father. He was an honest man. A just ruler. It was a blow to me when I heard the news." He shook his head. "This meeting has certainly gone in every direction, has it not?" He motioned for Ansel to take a seat, then put his fist to his heart . "How may I be of service to you?"

My heart nearly burst at what I had just witnessed.

"King Tynan," Ansel said, "I'm here to plead for your assistance in defeating Galtero. We are building our army, but with the addition of your select, we can assure a better chance to take back the throne."

One of the king's advisors stiffened. "Your Majesty, why would we interfere in the problems of another kingdom? Do we not have our own issues with which to contend?"

Without thinking, I leaped to my feet. "Your Grace, allow me to answer that question." Not waiting for his reply, I started, "The horror of Galtero's rule is not just isolated within Teravinea. I have personally heard him declare that he will march into Serislan. Your country is in as much danger as ours."

Ansel emitted a small groan that only I could hear. The king and his aides eyed me in shock. I did it again. I will not get used to being a silent female. No matter, I'd already committed myself. I didn't flinch.

"You would have us believe you spoke with King Galtero?" King Tynan asked.

"He spoke to me. I didn't say a word to him."

"You are an enigma, Rider Amáne. Please enlighten us." He leaned back in his chair and let out a exasperated sigh.

I told my story of how I had gone to the Hatching Ceremony disguised as a male and how I'd obtained a dragon egg to bring back to the Healer. Without detail, I went through my ordeal in the arena with the monster lizards and my subsequent rescue by the black lizard, Charna Yash-churka.

Ewan followed my narrative with rapt attention.

"I'm sure Galtero expected I would not leave the arena alive, when he told me, and I quote, 'There will be a new breed of lizard that will answer only to me. With them, I will bring power to my monarchy. Even the Kingdom of Serislan will fall to me.'"

I finished with a small curtsy, then lowered myself into my chair. I kept my eyes on the gaping mouths before me.

Young Ewan, once again, broke the spell. "Wow, Rider Amáne. I'm going to have to add a few more verses to my ballad."

The air lightened. King Tynan allowed a smile.

"Prince Ansel. I see you have the wisdom of your father. Bringing this rider with you was a shrewd move on your part. I would have granted your request for military aid in honor of your father's memory, but Rider Amáne has put it one step closer. I must grant you aid also for the sake of Serislan." He put his fist to his heart once again.

The meeting went on for a bit longer as they discussed details and other considerations. I couldn't stop my mind from wandering. Besides my uneasiness about the decision regarding my marriage proposal, my upcoming trip to Orchila had me on edge. My heart quickened its pace.

Finally, we took our leave of King Tynan with a promise to meet him in his private dining room for the evening meal.

Chapter Sixteen

Ansel and I made our way toward the guest wing where our chambers were located. Our rooms were next to each other. Two castle guards followed closely, so we refrained from conversation. I noted, by the colors they wore, these two were members of the elite guard. King Tynan must have assigned his best to us when he found out the identity of his esteemed guest.

I sensed Ansel was as anxious to have a word with me as I was with him. Arriving at his door, he said, "Rider Amáne, would you join me in my chambers?"

"My Lord, that would hardly be proper." *What is he thinking?*

He caught his error and shot me a mischievous smirk. I was thankful his back was to the guards. It was all I could do to try to keep my face neutral.

"Of course, my apologies my lady. I just need a word with you."

Ansel turned to the guards. "Please lead us to the gardens and leave us so I can consult with my aide."

"Prince Ansel," the lead guard responded, "my duty is to ensure your safety while a guest at Serislan Castle. I will be happy to show you to the gardens, however, we will not leave your presence. I can assure you your privacy. We will be out of earshot, but will remain in the vicinity."

"Very well, then. Please." Ansel motioned for the man to lead the way.

We walked in silence. My thoughts went again to my predicament. *How am I going to take my leave of Ansel without arousing suspicion? Maybe I should just tell him of my plans. I can't.* He would never let Eshshah and me go on any kind of reconnaissance without going through proper channels. I could see the importance of that if we were actually going the full distance and talking to the Ancient Ones. But Eshshah already talked me out of that plan. Rightfully so. This would be merely a fact-finding mission. No danger. Hardly any time involved. Just a matter of a few hours to find someone familiar with the Valley of Dragons. With that information, we could return at a later date with Ansel. I convinced myself it did not require any kind of discussion or permission from anyone. *But, how do I explain to Ansel that I wouldn't be flying back to Trivingar with him?*

"Amáne? Are you all right?" Ansel asked. I realized he'd been trying to get my attention.

I jolted from my musing, surprised to find we'd arrived at the gardens. The guard was out of sight and hopefully out of hearing. "Uh, I'm sorry. Yes, I'm fine."

"You didn't hear a word I said, did you? Why the worried look?"

I recovered quickly and deflected his question. "Ansel, what did you say to them when you sent me out of the council chamber? I'm assuming I don't have to deliver a marriage contract to the Healer?"

Silence. My head jerked to his eyes. He looked at me with an expression that froze my heart. My eyes went wide. He couldn't hold that look for long before he burst out laughing.

"I would strangle you here and now if those guards weren't around." I growled.

"I'm sorry, Amáne. I couldn't resist. You've been too distracted lately. I wanted to see if you were paying attention."

"You are not sorry."

A wave of guilt began to wash over me. I took a deep breath, and allowed it to pass.

His eyebrows first raised then came together as he eyed me curiously. "Why do I get the feeling you're trying to keep something from me?"

Why did he have to know me so well?

"Ansel, please tell me what went on in that room."

He shrugged. "I told them that not only are you a dragon rider for the Kingdom of Teravinea, but you ride a dragon from the Royal Dragon lineage. By law, you are duty-bound to the Royal Dynasty of Drekinn. You may not leave your duty, nor live outside of Teravinea. If Prince Ryant wished for your hand, he must denounce his crown, hand it to his younger brother and live with you in Teravinea — and play second to your duty to your kingdom."

"That would explain his reluctance to look me in the eye. And from Ewan's posture, it seems he was happy not to have the burden of the crown. How did you know such an obscure law?"

"Well, if it's not a written law, then I would be sure to make it one."

I shook my head. "You were taking quite a gamble. What if he'd agreed?"

"Then, I imagine you would be taking a betrothal contract to the Healer." He smiled.

I tried to work up an angry scowl without success.

"So, what are you hiding from me?" he asked.

His question took me without warning, but at that instant, I came up with a reason to leave in the opposite direction.

"All right, you win. I've been trying to decide how to tell you that I won't be going back to Trivingar with you tomorrow."

He blinked. "You'll be staying with Prince Ryant?"

"No!" I rolled my eyes. "Eshshah and I will leave here to visit Kira. She was the young girl from the slave ship. I promised her I would visit. Now is as good a time as any, since I'm so close. She lives just a short distance by dragonflight, north of here. I'll ask Prince Ryant or Prince Ewan if they can direct me to someone who knows her location."

"Sovann and I can go with you."

"No! ... I mean ... there's no need for you to spend more time away from Trivingar. I may stay up there a couple days. I'm sure there are more pressing things for you to do than go wandering around Serislan. Eshshah and I will be fine. Truly." My heart beat fast. I hoped he couldn't hear it.

*Ugh, I don't know if I can stand the guilt of my deceptio*n.

He eyed me sideways. After a quick sweep of our surrounding to determine where the guards stood, he put an arm around me, drew me in and stole a quick kiss. He pulled back with a soft smile. Concern shown in his eyes. A pain shot through my heart. *Did he doubt my story?* It was the truth — although a large part was left unsaid.

Chapter Seventeen

That evening we met in the king's private dining hall. The delectable fare was served in unlimited amounts and countless varieties. I wore yet another confining gown, designed by Fiona. This one, a deep red. Beautiful, of course, but I would have preferred to see it on someone else. Although I begged my attendants to go lightly on the tugging and tightening, it still prohibited me from enjoying the amount of food I could have consumed if I were in my usual tights and tunic. I cursed the latest fashion once again.

"You are in for an additional treat," King Tynan said. "After our meal, Ewan would like to recite his ballad for you."

Ansel and I both voiced our excitement to hear his poem.

Dinner completed, our plates were cleared and we were invited to large comfortable chairs near the walk-in fireplace. The fire blazed in red-orange heat, which of course made me think of Eshshah. I threw her a loving thought. I felt her hum in return.

At a nod from the king, Ewan rose from his chair and cleared his throat. His posture, straight and a bit stiff, he took a deep breath, and began in a shaky voice.

"The title of my poem is, *A Princess Brave and Bold.*"

Come hear my tale of adventure.
A tale of woe and strife.
A tale of a princess brave and bold,
Who was willing to give her life.

Two brothers born of royalty,
Boredom birthed their plan.
Disguised, they slipped from castle guards.
Into the city they ran.

Ignorant of the danger
Their plan had put them in,
They laughed when they found themselves
In an alley they'd never been.

An evil man approached them
A whip, his vicious art.
He bound them hand and foot with chains
And threw them in a cart.

Women and children chained like them
Partners to share their plight.
To a waiting ship they all were hauled
In the darkness of the night.

The ship did leave the dock at once
Human cargo filled its hold.
One more stop to load their prize,
A princess brave and bold.

Slumped over his broad shoulder
A burly mate did lug her.
Down the ladder the princess was hauled
To be locked in chains with the others.

A few hours under sail
The princess finally awoke
"Eshshah!" She screamed at the top of her lungs
The younger boy's heart nearly broke.

The princess revealed her warrior side
When the whip-man entered the hold
She stayed his arm from harming a girl
That princess brave and bold.

The young royal watching braced himself
To witness her demise.
Purple with anger, the man raised his fist
The glint of death in his eyes.

She stood there, defiant
She feared not a wee.
Before he could strike, an order was given
To hold and leave her be.

Docked at the final port
The slaves' fate did unfurl
The princess herself did brave the whip
To protect the same young girl.

Locked in a cart surrounded by guards
A cart more like a cage.
With a jolt it set out toward their next destination
It was the princess' time to engage.

She leaped from the cart
To make her brave stand.
As if by magic, when she reached in the air
A spear flew into her hand.

As lightning she struck
The guards were dispatched.
Withdrawing a key that hung from her neck
The shackles she deftly unlatched.

Like a specter she vanished
Her name never told.
Her fellow prisoners forever indebted
To that princess brave and bold.

The younger boy prince
Learned the hero's fair name
Amáne, with Eshshah, her dragon of fire
Their quests will be widely acclaimed.

So ends my tale of adventure
I beg you do not recoil.
I know this tale to be true, my friends,
As I was that young boy royal.

His recitation ended. Ewan locked eyes with me, smiled and settled back into his seat. *Truly, he is a charming boy.*

A silence filled the room. Somewhere in the middle of the poem, Ansel had handed me his handkerchief. There wasn't a dry corner left.

When I found my voice, I addressed the young boy. "Prince Ewan, you delivered your poem beautifully. The ballad was impressive and I'm truly honored. Thank you." Then in a low voice, I entreated, "Maybe now that you know me, you can change the part about me being a princess?"

"Oh, but Rider Amáne, you are a princess in my eyes. I think you'll be a great leader, perhaps queen. But not with my brother." His gaze went from me to Ansel. His knowing look gave me a chill. My eyes held Ewan's for a brief moment. *There is something special about this young prince.*

"Ha. The fancies of young boys," King Tynan dismissed Ewan's statement with a wave of his hand.

Then he turned to his nephew and with obvious pride said, "Bravo, Ewan. Very nice job. I want you to give a copy to the court musicians. They will put it to a tune. I expect it to be quite a popular ballad around Serislan."

A ballad about me spreading through Serislan seemed overwhelming. Suddenly, I found myself tired beyond reason. I couldn't stifle my yawn which was caught by the king.

"Well, I see that our guest has reached the end of her day. I wish you both a pleasant repose. I will see you off at morning light." He bowed his head at Ansel. We took that as our dismissal and rose from our seats, bidding good night to our hosts.

Ansel and I walked to our rooms, moving through the halls in silence. The elite guards shadowed us unobtrusively.

Ansel opened my door for me. "Good night my lady. Pleasant dreams."

I turned to him with a nod. "Thank you my Lord. Likewise."

Chapter Eighteen

We got off to a later start than I would have liked. King Tynan summoned us to break our fast with him. Not planning on dining with the royal family, I had already donned my riding gear. Tights and a tunic over a white shirt. My dragonscale breastplate under the tunic and my sword slung at my side.

I was uncertain how the king would react to my attire. I had no desire to confine myself in another gown. I'd had enough of those for a while.

Ansel waited for me outside my door. Before he could say anything about my choice of dress I said, "I'm sorry my Lord. I was dressed for flight before I received the summons. If it's all the same to you, I'll dine like this. Do you think it's disrespectful?"

"You're a dragon rider. It's only natural that you dress like one when you are about to take flight. The king should have the same expectations."

I smiled, grateful at how he always made me feel comfortable, even when I felt so out of place. I couldn't wait to leave the castle so we could drop our formal ways. *I imagine I'll have to get used to our public demeanor.*

Together with our shadow-like guards, we made our way to the king's dining hall.

We entered, and Ansel bowed to King Tynan and his nephews. The younger prince looked quite tired from our late night.

I didn't know if I should curtsy or bow. I decided a curtsy was more proper for this king. We moved to our seats at the king's gesture. Ryant and Ewan hadn't ever seen me in my riding clothes. The older prince recovered more quickly. Ewan stared with eyes wide open until Ryant elbowed him to mind his manners. I shot Ewan a quick smile. I was used to being stared at in my male clothing. Those stares were, by far, more preferable than the attention I received when in a fancy gown.

Before our meal was over, an attendant handed me a folded piece of parchment with the information I needed to get to Kira's home. She lived in Kep, a two-day ride on horseback north of Serislan Castle, less than a two-hour flight by dragon.

After our meal, the king and his nephews accompanied us to where Eshshah and Sovann waited, surrounded by onlookers, including what seemed to be most of the city's children. Eshshah had a special place in her heart for the little innocent ones.

Our saddles had been brought out and waited on stands in the field. Three horse saddles would fit in the space where one of Eshshah's sat. Ansel and I saddled up our dragons under the close watch of all whom had gathered for our departure.

King Tynan directed a series of compliments at our magnificent dragons, who nodded in thanks. He then saluted us, which we graciously acknowledged. We bid our farewells and mounted up. With one last nod to our hosts, Eshshah and Sovann launched into the air. I heard a collective exclamation from the people below.

"Amáne," Eshshah said, "Lord Ansel wants us to follow them until we get outside of the city. He and Sovann don't want us to turn north just yet. We'll find a deserted area where we can land."

I was excited that I could at last have a few minutes with Ansel without the watchful eye of the guards, yet nervous that he might question me about my plans to see Kira.

After a short flight, Ansel motioned us to an empty field. As soon as Eshshah alighted, I unbuckled and slid off. Ansel and I, relieved that we no longer had to hide our relationship, fell into each other's arms.

He kissed me warmly, then said, "Thank you for coming with me. I was right in asking you. I don't think King Tynan would have been so willing to lend his aid if you weren't there."

"I'm sure you would have done fine without me, but I'm happy I was able to help. What an uncanny turn of events."

"That, it was. The king's nephews seemed to recognize you right away."

"I know." I shook my head at how unlikely I would chance upon those two who had suffered the same fate as I.

I gazed up at Ansel. "Thank you for saving me from a betrothal contract." I shuddered. "I'm not sure even the Healer could have gotten me out of that."

"It was strictly selfishness on my part." He kissed my forehead and then my lips in a way that allowed no doubt — he wasn't about to share me.

"Are you sure you and Eshshah want to turn north? I hoped you could spend a couple more days in Trivingar. I thought I'd introduce you to hawking. We have a quite well-known falconer in Trivingar."

I wasn't sure how much more I could take under his scrutiny. Keeping him out of my plans was the hardest thing I'd ever done. *Should I just tell him and suffer the foreseeable rejection of my plan?*

I took a breath and decided I would stick with my objective. "It would be silly of me not to take advantage of the proximity to Kep. As for hawking, I'd truly love to take part, but it'll have to be at another time."

"So, you don't want Sovann and me to go with you?"

My stomach lurched. I hoped he didn't catch any change in my expression. *If he only knew how much I want to spend more time with him.*

"Ansel, it's not that I don't want you to go with us. You have more important duties to tend to than to go traipsing off to visit a young girl you've never met. I promised her I'd go, and so I must. I'm sure the Healer and the rest of the dragon riders are anxious to hear the results of our audience with King Tynan. You can't keep them waiting."

My mouth went dry.

His eyes narrowed as he gazed into mine. A shadow of sadness or disappointment showed briefly. My heart beat faster.

"Be careful Amáne," he said in a low voice.

Can he tell I'm hiding something from him?

"Please contact me the moment you get to a communication device," he said.

"I will. We'll only be gone a couple days. I'll contact you no later than three days time. I promise." Even though that was the truth, it was still difficult for me to look Ansel in the eye.

He opened his mouth as if to say something, but appeared to change his mind. Instead, he pulled me close and kissed me with an urgency, an almost desperation I couldn't ignore.

Before I broke down in front of him, I stepped back and attempted my most reassuring smile. “Don’t worry, we’ll be fine, Ansel. I’ll talk to you in three days. I love you.”

I turned and headed toward Eshshah willing my knees to not buckle under me.

Chapter Nineteen

Eshshah and I flew for a few long minutes before I finally let out a large sigh.

"Amáne, why do I get the feeling that I should have tried to talk you out of this mission of yours?"

"You did talk me out of my original plan, remember? I wanted to find the Ancient Ones myself and plead for them to join in our cause. You convinced me to lessen my goal, so we could return with Ansel and Sovann."

"I'm not sure if even your modified plan would be smiled upon by the riders, let alone the Healer or Lord Ansel."

I could feel her distress. "Eshshah, thank you for yielding to my wishes. Truly, you won't be sorry. Just think of our advantage when we have other dragons to help us win the throne. Galtero won't stand a chance."

"You're assuming Lord Ansel will have success convincing the Ancient Ones. I wonder if they care at all about humans and their problems."

I chewed my lower lip. "We can hope, Eshshah."

"True."

"We'll just stay the day, then be out of there by tomorrow evening. If you're up for it, we can fly all the way back home, or stop to rest somewhere along the way. That'll be up to you."

"The sooner we're home, the better I'll feel."

I felt guilty about dragging Eshshah into my plan, but it was a good one. Sure to succeed. I had no doubts.

In no time I spotted the small township of Kep. Eshshah and I decided she should not make herself known, but wait for me on the outskirts. We found a secluded field near a stream. Eshshah assured me she would be comfortable there.

"After my visit with Kira, I'll join you back here for the night. That way we can get an early start tomorrow to Orchila."

I said farewell and headed toward town.

It wasn't a long walk before I found myself at Kep's town center. Quite a few heads turned as I strode by — an obvious stranger in their midst.

"Who you lookin' for, young man?" was the question that prevailed. I didn't bother to correct them, but asked them to direct me to Kira's. That raised eyebrows. I could only imagine their assumptions that a "young man," a stranger, sought Kira. I hoped I didn't cause too much trouble for her and her mother.

At last I found her establishment. Kira's mother was a seamstress. They lived above her shop. A bell on the door jingled as I entered. Kira sat at a table, lost in concentration, stitching a hem on an extravagant gown.

She looked up and stared at me, hesitating for a brief moment before asking, "What can I do for you kind sir?"

I removed my helmet and smiled at her. Her eyes opened wide in surprise. She jumped to her feet and hurried toward me.

"Amáne!" she exclaimed, nearly knocking me to the ground

as she threw her arms around me.

Her mother rushed out from the back room, clearly alarmed. When she saw Kira was safe, she relaxed.

"Mama! Look, this is Amáne. The princess who saved us. She's here. She's here."

Tears came to her mother's eyes as she curtsied to me.

"Please don't. I'm not a princess. I am a commoner, from the far-away city of Dorsal in Teravinea."

I spent an enjoyable afternoon with Kira and her mother. It more than satisfied my concerns about her well being. She was delighted when I revealed I was a dragon rider.

That evening, I bid farewell to them. Kira insisted on accompanying me to where Eshshah waited. She showed no fear as she approached my dragon. I taught her the salute, and the proper way to address a dragon.

Kira faced Eshshah and said, "Eshshah, beautiful dragon on fire, my life will be cold until I meet you again."

Eshshah nodded in appreciation of her compliment. Both she and I in awe of the beautiful tribute Kira offered.

Kira wanted to linger, but I insisted she head back home before it got dark. We said our teary good-byes.

Chapter Twenty

The Valley of Dragons and our search for its location loomed before us. My excitement fought with my anxiety and guilt.

"Ansel will understand, won't he, Eshshah?"

Eshshah tilted her head, her version of a shrug, but didn't offer any opinion. I spent a restless night in the field with Eshshah.

The next morning we were up before the sun and soared on the wind currents heading north. We caught sight of the wild coastline of Serislan. I took in a deep breath at the imposing view as we flew low, just above the waves crashing on the rocky shore.

Another hour passed. We'd risen to a higher altitude over the ocean between Serislan and Orchila.

"I see the island, Amáne," Eshshah conveyed.

Her sight was far superior to mine, even with my enhanced vision. A few moments later, I spotted it.

If I thought the coastline of Serislan was striking, the island before us surpassed our wildest imaginings. A jewel to behold — a bright green emerald floating in a sea of turquoise. Strips of white sand beaches outlined the gem.

As we approached, I could make out palms reaching their

fronds to the sky. Not like our stubby grey-green palms in Dorsal, but kingly giants of verdant green. They covered the island for as far as I could see.

The town we sought appeared cut out of the jungle on the southwest side — a couple of ships docked in its small harbor. Eshshah and I wouldn't fly directly into it, but skirted more to the west until we found a suitable beach on which to land. We alighted on a small strand of coarse sand. The blue-green waves rolled in sets on the shore.

The heat and humidity suddenly hit me, like walking into a steaming bathing room. The air was stifling — a sensation I had never felt.

I dismounted and immediately stripped off my riding cape and my helmet, the sweat already dripping down my back. I was dressed for much cooler weather. My attire wouldn't do in this tropical climate. I was glad we were only here for the day. When we return with Ansel, I'll make it a point to bring the proper clothing.

I removed my dragon-scale breastplate and my outer tunic, then cinched my sword belt over my white shirt. Not certain how hospitable the town would prove to be, I decided to put on a more male appearance. It was too muggy to put my helmet back on, so I pulled my hair back and tied it with a leather thong at the base of my neck, the way Ansel sometimes wore his. It wasn't my best male impersonation, but would have to do for now.

My extra clothing, I stuffed into the satchels that were secured on the saddle. I debated whether to remove Eshshah's saddle to give her some relief while I went into the township. We both decided we should not let down our guard — she would remain saddled. I was disappointed she wouldn't be able to enjoy the water or do any fishing. She assured me she was satisfied to just lie on the beach and soak in the sun. If she felt like it, she could find shade at the edge of the jungle that pressed down toward the shore.

"Well, I guess I'm as ready as I'll ever be, Eshshah. Wish me luck. It looks like there's a pathway through the jungle that I hope will lead me into town."

"All I can say, Amáne, is please be careful. Keep your eyes open. We know nothing of this place. Just gather the information we need and come back quickly. It is beautiful here and I wouldn't mind returning with Sovann, but there is a dangerous feeling to it. Stay alert."

Her tone sent a slight shiver through me, but I shook it off and headed toward the settlement.

Chapter Twenty-One

After a half-hour walk, the jungle opened up to reveal the harbor we had spotted from the air. It was alive with activity as men unloaded the cargo-laden ships. No one paid me any mind as I walked past, heading toward the collection of buildings the same color as the jungle from which they appeared to grow.

I came upon a quaint little village. The style of which I was not familiar. The roofs were thatched with palm fronds, and the predominant building material was bamboo. I had read about that exotic plant, but had never seen it. It was, in reality a giant woody grass, but very sturdy. I'll have to remember to add a sketch and information to the journal that Leyna had begun.

I certainly turned heads — I wore more clothing than anyone in the village. Most villagers I saw were men who lounged on the porches of their establishments. They did not wear shirts, just white baggy trousers and sandals. Some wore light vests, unfastened and showing most of their chests. To my shock, I noted some men that didn't even wear trousers. They were as dark as Dorjan and had only a narrow strip of cloth — only enough to hide their private parts. Their brown muscular bodies glistened in the heat. I turned red and averted my eyes when those men strode by. They, however, didn't hide their curiosity at the stranger in town.

I passed only three women. Two walked together, dressed in white loose-fitting shirts and long light-colored skirts. They eyed me suspiciously. The third woman had on what looked like one piece of colorful cloth wrapped around her and tied above her breasts. No sleeves, no shoes. Her hair hung long and black down her back. Even though Leyna described the populace, truly, I didn't come prepared for such an unfamiliar culture.

According to Leyna's writings, there was a pub on the main path called Tavern of the Ancient Ones. The information I sought would be found there, keeping in mind Leyna wrote her journals many many years ago. She had left Teravinea before the Healer linked with Torin. Whether that tavern even still existed, or someone knowledgeable still lived, would be up to me to find out.

To my surprise, I came across the sign for the tavern after I had wandered about half way through the village. It had a carving of several dragons in flight and the words, Tavern of the Ancient Ones in a circle around them. The sign looked old and weathered compared to the relatively newer look of the building. The roof was thatched in palm fronds, like the rest of the village. Its front-facing side had only a half wall, from the ground up. Above that, the tavern opened out to the street. Even with the open front, it somehow remained dark inside.

The moment I entered, I wanted to turn and run back out. The stench of sweat and liquor mixed with smoke overwhelmed me. The noise was nearly deafening. The clientele were predominantly male. I cringed as I noted all eyes were on me. Drawing in a jagged breath, I pulled myself to my full height. It would not have impressed anyone, but it gave me confidence.

The best place I thought to start was with the barkeep. The man looked like he had put on a scowl at a young age and the scowl had stuck to his face. He stood behind the bamboo counter wiping a dirty tankard with a dirty rag.

"Good morning sir," I said, making sure my voice was low enough to sound at least like an adolescent boy.

He shot me a quick glance but returned to his work.

After a moment, I cleared my throat.

Again his eyes darted in my direction but his task drew them back.

"Excuse me, sir. I'm looking for information on someone who knows the location of the Valley of Dragons."

His dirty rag stopped mid swipe, but he didn't look up.

"Who wants to know?"

What kind of question is that? I'm standing before him having just asked. Who else would it be that wants to know?

I made sure my expression remained flat. "I would like to know, sir."

I would never have thought it possible, but his eyebrows came even closer together.

"Are you daft, boy? Do you have a name?"

"... er ... yes, it's Vann."

"That's it? Just Vann? No family name? No place of origin?"

"Vann of Anbon, sir. Anbon, in Teravinea."

He abandoned his activity and gave me a piercing stare.

"Teravinea? You're a long way from home. How did you get here?"

"I came across the water from Serislan." I hoped he assumed I meant by ship. "I need a name of someone who knows the Valley of Dragons."

"Teravinea?" he repeated in a booming voice, ignoring my request. Silence settled over the tavern. All eyes were back on me.

The barkeep changed his attitude and became almost friendly, if that were possible.

"It's been ages since anyone from those parts came in here. My grandpap told me about a Teravinean woman. A dragon rider."

My heart stopped. *Leyna,* I thought to myself.

He gestured toward an even darker corner of the tavern. "That man across the room. You might want a word with him."

"Thank you, sir."

He gave a barely perceptible nod. I could feel his eyes on me as I made my way through the boisterous room to the table he indicated. I wondered if I didn't have my dragon rider eyesight, would I have even been able to see the man who slumped at the table?

"Excuse me, sir. May I ask you a question?"

"You just did. The answer's no. Now leave me be."

Frustrated, I turned to my dragon in thought transference. "Eshshah, Orchila is getting more infuriating every minute I spend here. I can't wait to get my conversation over with this man so you and I can go home. Hopefully, Ansel will find better treatment than they've shown me."

Eshshah grunted her agreement.

Ignoring the man's rudeness, I said, "The barkeep thought that you would be able to help me. I need to know the location of the Valley of Dragons."

His head jerked up. With one eye squinting, he gave me a black look. I stood my ground and glared back, then pulled over a nearby chair and slid into it.

He relaxed his stare and gestured to the barkeep as if I had passed some sort of test. A woman brought two short pieces of bamboo and set them upright on the table. Then I realized the bamboo pieces were, in fact, small drinking vessels filled with a dark liquid.

The man pushed one over to me and lifted the other in a toast. "Drink."

I eyed the liquid and shook my head. "No thanks."

"It'll make a man outta ya. Put hair on your chest. Drink."

"What is it?"

"It's called dragon fire."

I pressed my lips together and didn't move.

"Ya want information? That what ya came fer?" He lifted the bamboo vessel, tossed the drink down his throat, and gave me his one-eyed stare. Again, he gestured toward the drink on my side.

I had no choice. Picking up the bamboo, I matched his action. The instant the liquid hit the back of my throat, I understood its name. I inhaled at the shock of the burning liquor. Big mistake. Inhaling magnified the burn. It threw me into a fit of coughing. My eyes watered. But I didn't miss the smirk on the man's face.

When I could breathe again, I glared daggers at him. "I need ... I need the location ... of the Valley of Dragons," I said in a raspy voice between coughs.

"Didn't make a man outta ya, did it?"

I didn't respond.

His hand clamped on my wrist. I jolted, but didn't make any effort to remove it from where he had it pinned to the table. I had to see what he'd do next. Mentally, I switched into fight mode.

"That's 'cuz you're not one. Isn't that right, boy?" he spat.

My eyes narrowed but never left his. I calculated my next move should I have to defend myself. I took note of my escape route.

He reached over and ran his rough dirty hand along my jaw. Leering, he said, "Truth bein', you ain't even a boy."

My heart beat fast. In the next breath, I flipped my wrist and seized his hand that had pinned mine. I grabbed the thumb of his other hand and twisted it back, slamming it to the table. Holding both of his hands firmly, I moved in close and said between gritted teeth, "Don't touch me again."

Releasing him, I leaped to my feet. My chair crashed backwards. I backed away with one hand on the hilt of my sword — fully aware of the eyes on me.

The man's face cracked into a smile. While I looked on in shock, he burst out laughing. He threw both hands up in a surrender, "Ya bested me, madam. I concede. Ya beat ol' Pratt."

He motioned with his hand. "Take yer chair back."

I remained standing. "Do you know how to get to the Ancient Ones?"

"What's yer hurry? Sit down and have another dragon fire." He signaled to the barkeep.

"I'm not having another." My throat still burned. My head felt light.

Pratt laughed.

I spun around and headed toward the exit.

"Hold on a minute. I know who can give ya what ya want."

Turning back to him, "I thought *you* knew where the Valley was."

"I know someone who can take ya there."

"I don't need to go there, yet. I just need to know it exists, and that there's someone who could take me."

"It does exist. He's been there. He can show you a map."

"Then take me to him."

"Come back in two hours and I'll acquaint ya."

Two hours! I don't want to stay in this place another minute. "Eshshah," I said in thought transference, "should we stay?"

"You have enough information. We know we're in the right

place. We can come back with Lord Ansel and Sovann. He would most likely fare better than you."

"I'm sure he would, but we've come all this way. Two more hours for a map might make it worthwhile."

"Suit yourself, Amáne, but the sooner we leave here, the better. This is not a friendly place. It doesn't feel right."

"I know. I feel it too. I'll get the map, then we'll leave immediately. I promise."

CHAPTER TWENTY-TWO

I decided to spend the wait with Eshshah back on the beach where we first landed. On my way out of the village I'd stopped at a shop to buy something more suitable to wear in this sweltering heat. The proprietor eyed me curiously as I bought a pair of light baggy leggings and a gauzy shirt. I found a pair of sandals that fit, so I bought those, too.

Eshshah had a chance to fish and enjoy the water. Relieved of her saddle for a bit she took full advantage of the bounty in the turquoise sea. Meanwhile, I repacked the saddle bags, adding my tights and tunic to my dragon scale boots, breastplate and helmet that I'd packed earlier. I decided to leave my sword, my dagger and my glaive in their places on the saddle. The only weapons I would take were two small knives that tucked into the sash at my waist.

Eshshah, well sated, joined me back on the beach. I re-saddled her, then grabbed her fangs, pulled her close and kissed her.

"Please be careful, Amáne. I'll follow you in thought transference. If you need me, I'll be there in a matter of minutes."

"I'll be careful, Eshshah. Thank you, but you don't have to worry. Nothing's going to happen. I'll meet Pratt and the man with the map at the tavern; give them some coins for their trouble and be back here in no time. I can't wait to see Gallen's face when we prove the Valley exists."

I turned for the trail that led back to the village. After a brisk walk, I arrived at the village in less time than I had on the first trip.

When I made my way to the Tavern of the Ancient ones, I saw that Pratt waited in front. A raised eyebrow and nod of his head was his only form of greeting. As I came closer, he gave me his one-eyed stare. I suppressed a shudder as he looked me up and down. I was glad I'd decided on leggings and not the wrapped dress the women here wore.

I stopped at a safe distance from him. "Where's this man I'm to meet?"

"This way," he grunted and took off at a fast walk toward the far end of the settlement.

This was not what I expected. I had second thoughts about following him, but decided a little further would be fine. We were still in the village, and Eshshah was only a short distance away. I had to practically run to catch up.

We passed the last building, but he kept going. The street narrowed until we reached the end of the cleared area. The edge of the jungle loomed ahead. It rose like a wall above us. My senses sharpened. I stopped. He stepped onto a small path. I didn't follow.

Pratt turned when he realized I wasn't behind him.

"You want yer map or not?" He sounded rougher than he had in the tavern.

"Where are we going?"

"A wee bit further. His shack is just a few paces down this path. Ya comin' or ya turned scared all of the sudden?"

I hesitated, so close to getting what I came for.

"Aw, yer just a spineless little girl after all. I knew you wasn't as tough as you pretended to be."

I glared at him. *How dare he call me a spineless little girl?* With Eshshah's venom running in my veins and the fact I could call upon her strength, I had no fear of this crooked little man.

"I just don't trust you, Pratt."

Pride got the better of me. "Eshshah, I'm going to follow him. If I don't see the shack soon, I'll turn around and head back."

Eshshah wavered. I could feel her reluctance. "If you must, Amáne. I'm with you."

I stepped onto the path, no wider than an animal trail. It certainly didn't see any amount of use. My hand poised near my knives, I followed at a safe distance behind Pratt. He turned around to eye me more than once. I'd give him a bit more time, then I'll end this trek.

We traveled a few paces more — the jungle closed in around us. The sun barely reached the ground. One minute the forest echoed noisily of insects, birds and other animal calls that weren't familiar to me. The next minute, complete silence. I stiffened, ready to draw a knife.

"Eshshah, I'm coming back. I don't have a good feeling about this."

Before I had the chance to turn around, two large men stepped out from behind the trees in front of Pratt, spears crossed. They were dressed like the men I'd seen in the village. Naked, except for a strip of cloth that barely covered them — their dark bodies a sharp contrast to the large green leaves behind them. I drew my blades, surprised Pratt didn't make any effort to defend us. Instead, he calmly stepped off the trail, allowing them a direct path toward me.

Another native emerged from behind a large plant to my right.

I spun on him and lunged. He blocked my thrust, but not before I drew blood as my blade raked his arm. I advanced, keeping my eye on the first two savages. *Why don't they make a move to help their companion?*

As I completed that thought a sharp sting on the back of my neck made me cry out in pain. I dropped one of my knives and reached for my neck. Fear chilled my spine when I felt what had caused the sting. I yanked out a miniature arrow, no longer than my finger. A pointed sliver of wood with feather fletchings on the end.

A sharp glance at Pratt showed a malicious smile on his ugly face. My jaw tightened, then my shoulders. My other knife dropped as my hand constricted, no longer able to hold it. The sickening realization dawned that the dart contained poison. A hot burn traveled down my body, paralyzing as it flowed.

"Eshshah," I cried in thought transference.

"I'm coming, Amáne."

"It would do no good. You can't get to me. The jungle is too dense. I didn't know trees could grow so close. You won't be able to fly in." I felt her distress. "I'm sorry, Eshshah, I should have listened to you."

She poured her strength into me. It was a great comfort, but it didn't stop the spread of the poison. Even with Eshshah's help, the effects of the foreign substance could not be reversed.

There was no pain. Only the terrifying claustrophobic feeling of being helplessly incapacitated. My vision became hazy, but not completely extinguished. The paralysis reached my legs and I toppled over on my side.

I watched as several more men came out from behind the trees. They spoke to Pratt in a language I couldn't understand.

One native handed the traitor a small cloth bag. He took it, hefted it to feel the weight, then turned back on the trail in the direction of town. As he passed me, he said, "These men will show you to the Valley, just like I promised. Give the ancient ones my regards." His wicked laughter echoed back as he retreated.

There were six or maybe seven natives. I watched, powerless, as they closed in on me. They circled — their spears at the ready. I summoned all of my willpower and strength to try to get to my feet. Even with Eshshah's help my muscles wouldn't obey. I couldn't use my voice. Thankfully I could still breathe.

One man had a long thick bamboo pole that he laid down behind me, against my back. Two others crossed my arms over my chest and wrapped a fibrous rope around me, securing the pole to my back. They bent my knees, and placing the bamboo between my ankles they tied them securely. Two of the natives grabbed the ends of the pole and lifted me. I was carried like a trussed pig as I watched the ground pass beneath me. The rope around my chest made breathing difficult. The pole between my ankles rubbed painfully on my bones.

We traveled like this for an interminable amount of time. The effects of the poison began to wear off, but I was tied so firmly, it was useless to struggle. I did, however get my voice.

"Let me go! Why are you doing this? Where are you taking me?"

They answered by jerking the pole roughly, causing me to grunt in pain. I remained silent for the rest of the trip as we wended our way deeper into the jungle. The light sifting down through the impenetrable canopy of trees came through as an eerie green cast.

Eshshah followed our movement, soaring high above the forest.

"Amáne, the jungle seems to go on forever. I see no clearing anywhere. Every once in a while, I catch a glimpse of water. It appears you are traveling alongside of a river. But, the trees are too close to its banks and hang over the water. I can't get close."

"Just your nearness is a comfort, Eshshah. If we ever get out of this, promise me you will whip me with your tail the next time I decide to go against your better judgment."

Chapter Twenty-three

At last we arrived at what appeared to be a small settlement built between the trees. The savages lowered their burden, not too gently. My lungs emptied when I hit the ground. It was impossible to take a deep breath because of the ropes that bound my chest. I lay helpless — my back to the main activities. I tried to roll over so I could see what was happening. A sharp kick to my ribs discouraged my efforts. All I could do was listen to their indecipherable discussion as it became more energetic. I had no doubt the conversation involved me.

The exchange ended abruptly. A native stood above me with a long knife. I braced myself for the blow, but instead he cut the ropes that secured me to the bamboo pole. Gathering my strength, I made an attempt to leap to my feet and assume a defensive stance. The effects of the poison, as well as my method of transport left me weak. I toppled over before I could find my feet. I landed in a sitting position. The natives laughed.

Surrounded by warriors, and with my debilitating condition, I decided I wouldn't be fighting my way free any time soon. My best option was to try to remain calm until Eshshah and I could figure something out. I could see there was nowhere for her to land — no way for her to enter the close-packed forest to reach me.

Several bamboo huts rested high up on stilts, their roofs thatched in palm fronds. The structures looked like they were woven in with the tree trunks, blending in above the forest floor, maybe about the height of one-and-a-half men. A notched log leaned from the ground to the entry of each hut. I watched as a small man descended from one of the lodgings. His angry words filled the air as he rushed down the pole. The natives around me tensed up. The man, though gray and thin, was obviously their leader. Around his neck he wore countless strands of beads, animal teeth, bones and coins. So thick was the ornamentation, it looked like a breastplate.

Berating all those that stood around me, he shoved them out of his way. They moved quickly to avoid his wrath. The chieftain, as I assumed him to be, studied me with great interest. He shouted to someone over his shoulder. From behind the onlookers a young girl emerged, maybe about my age, or a bit older.

The chieftain's voice became more subdued as she approached. She walked confidently toward me. Her dark long hair hid her partial nudeness. Almost all of the females wore nothing above their waists. They were covered only with their hair and multiple strands of beads. Most were dressed in grass skirts, but some were wrapped in colorful fabric, similar to what I saw in the town of Orchila.

The chief spoke to the girl, who turned to me and in a thick accent said, "I am Lia'ina. Our Chief Father say to you, welcome."

I huffed. The irony of the situation was nearly laughable. They had kidnapped me and carried me like an animal to their encampment, yet they welcomed me?

"What do you want with me?"

"You will know soon. You are called?" she asked.

I remained silent, but then decided I would probably do better if I cooperated.

"Amáne."

The Chief Father barked orders at the men who had brought me here. I cringed as two of them reached for me.

I felt Eshshah's strength flow into me and at last overcome the effects of the poison dart. "Thank you, Eshshah," I said in thought transference.

"I'm with you, Amáne."

As the men touched my arms to help me up, I swatted them away and sprang to my feet. My eyes shot daggers at the two. I felt a small bit of satisfaction at their hesitation. One man actually jumped back — the same one I had slashed with my knife. For some reason, their leader found humor in this and issued what sounded like a string of mocking words at his men.

"He say you brave warrior. It show in your eyes. They are weak women before you," Lia'ina said.

Resentment reflected in the face of the one who had stepped back.

"So sorry, but because you warrior, cannot remain free. With respect, you must be roped ... uh ..." She pantomimed being tied up.

Until I figured out what their intentions were, I thought it best not to resist. There were far too many of them, and only one of me. Under the old man's scrutiny, they tied my wrists and hobbled my ankles. I was thankful they allowed my hands in front of me.

They led me to a stump off to the side and motioned for me to sit. The clan bustled about as if preparing for a feast. I could feel the excitement that ran through the entire camp. It grated my nerves the way they looked at me.

Maybe a couple of hours passed as I sat on that stump. I noted every member of the tribe, including the children, had a job to do in putting together the meal.

Someone started beating a rhythm on a log. He was joined by a drum and then by sticks banged together, increasing to an urgent tempo. Women began to dance with bells on their ankles, and the mood quickly became festive. The aroma of whatever they were roasting was enticing. I relaxed a bit as I decided it wouldn't be me being be put to the spit. At least not yet.

The music subsided and a large leaf, stacked with food, was placed on my lap. It included the roasted meat. Next to the meat, they added a serving of mush, possibly some kind of grain. Another dark pile of unidentifiable fare lay on my leaf plate. I saw insect-like legs intermingled in the unknown serving and decided I would not be sampling that portion. The flavorful smells rising from my meal reminded me I had not eaten in a long time. My stomach growled.

The natives surrounded me, with an air of expectation. They hadn't served themselves, but leaned in toward me.

Are they waiting for my reaction to their meal?

I hoped this wasn't their way to finish me off with more poison, but Lia'ina nodded at me with a smile, encouraging me to try it. She took a piece of meat from my serving and ate it. Unless they had an immunity to poison, she proved it wasn't tainted. No utensils were offered and they had confiscated my knife, so I grabbed some meat with my bound hands and took a bite. The juiciness and the subtle spices surprised me. I found it very tasty and bobbed my head in approval.

They exploded into laughter and clapping. The drums resumed their beat, and leaf plates laden with the unusual cuisine were passed around to the rest of the village. In another setting, I may have found the situation enjoyable, but I was here as their prisoner. I found no amusement in that.

Chapter Twenty-Four

My head jerked as I forced my eyes open. The night dragged on, and still I sat on the stump. How I stayed upright remained a mystery — I was exhausted and starting to feel ill. It was hard to believe the revelry still continued as the natives danced and caroused. The men passed around a gourd full of what I guessed was a strong ale or liquor. The drums beat at a frenzied pace.

At a late hour the chieftain stood up and banged a gong for attention. He finally called the festivities to an end. From the ones left standing, or more like swaying, there was a collective sigh of resignation. With additional words, he turned and gestured toward me. This brought a loud round of cheering and applause. As they stumbled to their huts, they passed me and bowed. It made me very uncomfortable.

Eshshah, much to her distress, could do nothing for me at this time. The settlement was built so tightly between the trees, there was not enough room for her to land. We had to wait.

"Amáne, I've found a spot where I can land. It's near the river we followed after your capture. It's not far from where you are."

"Eshshah, I'm glad you didn't have to soar all night. I am so sorry I got you into this mess."

"No matter, Amáne. Don't spend your night in regret. We'll know more tomorrow about their plans for you. Maybe there will be an opportunity for you to reach this clearing. At least we're close.

Lia'ina slipped next to me and sat on the ground near the stump. "Amáne, stay tonight in hut with Lia'ina?"

Do I have a choice?

"Lia'ina, what is this about? Your people tie me up as a criminal, yet offer me a feast as if they honor me."

"Stay in my hut. Amáne learn at morning light. Come."

She called to someone in the group. A large native approached and bowed to her. Before I realized what was happening, he bent down, picked me up and threw me over his shoulder. I struggled to free myself, but he held tighter. With Eshshah's help, I could have overtaken him, but again, where would that have gotten me? I was deep in a jungle with enough warriors to make any escape at this point impossible. Not to mention their blowguns with that incapacitating poison they wielded. I could still feel its effects. I wouldn't want another dose.

I closed my eyes as the native carried me up one of the long single poles that led to a hut. Thankfully, he was sure-footed and ascended the log ladder without missing a step.

"So sorry," Lia'ina said as she motioned for me to sit on a mat in the corner of the hut. The man tied my hands to a pole.

It turned out to be a very uncomfortable night. I hardly found any sleep. At least I wasn't plagued with nightmares. Instead, the slight illness I felt earlier exploded into a burning fever. I tried to keep up a conversation with Eshshah, but it proved too difficult.

"Amáne, I can hear you, but you don't sound like yourself.

It's almost like your voice is fading."

"I know, I don't feel right. I just need to sleep, Eshshah." My mind drifted.

Just when it felt like my eyes finally closed, Lia'ina's soft voice sounded behind me. "Amáne, morning time. You must awake."

My body screamed in protest. My head throbbed; my eyes felt like I had rubbed sand in them; my tongue was thick. I could barely swallow. Maybe it was the unfamiliar food I ate last night. I shrugged the native girl off with a jerk of my shoulder.

"Leave me alone, Lia'ina."

She put her hand on my forehead. It felt cool against my skin. "Did no one give nápoj to drink when they bring you?"

"What's nápoj? All I got when they brought me here was pain. Now just leave me alone." I closed my eyes.

She spoke to someone else in the room. I heard footsteps as that person rushed from the hut.

"Nápoj drink is take away the poj ... the poison ... when they catch you. My father not smile when Lia'ina tell him they did not give."

Footsteps again as someone entered. Lia'ina cut my bonds and pulled my shoulder toward her so I would roll onto my back. One of her attendants lifted me to a sitting position. The room spun around me.

"Drink," Lia'ina said with an urgency in her voice. She held a gourd to my mouth. I pressed my lips together and turned my face in protest.

"Amáne, so sorry. Must drink. It take away the poj, the poison, or you die. You very strong, or very lucky you not wake up dead."

I did as she bade. The drink was sickeningly sweet, with a bitter aftertaste. I could feel it burn its way down my throat. A girl at my back kept me in a sitting position. I opened my eyes and saw

Lia'ina and four other women, probably her maids, staring at me. Concern filled their faces.

The nápoj worked swiftly. My head cleared, moisture restored in my mouth. The girls relaxed their strained looks, and Lia'ina sighed in relief, as did Eshshah.

"Amáne, I was just ready to come crashing through the trees to get to you. I almost couldn't feel you anymore."

"I think I'm fine, now, Eshshah. You wouldn't have been able come through the trees, even with your strength. They're too thick."

"I would have tried anyway."

"Your wings would have shredded if you weren't impaled first. You don't have a breastplate on to protect you. Eshshah, whatever happens to me, please you must make it back to Ansel. This is my doing. I know now that I've jeopardized your life and my duty to Teravinea. I think if I live through this, the Healer will send me to my ancestors anyway."

"We just need to get off of this hateful island," she said.

Chapter Twenty-five

Lia'ina watched me closely for a while longer, then said something to her maids. They bustled about. A few left the hut and one returned with a large water jug balanced on her head. I couldn't believe she could carry it like that and climb up the ladder pole. Others came in with baskets of sweet-smelling herbs and other items I couldn't identify.

After checking to make sure I was fully recovered, they pulled me to a standing position and herded me to the opposite corner of the hut. They motioned for me to sit on another mat. When they reached for my shirt like they wanted to remove it, I shoved their hands away and glared at them. The frightened girls retreated.

"They will help, not hurt you."

"I don't need anyone's help."

"Prepare Amáne for ceremony. Must wear ceremony cloth called kikoi. Please to not make me offend and ask man or many men to hold Amáne quiet."

The last thing I wanted was for one of those savages out there to touch me. Once again, I saw no other option than to comply with her wishes.

I closed my eyes and pressed my lips together, trying to control my desire to knock all these native girls senseless and run out of here. It started to look like a more desirable plan as each minute passed. However, I didn't miss the fact two large guards waited at the bottom of the ladder pole — armed with their poison darts.

"What do you want with me?"

"Know you have great honor in our village. Amáne be one who save us. Must say no more."

"Save you? From what?"

"Patience, Amáne. Soon."

A colorful cloth was handed to me. I removed my clothing and wrapped it around myself immediately. Forgetting, themselves, the girls laughed.

"No, Amáne. It only for ... skirt, like this." She gestured to her wrap and those of her attendants.

I gasped. They wore no tops.

"No!" I said.

One of the young natives ran to another part of the room and brought back a smaller piece of cloth. She folded it lengthwise. Using a sort of pantomime, the girl indicated it could be used for a top. After moving the kikoi to my waist, I allowed her to proceed. With surprising skill she wound the folded sarong around me, leaving my stomach bare. She brought the ends to the back of my neck and tied it securely. The girl then re-wrapped and tied my skirt.

A maid dipped a sponge in the water mixed with the herbs and handed it to me. She indicated to wash my face and arms. They brushed my hair and left it straight down my back, then put a wreath of flowers on my head.

Next, a girl stepped up with a tray that held several bowls. Each contained a paste-like substance ranging from earthy shades of reds, to browns and near-blacks.

"Decorate Amáne with henna. Not hurt. Look beautiful,"

Lia'ina explained.

I nodded reluctantly and sighed. The girl took up her brush and dipped it in one of the bowls. She started at the corner of my right eye. I felt the soft strokes of the brush as she made swirling designs on my face and down my cheek. She proceeded to my jaw, then my neck, continuing with the intricate design across my shoulder, adding leafs and other shapes in the different shades of henna. I watched as she wound the vine pattern around Eshshah's linking mark, then down my arm, finally ending at the nail on my little finger. For such an elaborate pattern, she completed it in a remarkably short time.

Lia'ina studied the design. Satisfied, she smiled and said, "Noa'ina make Amáne more beautiful. Ready for journey. Come, Father waits."

"What journey? Why won't you tell me?" I knew it was useless to ask. She wasn't going to give me an answer.

With great care, I made my way down the ladder pole. When I reached the bottom, the two guards flanked me. Lia'ina took my hand and led me to where the villagers had gathered — the men on one side and women on the other. The women chattered and pointed at me. They stared in awe. I caught glints of admiration in their eyes. Those whom I walked near reached out to touch me. They touched my arms, stroked my hair. The henna tattoo received a lot of attention. My skin was much lighter than theirs which made the design stand out. They paid extra attention to Eshshah's linking mark.

The chief nodded at me. I didn't return the gesture.

I noted where I stood in relation to my surroundings.

"Eshshah, this might be our chance. I'm not tied up."

"Can you get to me?"

"I can feel the direction you're in. There's a path through the trees that heads that way."

I marked the positions of the men who had weapons. "I could use the crowd to shield me from the poison darts."

"I'm with you, Amáne."

I felt her strength flow through me. My heart beat fast. I inhaled and prepared to bolt toward the path.

At that moment the chief took my arm and pulled me to the front of the crowd, to the empty space beside him. He turned me to face the villagers and began to speak — a tight grip on my wrist. I'd missed my chance.

Lia'ina stepped up next to me and translated. "Chief Father say 'Amáne great warrior maiden. She powerful sacrifice — more mighty than other maiden before. Will save village."

"Sacrifice?" I asked.

I tried to pull my arm free, but two other tribesmen rushed in and held me. The chief gave me an angry look.

Lia'ina continued translating. Her father had to slow down and repeat some of his narrative so she could put her words together in a way I could understand.

"Before sacred journey Chief Father must fix evil done. Ancient ones will anger if deed not punished."

The chief called out an order and three natives dragged a man to the front. He was close enough to me that I could hear his ragged breath and beating heart, and smell his fear. His eyes wide, he looked at me with a mixture of hatred and apprehension. He was the one who had jumped back when I regained my strength — the one I'd humiliated.

The chieftain turned to me. Lia'ina conveyed his message,

"This man had duty. Must give Amáne nápoj when arrive. Did not do. He dishonor tribe and Amáne, our sacrifice."

Murmurs came from the villagers.

"We avenge Amáne for his wrong. Man must die."

I whipped my gaze to Lia'ina. "Die? They're going to kill him?"

She gave me a slight nod, as casual as if I'd asked if she'd like some tea.

"I don't want to be avenged! I will not have this man's blood on my hands."

Lia'ina scowled at me, as if embarrassed by my outburst. She didn't translate it to the chief.

"Tell him, Lia'ina. This man does not need to die because of me."

She stayed silent.

I yelled at the chief, "Let the man go!"

"It is our way, Amáne," Lia'ina whispered to me. "What Father say, must do."

At the chief's word, the three large men dragged the offender away. The man thrashed and yelled. The huge natives overpowered him, then hauled him into the forest. My heart beat fast, my stomach churned as the man's screams became more desperate. I swallowed hard at the blood-curdling howl. Then silence.

CHAPTER TWENTY-SIX

I stood in shock. The world receded. I felt like I was in a tunnel, moving backward. The chief's voice echoed in my head, wrenching me back to reality. Fighting my tears, I pushed the event of the man's execution to a dark place in my mind. Eshshah hummed to help me. I took in a deep breath and focused again on the chief. He went on as if there had been no interruption with the brutal killing of one of his clan.

Lia'ina continued to translate as the chief began his story.

"Many many season ago, our ancestor live in valley. Live in harmony with Ancient Ones. One bad bad night, crazed dragon fly close, breathe fire and death on our village, kill our people. Only few escape to jungle. Run deep in forest to this place we live.

"Wise man say must offer up maiden each seven season — sacrifice to appease Ancient Ones. If not do this, dragon come in many numbers and breathe fire through trees. All our people die. He say offering must continue until pale maiden from across water come. She last sacrifice. After you give your heart, our people can return to valley and live in harmony with many dragon."

A chill went up my spine.

"Eshshah, could dragons truly have a taste for human flesh?"

"Things are different here, but my memories recall nothing of human sacrifice to dragons. It has to be a superstition they've passed down through their generations, but that doesn't lessen your danger."

The chief faced me. Through Lia'ina he said, "On sacred journey you travel until moon in sky. You arrive at Valley of Dragons. Must pour ashes on stone table." He handed me a small cloth bag, filled with what I assumed were the ashes he spoke about. "You lay on stone table. Medicine man use sacred knife." With that the chief made a stabbing motion at my heart. I gasped. My hands shot to my chest. He pantomimed taking my heart out, then raised his open hands above my head and said, "Go. My blessing on sacred journey. You must pride this great honor, warrior maiden."

The villagers cheered. Music and dancing started. My hands were bound again. I started to resist, but one of the natives raised his blow gun in warning. A rope was tied around my waist — the ends left at about a man's length in front and behind. It was decorated with leaves and beads. Two large natives emerged from the crowd. They had henna decorations on their bodies similar to mine. In an exaggerated ceremonial ritual, the chief handed each an end of the rope, which they tied around their wrists. The rope would keep me equal distance between the two, which would prevent me from overcoming either of them. Another tribesman, who was probably the medicine man, led the procession. They guided me out of the village.

To my surprise, we took the path that headed toward where Eshshah waited. My heart lightened.

"Eshshah, be ready. Once I see you, I'll yank the rope and try to pull these two down. You take care of the medicine man and then help me with whomever is left. This will soon be over."

The light of the sun filtered down through the trees a little more brightly. I allowed a small sigh of relief. But before we came close enough to Eshshah, our little procession turned sharp right — away from my dragon and back into the dense forest. I nearly collapsed.

"Stay brave, Amáne." She tried to hide it, but her disappointment matched mine. "I could crash through the trees now, but they may harm you before I could get to you. We must be patient. There has to be another opportunity soon." Eshshah took flight and followed from high above.

The rain started as small drops that made their way through the canopy of trees. In no time the drops increased until they pelted down upon us, even through the foliage. Hours later the downpour continued as we traveled on a precarious trail by a river. I could hear the rushing water far below to my left. A steep slope rose up on our right. We followed a narrow ledge. As the water cascaded down, it brought mud sliding onto our path. The trail washed away before us in several places. We lost our footing a number of times, causing us to slide down the embankment before one of the men could grab something to stop us. After which we had to make the difficult climb back up to the trail. They practically dragged me each time. I didn't have full use of my hands.

The mud clung to my body. My hair matted with it. I couldn't remember a time I'd felt more wretched.

The medicine man stopped our small group and said something to the rope bearers. They cut the rope from their wrists and from around my waist, then unbound my hands. My skin had been rubbed raw. Free of the ropes, I felt an unbelievable relief.

The trek would be much easier. I thanked them.

We continued on our miserable way for an indeterminable amount of time. The rain didn't let up, but came down heavier. I'd never seen such a deluge. Our path headed downhill, now. The sound of the river we followed became louder, although it still flowed a ways below us.

The man behind me cried out as he lost his footing. I turned to see the ledge collapse from under his feet. He desperately grabbed for something to stop his fall. That something turned out to be me. He hooked my leg on his way down and dragged me with him. I plowed feet first down the hill, sliding out of control. A jolt of pain shot through me with every rock I hit, with every bush I crashed through. I was unable to find anything solid to slow my momentum. The native careened down the hill in front of me. He hit a tree and lay still. I slid past barely clearing the tree, but I couldn't grab it either.

"Eshshah," I called out loud. There was nothing she could do but to offer me her strength. I accepted it gratefully. The slope ended. I plunged into the raging river.

The rapid waters swallowed me and pulled me down into their depth. I tumbled and rolled beneath the surface. Panic set in. *Which way is up?* I pumped my arms in powerful strokes. My head struck a rock. Pain shot through me. It was the wrong direction. I gathered my feet under me and pushed off what I hoped was the bottom. My lungs burned. The turbulent water thrust me up above the surface. I gulped in precious air before it pulled me under again.

"Amáne, I'm following you, but I can't get in yet. The river is narrow here and the cliffs and trees are too close. Stay with me!"

Even with Eshshah's strength, my efforts to survive the rapids and avoid the rocks began to fail. The river shoved me under one last time. My lungs couldn't hold any longer. My sight blurred.

A pressure constricted my body as if a giant hand were squeezing the life out of me. My head spun and darkness took me.

Chapter Twenty-seven

I coughed and sputtered as I heaved. Eshshah sat behind me and pushed her nose on my back. Breathing her healing breath, she forced the water out.

The sound of the river raged nearby, as if it had already forgotten me and its failed attempt to take my life. I lay on the rocky beach and filled my lungs with air.

Turning on my back, I looked up at my dragon. "How did you reach me?"

"The river widened. The trees thinned. I spotted you immediately, but almost too late. Once I could get in, it was easy to pluck you out of the water. I've caught fish much larger than you." She rumbled her laugh, but it sounded flat.

I smiled. "Thank you Eshshah."

She breathed on me once more. I inhaled slowly and sat up to assess the damage to my battered body. Without the powerful healing gift of my dragon, I don't think I would have been able to move. But the pain subsided as my bruises began to heal. My skirt and top had been washed away. There was not much left of the henna tattoo.

Holding on to Eshshah's foreleg, I stood slowly.

"Take it easy, Amáne. You should probably lie still for a bit longer."

"I just want to get out of here, Eshshah. It's time to go home."

Pulling myself up on her leg, I reached for my clothes in the saddlebag. I threw on the first things I found.

As I tightened my belt over my shirt, I felt Eshshah stiffen and come to full alert. Before I could ask her what was wrong, a shadow fell upon us. Three dragons flew overhead. Eshshah covered me with her wing ready to defend me. The dragons bellowed. Eshshah answered the call. A sound I had never heard from her. Like a trumpet of thunder.

A fear gripped my heart. If these dragons were aggressive, we would never stand a chance against them.

A conversation ensued between Eshshah and the three dragons. They communicated in a language I couldn't understand. It sounded similar to Charna Yash-churka, the black lizard who rescued me from the arena of death in Castle Teravinea — only more refined.

"They feel your presence, Amáne, but they won't hurt you. They've ordered us to follow them. Mount up."

"What now, Eshshah?"

"I don't know. Please hurry. They seem a bit apprehensive about us."

Wincing, I pulled myself up to the saddle. As I buckled in, Eshshah thrust off the ground. One dragon led us, a dark emerald green one. He was quite large. The other two trailed us. Both were brownish gray and smaller than the green, but larger than my dragon. Regardless of my trepidation, I couldn't suppress my pride. Eshshah, by far, surpassed them in grace and beauty.

We flew with them for a short distance. I started to relax as I felt Eshshah calm down. Up ahead I saw a beautiful valley spread out below us. I could see dragons circling in random patterns over the vale. The sight was beyond magnificent. I forgot to breathe.

"Dragons, Eshshah! Hundreds upon hundreds of them. We've reached the Valley of Dragons."

We landed in a large field in front of a cave that opened at ground level. A rock cliff rose above us. Other caverns dotted the face of the cliff. Dragons of various sizes and colors exited and entered. Several landed nearby. I had no fear of these magnificent creatures. There was no feeling of hostility. In fact, I had the impression they were as fascinated with Eshshah and I as we were with them. I remained in the saddle and gazed in wonder.

A few curious young-looking dragons approached. They brought their great heads close to me and sniffed. I sensed they'd never encountered a human. I smiled at them and tried to convey a friendly sentiment. I didn't know their language. Eshshah was engaged in dialogs with others that approached and couldn't translate for me.

I cocked an eyebrow as the young dragons around me parted to open a way for an older-looking silver-scaled dragon who came toward me. It drew close and bowed its head.

"Greetings, young rider," she said, "I am Sitara. Leyna was my rider."

My jaw dropped. I saluted her as Eshshah turned and nodded a salutation.

"Sitara," I said, "your scales still shine brightly here and in Teravinea. It is truly an honor to meet you."

She nodded acceptance of my compliment.

"It has been long since I've seen a rider." She brought her face close and inhaled. I felt her joy. She moved aside as another yellow dragon approached.

"This is Dinesh. His late rider was Hajari."

I saluted him and uttered a compliment at which he nodded his appreciation.

The two dragons that had been at the root of my search for this place stood before me. It made our entire ordeal almost worth it. Almost, because only one thing would make it entirely worth it — that would be to confirm their support in our fight for the throne.

There was so much I wanted to ask these two. Trying to decide how to begin, I opened my mouth when Sitara stopped me. She glanced over my shoulder and then brought her head down to the ground in a deep bow. I noted that all of the other dragons took the same posture.

"Senolis, the Ancient One," she told me in thought transference.

I turned in the saddle to see a dragon emerge from the cave. An awesome air enveloped him. It caused me to bow my head in respect. Eshshah already had touched her nose to the ground. The Ancient One's gray scales lacked the luster of Eshshah's and the others. He embodied his name, Ancient One — as if he had seen this valley when it first formed. His wings were folded but dragged on the ground as he approached. He probably hadn't used them in ages, and for that reason, his cave was on ground level.

Senolis gazed intently at Eshshah and then at me with eyes wizened beyond belief. I could have lost myself in their depth if he had wanted to pull me in.

He conversed with Eshshah in an ancient language I couldn't understand. She conveyed his dialog to me.

"Greetings, young dragon and human child. What brings two youngsters from such a distance?"

Eshshah bowed her head to him. "Ancient One, we are

honored to be in your presence. My rider is Amáne and I am Eshshah from the Kingdom of Teravinea. An event beyond our control has brought us to your Valley."

He tilted his head. Switching to the common tongue, he spoke in thought transference so I could understand. "Perhaps, but I sense it was not beyond your control to seek our island." Senolis rested his gaze upon me. I cringed in shame.

His eyes released me as he said, "Teravinea? I have not heard any news from that kingdom since Leyna rode in on Sitara." He glanced at Sitara, at which she nodded in reverence at his attentions.

"An event beyond your control? I hunger for a good story." He lowered his great body and lay in front of us, looking expectantly at Eshshah. She obliged and relayed our story of how we had flown in to Orchila to inquire about directions to this valley; about the natives' attempt to use me as a sacrifice; and my harrowing ride on the white waters of the river. He listened intently, interjecting questions here and there.

When his curiosity was satisfied, he said, "Well told. Thank you, Eshshah. First, let me assure you that we never have, nor ever will condone any human sacrifice. Those mortals and their superstitions have created their ritual. By the time those poor females were left on the stone table, their lives had already been ended. Their deaths were useless and wasteful ... humans."

He lay still for a time, staring at the valley behind us before turning his golden eyes on me. "Now, Amáne, tell me why is it a dragon and rider from Teravinea seek the Valley of Dragons?"

I inhaled sharply, my mouth went dry. *Why would he decide to address me?* I cleared my throat and began to speak out loud without realizing.

"Ancient One —"

He rumbled deep in his chest. The same sound Eshshah made when she was amused. Their version of what I would relate to laughter.

I caught myself. Embarrassed, I switched to thought transference.

"Excuse me, sir, uh, lord dragon ... uh ... I too am honored to meet you."

He nodded.

"We had hopes of bringing the heir to the throne of Teravinea to petition assistance from the Ancient Ones. With your support, we could win the throne back from the usurper who'd seized it from King Emeric Drekinn."

"I recall the Drekinn name favorably. Tell me about the usurper."

I proceeded to tell him of Galtero and how he had sent the king and queen to their ancestors, and how the heir escaped harm. Because of Galtero, there were no longer any dragons in Teravinea, only Eshshah and Sovann.

I startled at the vibration in his chest. This time it sounded angry, dangerous.

"This human, Galtero, has destroyed dragons?" He switched back to the ancient tongue. Eshshah translated for me, but I didn't need her help to feel his burning anger.

I nodded. It took several minutes before Senolis managed to compose himself. He looked at me again and indicated for me to continue.

The hours passed as Eshshah and I answered his questions into the night. Sometime early on, I had dismounted. I had a feeling we would be speaking to the Ancient One for longer than I cared to stay in the saddle. It proved to be a lengthy audience. My anxiety grew with my desire to leave. But the old dragon relentlessly directed queries at us. There was no way we would deny him his satisfaction.

When it seemed like he had exhausted all the information he could extract from us, he went silent. Time passed. I wondered if he'd fallen asleep.

At last he broke the silence. "What is it you expect from us?"

His question puzzled me. I thought he understood what we were asking.

"We hoped you would join forces with us to overcome Galtero. That this valley's dragons would fly into battle. Perhaps some would carry a dragon rider. With your assistance, we can win the throne and assure more dragons will hatch and choose riders."

Again silence from the ancient creature. More time passed. I just wanted to head home. By now Ansel would be worrying about us. I had promised him we would be back in Dorsal no later than three days time. At this point, if we left now, it would be over four days he hadn't heard from us. An uneasiness filled my chest.

"Eshshah and Amáne," the old dragon said, "thank you for your engrossing story. It's been too long since I've heard from your world. I take pity in your plight and wish you success in uprooting the usurper.

"As to the eggs that will not hatch, it appears where they are held is cursed or polluted in some way. If you remove them from the area, they will recover.

"But the concerns and squabbles of humans have rarely been events in which we have taken part. Our last human contact came when Sitara arrived with Leyna, who has since met with her ancestors. Leyna's company was delightful, her passing saddened me. Perhaps it was Leyna's information you followed to find this island. I see no reason for our involvement in your affairs. The dragons of Teravinea have passed." Another angry rumble quaked in Senolis' chest. "Our interference will not bring them back."

My heart sank. All this time, I thought his questions and interest in Teravinea were to solidify his decision to come to our aid. It served only to gratify his curiosity of the outside world.

"Don't be discouraged, Amáne. I see your cause to be as worthy as you believe it to be. You will find a way to succeed — with or without the valley's dragons. I can sense your strong character and your sincerity of heart. You must persevere and continue to accept whatever befalls you. Remember to be patient when you come upon great misfortune, because it is in fire gold is refined."

My breath left me. His words nearly matched those my mother had uttered on her dying bed.

He continued his prophetic words. "Through your trials you have brought hope, and through them perhaps attainment of that for which you fight. I see that one day you could be a leader, but you have two weaknesses that may be your undoing. Your stubbornness and your pride. In truth, at this moment, your fate hangs by a thread because of your flaws. I only see what may be. It is up to you to direct your life."

My stomach twisted at his foretelling. There was nothing for me to say in response. I simply bowed in respect.

Senolis turned to my dragon. "Eshshah, your duty and devotion to your rider is noble. Notwithstanding, my advice to you is to remain strong in your convictions and guide Amáne away from imprudent decisions. Mastering this will ensure a long life together."

Eshshah touched her nose to the ground.

"Go in peace, young ones. You are welcome back when you so desire. Bring the Drekinn with you."

With a nod to Eshshah and I, he turned and disappeared into his cave.

Utterly defeated, I couldn't stop my tears as I mounted the saddle. I turned to Sitara and Dinesh. "We are honored to have met you. I hope one day our paths cross again. We have much to talk about. But now we must take our leave."

I gave Eshshah the word to at last head for home.

Chapter Twenty-eight

We flew swiftly — straight south, a more direct flight than if we'd gone by way of Trivingar. I decided to fly to the Dorsal Outpost and contact Ansel from there, rather than approach him in person. I would also get hold of the Healer from the outpost. I was a little afraid of facing her, too.

Ansel always tolerated my poor decisions, but something ate at me this time. As much as I longed for his embrace, I feared confronting him in person. *Why didn't I think this trip through? Or listen to Eshshah and reason? Senolis is right — because of my pride and stubbornness.* Nonetheless, I convinced myself Ansel could be persuaded to see my intention. He would appreciate my effort.

Even at the speeds at which Eshshah flew, it was still about nine or ten hours of travel before she spotted the outpost. I put my misgivings behind me and looked forward to telling Ansel, Gallen and the Healer of our findings.

At last, familiar territory. I could see the scattered islands in the blue waters of our bay.

"Amáne! Sovann and Lord Ansel are at the outpost!"

My heart skipped. At once I was excited to see him, but in the next beat, a twinge of apprehension shot through me.

"What are they doing there?"

"I don't know, but Sovann says Lord Ansel is angry."

I took a deep breath as the outpost came into view. I could just make out the small figure of Ansel, pacing — watching our approach. As we came closer I gasped at the sight of him. He looked a wreck, disheveled. The desperate look on his face stopped my heart.

I unbuckled myself before Eshshah touched down. Sliding off I ran toward Ansel, anxious for his comforting warmth, but stopped short. The wild look in his eyes frightened me.

"Ansel? I ..."

"What do you mean by this, Amáne?" he shouted only inches from my face.

He had every right to be angry, having no idea what had become of Eshshah and me. My heart hurt thinking of the anguish I'd put him through.

"I'm sorry, Ansel. I was only trying to ..."

"Did you, or did you not go out on your own decision to chase after some legendary dragons?"

I wasn't surprised he had figured it out. "They're not ..."

"Do you know what you've done?"

Without waiting for my answer, he repeated, louder, "Do you know what you've done, Amáne?

"I haven't done anything. I'm sorry if I went without telling you or the Healer. I just wanted to ..."

"You don't get it, do you? You have no idea."

"What, Ansel? You're scaring me."

"You should be scared. You, a sworn dragon rider, have decided you know better than the Council. That you can make up your own quest without so much as conferring with anyone —

without going through the proper channels and discussions on your safety and that of your dragon. You went rogue."

"No, let me explain ..." but my words froze in my throat.

He looked closely at me. His eyes focused on my right cheek. My hand went to my face. *There must still be some henna tattoo left.*

He shook off whatever question he seemed about to ask, turned his back on me and cursed.

Ansel stalked to the fireplace at the far wall. His breath released in a sound of agony. He pounded his fist on the mantelpiece.

"Do you know the extent of your violation, Amáne?" He began to pace the floor. His hands raked through his hair.

"Violation? No," I whispered.

He pulled up and faced me, his eyes piercing. "It's called insubordination." The word came out slowly, each syllable pronounced.

His anguish and tone confused me. "I said I was sorry, Ansel. I didn't mean to be gone so long. I didn't mean to do this to you."

"Insubordination, Amáne! This is not just about what you did to me. You obviously don't realize the seriousness of this charge."

I shook my head.

He took several strides before he spun around and came back. Stopping directly in front of me, he put his hands on my shoulders, gripping tighter than necessary. I stood terrified.

Barely in control of his voice, it quavered as he whispered, "Amáne ... the maximum penalty ... for this crime ... is ... *death* ..."

My knees went weak. I felt the blood drain from my face.

Ansel let go of me and cleared his throat. "I'll go before the Council and plead leniency for you. I'll do whatever I can, but your fate will be decided by a majority vote. It's not my sole decision."

He began his pacing once again, pulling his hair and cursing. My stomach churned. My body shook.

"If I ever gain my throne," he went on almost to himself, "how would it look for a king to not know the whereabouts of his queen — if she takes it upon herself to go off on a whim?"

I froze, *queen?* I hoped one day I would marry him, but the thought never fully formed in my mind — *I would be queen.* But now, it may be a future no longer attainable. I'd overstepped my bounds. I've lost his trust. That, in itself was worse than the penalty of death. He must have felt betrayed — as if his love for me didn't matter. *It does.*

I took a deep breath and stepped toward him to try to salvage a thread of whatever faith he had left in me. I opened my mouth. Ansel's hand commanded me to stay silent.

His eyes filled. "I'll always love you, Amáne, but you were right all along." He tried in vain to blink back his tears. "You can't mix duty with desire. It just doesn't work." He backed away.

"No, Ansel. Please don't. Don't do this!"

My knees gave out. I sunk down and sat on my heels. My hand started to reach out toward him, but went instead to my breast. I felt as if my heart would fail.

The pain showed in his eyes. He squeezed them shut. When he opened them, his jaw clenched. Taking in a deep breath, his voice became cold and authoritative. "You will remain here until the Healer contacts you. That is a direct order. Is that understood, dragon rider?"

I bowed my head, and gave a nearly imperceptible nod. My eyes followed him as he turned and strode briskly to Sovann. He mounted. Sovann pushed off and dove from the ledge.

"Ansel," I whispered.

Chapter Twenty-Nine

I sat on the floor in utter disgrace as Sovann and Ansel grew smaller in the distance. I had to turn my back until my darkness passed. But it wouldn't pass. My life, or what was left of it, would be ruined by my stubbornness and my pride. The words of Senolis, the Ancient One, echoed in my head.

A shock went through me. "Eshshah, please tell me that Sovann hasn't dismissed you as well." That, I would not be able to take.

"No, Amáne." She trudged over to me, as devastated as I, which added to my wretchedness. "I will, more than likely face punishment for insubordination, but this separation is between you and Ansel."

"This is all my fault. You shouldn't have to suffer a bit of punishment. I'm going to make certain that everyone understands you can't be held to blame."

"No matter. Whatever you must suffer, will affect me just as much."

My remorse couldn't bore any deeper. Devastated, destroyed,

I slumped forward. I rested my head on my arms on the cold stone floor, and cried until I succumbed to fatigue.

Between waking and giving in to exhaustion, I struggled to keep from falling off the edge of my despair. The last time Ansel was angry with me — I shook my head at that thought, *No, Ansel isn't angry with me, he's done with me* — my depression had affected Eshshah. I couldn't repeat that selfishness. I had to hang on ... for her. Privately, I panicked when I thought what my death would do to her. Surely they'd allow Eshshah to live. But, she's bound by duty to the Drekinn throne. That and her commitment to Sovann would force her to remain in Teravinea. *What have I done but ruin the lives of all those I love?*

Thinking back to Ansel, I forced myself to face the fact his life would be miserable if he stayed with me. I'd never make a good queen. The truth was easy to see. I had to accept I would be living my life without Ansel — *if I'm even allowed to live.*

The days went by and still no word from the Healer. Maybe I should be the one to contact her, but my shame prevented me. I couldn't bear to see the disappointment on the face of another person I loved. Besides, I had orders to wait until she contacted me. I might as well start obeying orders.

Each day I made an effort to drag myself out of bed; to get dressed; to face the day. In order to fight my depression, I had to keep myself busy, and make no time for thought. I awoke early one day and put myself to the task of scrubbing the entire outpost. From the library to the entry cavern, I oiled every piece of wood, washed or aired every item of bedding in the three bedchambers. Another day, I brought all forms of weapons outside — spears, swords, daggers, throwing knives, crossbows, longbows and I practiced relentlessly. The trees on the island suffered dearly that day. Eshshah and I went on many flights, and worked at consoling each other.

My efforts were only partially successful. I couldn't shake the burning reality that my crime could be punishable by death. I hoped with every fiber I wouldn't have to pay that price. But right now not knowing our fate was the worst punishment we could have been given. I deserved this, not Eshshah. She had tried to talk some sense into me. I didn't listen. I had shirked my sworn duty.

Our days moved slowly forward at the Dorsal Outpost, until one dreary day — it may have been the fifth day, or maybe the sixth. At early light I jerked awake from a nightmare when I felt Eshshah's alarm.

"What is it, Eshshah?"

"Someone's out there."

"Is it Sovann and Ansel?" *I must be mad to even think that.*

"No!" She got up quickly and headed to the entryway. My heart beat wildly as I threw a tunic over the sleeveless chemise I'd slept in. Pulling on my tights, I stumbled down the corridor to the entryway. In the next breath, a deafening boom echoed through the cavern. I was thrown against the wall as the outpost quaked.

"We're being attacked, Amáne!"

I made my way to the entry. We'd left the large stone door open the night before. My heart froze in my chest. Anchored in the deeper water was a great galleon, its port side angled toward us, cannons smoking. The open entry must have attracted their attention. Several rowboats were holding just outside the shore break, awaiting the end of the assault before heading in to our beach.

"Quickly, Eshshah, to the library! I need to contact the Healer. We have to get geared up. If we can't stop the galleon here, its next destination will be Dorsal."

I closed the entry, hoping the massive door would sustain another barrage. We raced to the communication disc.

Placing my hand on the knob that protruded under the glass disc, I said, "Gyan," and then "Nara." I tried to even my breathing and stop my tremors as I waited impatiently for the Healer to answer. After an everlasting moment, her face shimmered into view.

Without any greeting or formality I shouted, "Healer, we're being attacked! They're firing on us! A galleon. I don't recognize its markings. If we can't stop it, Dorsal might be next."

"Amáne," the Healer exclaimed in alarm, "you need to —" Before she could finish, the outpost shook with the next volley. The impact flung me from the communication disc. Her image disappeared.

Angry at losing the connection, I tried to get her back again, but the device had been jostled. There was no time to figure it out. We rushed to the tack area where I chose the smaller fighting saddle. I flung on Eshshah's breastplate then saddle, thankful that Gallen had drilled us repeatedly on the importance of speed.

I buckled my breastplate and tugged on my dragon-scale boots, gauntlets, and helmet. Grabbing some spears, daggers, a bow and a few quivers, I jammed them in their places on the fighting saddle. I yanked a shield from the wall.

Our hearts quickened as we switched into fight mode. We charged out of the library. The outpost shuddered with another bombardment. We bolted down the corridor to the entry cavern. Eshshah held her step for a brief instant so I could climb her leg and hoist myself up into the saddle. She hardly missed a beat. I buckled into the boot pegs as we arrived at the ledge. We hoped our timing was right to avoid the next barrage.

The door slid open and we dove off.

Eshshah and I headed straight for the soldiers in the rowboats. We took them by surprise. My dragon roared, causing several to throw themselves off the boats. More men tumbled into the sea as they were pitched off balance. The braver ones stood as if they would fight her with their spears. Some went for their arrows.

I took in a deep breath. "Go ahead, Eshshah, we have no choice. Flame them."

She belched a massive inferno. Their screams were cut short as the men and rowboats went from flame to ash in seconds. The smell of burning flesh rose on the steam that came up from the churning water. I closed my eyes and wished them to their ancestors.

Racing toward the galleon, I could see alarm in the faces of the soldiers on board. Their beliefs instantly disproved if they thought there were no such creatures as dragons.

Eshshah and I worked as one. We dove and dodged. Searching the deck for the commander, I let fly my arrows. Eshshah flamed at every pass. The sails were ablaze. More soldiers met their ancestors. Some had already abandoned ship, not dedicated enough to stand their ground.

Dragons' ability to belch out flames was not inexhaustible. Eshshah needed to take a few minutes respite to replenish her combustion. On our next pass, I hurled all of the daggers I'd collected. Many found their mark. Arrows flew around us, bouncing harmlessly off Eshshah. Her tough scales and her breastplate made them useless. Only her wings were susceptible. She jerked when one would find its way through the leathery membrane. She assured me the pain was minimal. We would work to heal them once we returned to the outpost.

My shield was indispensable as a sea of shafts rushed toward us. The odds were against me, however, that I could fully protect myself from the onslaught. I yelped out in pain as one got by and lodged itself in my left upper arm. It penetrate my bone. Eshshah flinched.

"I'm all right, Eshshah."

Ignoring my pain, I melded with my dragon. We continued to dive and flame the ship. I regretted the fact we had not been trained in aerial battle. We both knew we were sorely missing in technique and strategy. If we survived this day, and if my life were not forfeited for my insubordination, I wanted that training without delay.

As we flew over the bow, I noted some activity in the forecastle — the high deck at the front of the ship. Soldiers clustered together. I didn't give it a second thought.

Eshshah and I had gained the upper hand. The vessel listed dangerously. One more pass and it would be completely incapacitated. Victory.

We dove at breakneck speed for our final onslaught. Only the soldiers on the bow remained — the ship almost consumed by flame. My blood ran cold when I realized what they had concealed. It was a cannon, smaller and thinner than those on the port side that had fired on the outpost. I screamed at Eshshah when I realized our danger. But too late. They fired off a harpoon. Our only advantage was the inaccuracy of the weapon. Eshshah dodged the projectile hurtling straight at us. She couldn't get completely clear. The harpoon whizzed by to our left and raked a deep gash in Eshshah's thigh. She howled in pain. I screamed in anguish for my dragon.

"Sovann!" Eshshah cried. I thought her pain brought on her plea for him. A movement to my right caught my eye. Sovann and Ansel arrived in a fury.

"Retreat, Amáne!" Ansel commanded.

I didn't need to be told again. Eshshah was my only concern. Her leg hung limp as her agony increased.

"Come on, Eshshah. Hang on!" I merged with her. We

gathered all our strength to make the entry to the outpost. Memories of our ordeal, when we fought the Valaira, came back. We strained together — the safety of the cavern just ahead.

"We're almost there. You can do it, Eshshah!" My heart raced out of control. I feared for her life. It was a fear I had to block from her.

Her strength waned, but she managed to maintain her glide to the cavern's mouth. My teeth clenched. The entry approached. We were on a collision course. At the final moment she pulled from the last of her strength in a weak backstroke. It slowed us down just enough. We careened into the entry. She stayed upright but we skidded the length of the room. Eshshah met head-on with the back of the cavern. My head jerked forward — my face slammed into the back of her neck. I bit through my tongue. An explosion of stars scattered around me.

Eshshah lay motionless. I released myself from the boot pegs and leaped to the floor. Spitting the blood out of my mouth, I ran back to her rear leg. Panic filled my chest — like a weight that bore down upon me.

Think, Amáne. Act!

I threw off my breastplate. I tried to pull off my tunic to use on her wound, but winced as it caught on the arrow lodged in my upper arm. Twisting my left hand, I grabbed the base of the shaft, then reached over with my right and snapped it off. The point remained in my arm. I removed my tunic, leaving only my thin sleeveless chemise. No one was here. Even if there were, my clothing, or lack of, would be the least of my concerns.

I climbed up on her rear foot to reach her wound, just over my head. It was a gaping laceration that spilled out her precious dark blood.

"Eshshah!" I screamed. "Don't you leave me!" I could feel

her presence, but it was weak. She had lost a lot of blood between the galleon and here.

Rolling up my tunic, I reached up, stuffed it onto her gash and pressed as hard as I could. Then closing my eyes, I concentrated and hummed her healing tune. I pushed my weight into her as I felt the restoring warmth radiate from my hands. With all my might, I willed her to heal. My hands, at first just warm, heated with an intensity that surprised me. I strained from my effort. Sweat streamed down my body. My legs became weak, but I could not let up. The bleeding was not under control.

I felt a pressure on my back. *Sovann.* I hadn't noticed he and Ansel had glided in. His power flowed through me, allowing me to redouble my efforts.

I opened my eyes briefly to see Ansel freeing Eshshah of her saddle and breastplate.

"Amáne," Eshshah faintly entreated, "enough. You'll exhaust yourself. You've done plenty for now. Please, you will make yourself ill ... or worse."

"Just a bit more, Eshshah. With Sovann's help I can stop the blood flow completely and begin the healing. I'll be all right." But I was nearly spent. My sight dimmed; my legs shook; my palms erupted into blisters from the healing heat they'd generated.

"Amáne!" Ansel's voice echoed as if from far away. "Stop. Sovann can finish for you."

In one last burst, I poured myself out, my hands nearly on fire. Finally, my legs gave out. As I slumped forward, my hands slid down her leg. Her scales ripped open my burning palms. Ansel caught me before I hit the ground.

As if in a dream, I felt him lay me down on my right side,

my back to Eshshah. He had spread quilts by Eshshah's neck, so I could be close to my dragon. Ansel knelt by my side and gently pulled a quilt up over me. Lifting my injured arm, he tucked the covers under it. He groaned as he inspected the point embedded in my bone.

"Sovann, when you're done there, I'll need your help." He tied a cloth around my arm, above the arrow point. With Sovann's healing breath, he worked the point from where it had lodged. I squeezed my eyes shut and clenched my teeth from the pain. Sovann's assistance was immense, but I couldn't help notice he didn't have the same intensity as Eshshah. All dragons have healing powers. But Eshshah's were extraordinary.

As Ansel finished wrapping my wound, my body began to shake in spasms. Violent tremors erupted from my legs to my shoulders, and up to my clenching jaw. Before I could hurt myself with my thrashing, Ansel wedged himself at my back, between Eshshah and me. Molding his body to mine, he put one arm around my waist and held tight. With the other, he cradled my head.

My body jerked so uncontrollably, it frightened me.

"Breathe, Amáne. It's muscle spasms," Ansel said.

The warmth from his body and his strong arms wrapped around me, eased the tremors until they finally ceased. A new fear washed over me. I realized after this, Ansel would no longer have cause to hold me. His closeness was temporary — a mere necessity. I closed my eyes and memorized the feel of his embrace as I breathed in his scent. I lamented the times I'd kept him at arm's length. I regretted dismissing his attentions because of my stupidity. The pain in my heart would not let up as I reflected upon my disloyalty. If one last time I could feel his lips on mine, then I could make it last for the rest of my life — no matter how short or long that proved to be.

I tried to turn my face to him, but he tightened his hold, prohibiting any movement.

Devastated, I exhaled, "Ansel?"

"Shh," he soothed as if to a baby.

"But —"

"Shh. Rest, Amáne. I'm right here."

I bit my lip as the tears soaked the quilt beneath me.

Chapter Thirty

Half awake, I felt Eshshah's awareness. Her lack of pain touched me first.

"Eshshah, you're healed?" I said in thought transference.

"Sovann treated me. Another few healing treatments and all that will be left would be my memories and a scar. Thank you, Amáne. But please, you must learn when to stop. You spent yourself once again."

"I know. I'm sorry, Eshshah. I was scared for you. I'll be more aware next time I use my gift."

My bodily pain was gone. I thanked Eshshah for treating me as I slept. The pain in my heart, however, remained. Our recent drama replayed in my mind.

Expecting to be alone with Eshshah, I opened my eyes to face another day. The sight of Ansel gave me a start. He sat across from me, leaning back on Sovann, watching me sleep. A ripple of anxiety went through me. I met his eyes. My throat tightened at the pain they reflected.

Scooting over to where he sat, I crawled into his lap and lay my head on his chest. He didn't reject me. Instead, he put his arms around me and rested his chin on my head. We sat in silence for a long time. I wasn't about to interrupt the moment, afraid if I moved, I would awaken from this dream.

"Amáne," Ansel broke the silence, "will you forgive me?"

Bewildered, I pushed away from his chest and looked up at him. I was afraid my imagination had run amok. But no, it was truly Ansel — and I'd heard correctly.

He took a deep breath, his voice full of emotion, "I would rather be sent to my ancestors than live without you."

My eyes filled as I whispered, "Forgive *you*? I'm the one who should be begging your forgiveness."

Our eyes locked. A corner of his mouth turned up. "Always the stubborn one."

He ran his fingers through my hair as he brought his face to mine. Our lips met. My anxiety dissolved in his passionate kiss.

Ansel and I sat for a while longer, each in our own thoughts. *How many chances is this man going to give me?* I didn't deserve him, but needed him as much as he needed me. Our fates were woven together. Regardless of what we did, we were part of the same tapestry.

I hope I live long enough to make it up to him.

His voice brought me out of my musing. "The Healer's waiting to hear from you," he said quietly.

"Is she going to tell me my fate?" My body trembled.

"She's waiting," he repeated. Moving me off his lap, he stood and held his hand out to me. He gave me a kiss on my forehead and with a jerk of his head, motioned me to go contact the Healer.

As I headed out of the entry chamber, he said, "Uh ... Amáne."

I stopped with a questioning look.

"You might want to put on a tunic before you contact her." He indicated my flimsy chemise and then politely looked away.

I gasped and threw my arms around myself as I rushed out of the room.

Chapter Thirty-one

My hand shook as I placed it on the brass knob of the communication device. Ansel had repaired the damage from the attack. My mouth went dry as I worked up my courage. *I'd let the Healer down. My mentor. What a frustration for her I must be.*

In a hoarse whisper, I said, "Gyan," then, "Nara."

The Healer's face shimmered into view in the glass disc. I noticed her eyes, first. Her suffering and pain read clearly. Gallen slid into view beside her with the same stricken look. I stood mute.

"Amáne," the Healer said, then fell silent. In that one word, her disappointment and concern echoed in my ears.

"Healer, I've failed you."

She could have unleashed her wrath upon me. I wished she would have. Her silence was worse than anything she could have said.

After a torturous moment enduring her scrutiny, she said, "I'm pleased to hear Eshshah has recovered. Your healing powers are a remarkable gift. Let me caution you again to learn your limits."

I nodded. It was not the first warning on that subject I'd heard that day.

The Healer continued, "When we lost our connection, I was

about to order you to abandon the outpost and head for home. I tried to reconnect, but you didn't answer."

My shoulders dropped. "I tried too. The device was damaged. Will our decision to fight be added to the charge against me?"

"No. You made the right decision. To our advantage you destroyed the ship."

"Ansel and Sovann destroyed the ship."

"He told me there wasn't much left to do. One flaming pass and the ship sank. We have you and Eshshah to thank. That fact will be considered by the Rider's Council when discussing your sentence."

I hung my head.

"Healer, what will happen to Eshshah if I receive the max ... if they decide ..."

"My fervent hope is it won't come to that. We're heading into a time of war. You and Eshshah are a great asset to our cause. If you can be trusted."

Her eyes focused on mine. Her wrath began to show. "When are you going to understand, Amáne, that we riders rely on each other for our lives? There needs to be a trust that does not waiver, that is not questioned. You've broken that trust. You took it upon yourself to decide what was best for the kingdom. That was not your call to make."

I bit my lip and fought my tears.

"Ansel spent days trying to verify your whereabouts. He figured you'd followed Leyna. If you hadn't shown up when you did, I was afraid I couldn't have stopped him and Sovann from going after you — the kingdom put on hold because of you."

That thought nauseated me.

"He knew you were keeping something from him when you parted in Serislan. He blamed himself for not pressing you."

My knees went weak.

"I've told you before, it's not all about you, Amáne. You are but a small part of a team that needs to work together, if it is to work at all."

I wiped my nose with the back of my sleeve.

The Healer closed her eyes and took a deep breath. More calmly she said, "You have many points in your favor that may lighten your sentence. The esteem in which Ansel places you counts for more than a lot. All of the riders are witness to that truth. The fact of your youth, and yes, whether you care to hear it or not, the fact that you are a girl will play a part in the riders' decisions. You made a favorable impression, I'm sure, with your entry at Ansel's birthday feast. You met and interacted with all of them at the ball. Most importantly, the riders will factor in the accomplishments you and Eshshah have already achieved.

"I'll make no false promises. You will be punished. That much is certain. To what extent, is not yet known. A Rider's Council will convene here in Dorsal. You will stand before the Council to plead your case."

She paused to let that sink in. My tears flowed freely; my hand trembled on the brass knob.

"It'll be dark soon. I understand Eshshah will be well enough to fly. I'll expect you here no later than an hour after dark."

"Yes, Healer."

She saluted me and signed off. My hand was still poised at the end of my salute when her image faded and I found myself alone.

I slumped to the floor and sobbed. Eshshah hummed to me in thought transference.

Chapter Thirty-two

As soon as darkness fell, we left the outpost. Gallen, the Healer and Dorjan stood waiting as Eshshah and Sovann spiraled down into the Healer's courtyard.

I returned their salutes, unbuckled and slid off the saddle. Full of remorse, I hesitated to approach the Healer. She held out her arms and I fell into them straightaway.

"I didn't know it would be a crime, Healer. I only wanted to help. We were just going to verify the Valley's existence. That was it. A matter of a couple of hours, then we'd come back with our report. I didn't expect to be betrayed and captured to become their human sacrifice."

"Human Sacrifice?" Ansel said. "You didn't tell me anything about a sacrifice or about being captured."

"I'm sorry, Ansel. I didn't know where to start. I didn't want to burden you more than I already had."

"All right," broke in the Healer. "Let's get Eshshah and Sovann taken care of, then you can tell us everything we need to know."

A short time later, we sat at the Healer's kitchen table. A plate of smoked fish before us, a pitcher of ale for them and chamomile tea for me. I ate so ravenously, the Healer fetched the salt pork and a loaf of bread. When she took her chair again, all eyes turned to me.

In a shaky voice, I told our story. I made it clear it was my idea. I'd gone against Eshshah's better sense. I told of meeting Pratt, and of his betrayal. When I came to the part where I was shot by the poison dart and transported like a trussed pig, Ansel went pale. They all listened intently to my description of the natives and their encampment. My near-drowning brought on groans of distress.

Gallen leaned in, eyes wide with awe as I described the Ancient One, Senolis, and our extended conversation.

"Senolis shared his thoughts about the eggs at the Hatching Grounds. He said where they are held is cursed or polluted in some way. If we remove them from the area, he believes they will recover."

The Healer nodded.

"He also invited us back and told us to bring you, Ansel."

He raised his eyebrows.

"Then to me, he repeated almost the same words my mother had said on her dying bed. That I must persevere and continue to accept whatever befalls me; to remember to be patient when I come upon great misfortune, because in fire gold is refined. Through my trials our goals may be attained. But, Senolis warned me my stubbornness and pride may be my undoing. Because of these weaknesses, my fate will hang by a thread." I finished in a whisper.

"To Eshshah, he said she must remain strong in her convictions and guide me away from imprudent decisions."

My voice cracked as I added the old dragon declined our plea for help.

Silence descended around the table as each digested our remarkable story. Then their questions came at me in an unrelenting bombardment. Finally, exhaustion from the long day hit me like a Valaira. At a lull in the conversation, my eyes became heavy. The Healer sent me off to my chambers. I fell into bed fully clothed.

Chapter Thirty-three

The following morning, the Healer came into our chambers.

"The decision has been made to convene the Rider's Council here in seven days' time," she said.

I pressed my lips together and hung my head. It overwhelmed me that one thoughtless decision could affect so many people. It was like a stone thrown into a pond. The ripples get wider and wider.

"With Eshshah's permission," the Healer continued, "we need you two to transport the riders to Dorsal. You'll leave at dark tonight. Ansel and Sovann insisted they help. Between the two dragons, you could have all the riders here before the end of the week."

The week went quickly. We actually enjoyed our night flights. That is as long as I put out of my head the reason for which the dragon riders gathered. I wasn't allowed to engage in any discussion with the riders during flight, or at the Healer's. I spent most of my time in my chambers or on the other side of the barn practicing on the pell.

The Healer had told me to write a statement to read in front of the Council. She said to be sure I summarized my story, and that I included my intentions of why I decided to go on my own. In other words I was responsible for my own defense.

The day of my hearing arrived. The riders made their way to the Healer's library. Several tables were pushed together to seat twenty-seven of us.

My stomach would not be still, my breathing became shallow and quick. This was worse than preparing for any of my quests. My life hung in uncertainty.

Ansel came into the kitchen where I awaited the order to enter the library. He took my hand and pulled me to him. He pushed my hair back. Locking eyes with me, he said, "I know you had no idea of the gravity of your offense, Amáne. Unfortunately, it doesn't lessen the severity. I'll stand behind you and support you. Stay strong when you read your testimony. Hold your emotions in check. State the facts. The riders will have a chance to ask you questions after you make your statement." He paused, then added, "I love you."

He tightened his arms around me and kissed me passionately. I drew strength from his confidence and from his love. Whatever happened to me would be more bearable knowing he stood by me. And yet less bearable knowing he suffered with me.

"You can go in now," he said.

I nodded, my lips pressed together. I breathed in deeply and let it out slowly, trying to wrest control of my heart and my anxiety. I entered the library slowly. My eyes met those of the men gathered there. It was a mistake. I should have kept my head down. Avano didn't hide his disappointment or the worried look on his face. The others showed similar expressions. My heart sank. I struggled to recover as I took my seat.

When Ansel came in, we all rose and saluted him. He gave a crisp return salute. Taking his chair, he wasted no time getting started.

"Thank you, riders. The Council has been called to a special meeting to hear and discuss the charge of insubordination against Rider Amáne."

I felt his eyes on me. I didn't look up.

"Amáne, are you prepared to give your declaration?"

I rose to my feet. "Yes, Lord Ansel."

"Very well, then. You may proceed."

"Riders." My voice came out unsteady. "I stand before you charged with the crime of insubordination. Let me first start with a sincere apology for my thoughtless action. I do admit, because of my pride, I went on my own to gather information. I thought I could succeed in an action that was, in my opinion, for the good of Teravinea. That I did this without the approval of the Council was wrong. I now see the magnitude of my decision."

I raised my eyes from the piece of parchment from which I read, meeting Eben's troubled expression. Returning to my notes, I said, "I assure you riders that my purpose was in no way intended to undermine your trust, nor go against the rules of the Council.

"I planned only to find the island of Orchila and verify the existence of the Valley of Dragons. An hour or two was all I needed. I intended to take the information back to the Healer and petition Lord Ansel and the Council to consider a quest to plead assistance from the Ancient Ones. This would give us the advantage over Galtero. That was my sole intention. I now see my behavior put my dragon's life in danger, as well as my own. My actions jeopardized the safety of the kingdom. If something had happened to her, or me, it would have set back all your efforts thus far to gain the crown.

"I take full responsibility for my decision. In no way would Eshshah be to blame."

I felt Eshshah's protest, but continued.

"Please hear our story so you can understand my true objective — and my ignorance."

I proceeded to give them an account of our experience in Orchila, keeping all unnecessary emotion from my story. There were gasps and exclamations from the various riders at certain points during my narrative. I told them of our conversation with Senolis, of his reprimand about my pride, and his decline to assist us. I swallowed hard when I reached the end, thankful I hadn't allowed a tear in the entire recounting.

Similar to the first time I'd finished my story, the room filled with silence. And like then, once my listeners had absorbed it, all manner of questions were shot at me. Most of their inquiries centered on the Valley of Dragons.

The Healer spoke up, "It seems there is a great interest in the Ancient Ones. In order to avoid taking up any more time in this proceeding, Rider Amáne will write a full account of all that she saw in that valley."

Finally, the questions ended. They had all the information they needed. Avano's eyes met mine. My throat closed. A corner of his mouth raised as he gave a slightly perceptible nod. I read it as a silent *stay strong, good luck*. I took my seat before my knees gave way.

Ansel took over. "We'll move forward, now to discussion. Rider Amáne, you are dismissed. We'll call you back in three hours time."

"Yes Lord Ansel."

Thoroughly exhausted, I trudged out of the library to await deliberations. I headed for the courtyard to join Eshshah where she lay in the sun.

I slid to a sitting position and leaned my back against her foreleg in the shade of her body. Tears streamed down my face as

Eshshah and I waited in misery for the riders to discuss my fate. The wait became excruciating. I mused on the properties of time. Why, when enjoying a flight with Eshshah, did the time pass so quickly? An hour seemed like five minutes. Conversely, why, when I suffered from pain or anxiety, did time appear to stand still? Five minutes seemed a lifetime.

I rotated between pacing and sitting. Maybe I should have kept myself busy with some chores that needed to be done, but couldn't bring myself to stray far from Eshshah's side. We needed each other's touch.

When I thought I would go mad from the pressure, Ansel came out to summon me back to the library. He held out his hand to help me up. I searched his face but could read nothing. He'd had years of practice in keeping his expressions indecipherable. His eyes wouldn't meet mine.

My heart pounded out of my chest.

Hand in hand we walked back to the library.

"Ow, Ansel, you're squeezing my hand."

"Sorry."

My panic increased.

Ansel seated himself. I lowered into my seat and looked at the faces around me. Like Ansel, the others managed to keep all emotion from their countenance.

"Ansel asked that I facilitate this portion," the Healer said in a low voice. She turned to me. "Please stand."

My breath stopped. I rose to my feet.

The Healer cleared her throat. "After careful deliberation, we, the twenty-six members of the Dragon Rider's Council, find you, Amáne of Catriona of Teravinea, guilty of insubordination, as charged."

The blood drained from my face. My fingers clamped on to the edge of the table until my knuckles went white. The room spun.

"As a sworn rider, you are required to confer with the Council or Lord Ansel for approval for any matter that involves the well-being of the kingdom. Regardless of your intentions, you went without approval to seek information you, and you alone, felt necessary to attain the throne."

The Healer took a deep breath. "However ... the Dragon Rider's Council has agreed unanimously that you will not receive the maximum penalty of death."

Somehow, I managed to choke in a breath.

"Furthermore, the Council has agreed unanimously that you will not get a second chance; unanimous that for your punishment you will be grounded indefinitely from any flight with Eshshah, unless you have permission or orders from either Lord Ansel, myself or a ruling from the Council."

Grounded? — Unanimous? Eshshah and I silently screamed. This was a severe punishment for a dragon and rider. They might as well have thrown me into prison straightaway. I flashed a look at Ansel. I knew he felt my glare but didn't look at me. Without thinking, I opened my mouth to protest. Upon seeing the stern look on the Healer's face, I quickly shut it and lowered my eyes.

The Healer continued, "Amáne, do you understand each of these dictates?"

"Yes, Healer."

"Do you have anything to add?"

"No, Healer, except that I am truly sorry. Not just because of my punishment, but because I've failed in my duty to my fellow riders and to Teravinea. And, I've disrespected my dragon."

“Amáne, please don’t,” Eshshah said.

The Healer nodded in acceptance. “Does anyone at this table have anything they wish to say before this dreadful meeting is adjourned?”

All voiced their nays.

“Very well then, Amáne, you are dismissed. Go dress for fighting practice. Work on your own until someone can come out to work with you.”

“Yes, Healer.”

Chapter Thirty-four

A few weeks had passed since my hearing. Ansel had remained at the Healer's and planned to stay a while longer. My life would have been nearly impossible if he had left after I'd been pronounced guilty. It was as if he sensed his leaving would have pushed me into a deep depression. I was full of remorse for what I had done. But denying me any flight with Eshshah proved almost more than I could take. My punishment affected Eshshah, which she didn't deserve. Ansel's support became my life line. Sovann was a comfort to Eshshah. Even with our busy schedule, Ansel made it a point to spend some personal time with me every day, if only briefly.

Sitting around the Healer's kitchen table early one morning Ansel, the Healer, Gallen and I discussed the young men and few women who came each day to our weapons training.

"Bern said to expect one of his trainees to arrive within the next few days," the Healer said.

"Why is Bern sending a man down here?" I asked.

"He thought it was best. The recruit is young and has become restless in their mountain hideout. He's a quick learner but is prone to cause trouble with the others and with many of the girls. Bern proposed sending the young man to train under one of the other riders. The trainee requested Dorsal."

"That's odd. Who would request to come to Dorsal?" Something tugged at my memory. "Did Bern mention the man's name?"

"Yes, he said it was Darqin. That's an unusual name, isn't it?" the Healer said.

"Darqin?" My voice betrayed my uneasiness. He was that obnoxious young man who showed so much disrespect to Eshshah, and had a habit of calling me Sir Amáne.

Ansel cocked an eyebrow. "You know him?"

"I've met him."

"And ...?"

"I'm going to keep my opinions to myself so I won't influence your first impression of him. I'm sure a change of scenery will do him good." ... I hoped.

I took a sip of my tea to have an excuse to look somewhere other than Ansel's eyes. I got the feeling he'd already formed an opinion of Darqin.

The following morning the Healer sent me on an errand into town. I returned in time to start training my first class. I'd been put in charge of recruits who, for various reasons, hadn't had much in the way of weapons instruction. Since I was new at training, I taught those less skilled in the defensive arts.

I gave my full attention to my young group, taking seriously to the task of preparing my students well. They would advance to either the Healer, Gallen or Dorjan once they proved their skills from my instruction. I wasn't about to let one go without the knowledge and mastery necessary for their next level.

At a break in our workout, I stood at the laver outside the

kitchen splashing the cooling water on my face.

From behind me, I heard, "At last, Sir Amáne, we meet on your turf."

I spun around, eyes wide. "Darqin."

"You could at least be a little more happy to see me. You were all I could think of my entire trip."

Before I could stop myself, I grimaced.

"No need to hide your emotions any longer. I know deep down you're glad I'm here. Maybe we can spend a little more time together than we did in Anbon."

"Look, Darqin —"

"I would introduce you two," Ansel said as he approached, "but I see you already know each other."

Ugh, he'd heard our exchange.

Ansel and I had agreed to keep our relationship on a professional level in front of our students. This moment would be no different.

"Yes, Lord Ansel," I said, "we met when Anbon was attacked and Eshshah and I flew there to help Bern."

"And don't forget the next time we met." Darqin turned to Ansel. "I know she couldn't wait to bring Sir Bern back to Anbon so she could check in on me." His eyes swung back to me, "I enjoyed your company that last time," he added.

I glanced sharply at Darqin. Ansel threw me a questioning look. Shaking my head, I excused myself, spun around and stormed into the house. Poor Ansel, but there was nothing I could say to him in front of Darqin. I took in a deep breath and let it out slowly. My jaw unclenched.

During much of the afternoon training session I could feel

Darqin watching me. He trained under Dorjan. Out of the corner of my eye, I noticed he had some skill with a sword, but I also noted the anger that boiled in him during a sparring bout.

There were several recruits who lived some distance from the Healer's. She'd made arrangements to house them at an inn just a couple blocks away. I breathed a sigh of relief when Darqin left the grounds for the evening.

After our meal that night, Ansel and I wandered out to the courtyard and sat close together on a bench by the herb garden. The aromatic scent of rosemary floated in the night air.

I leaned back and enjoyed his company, even if he seemed a bit pensive. He took a strand of my hair and repeatedly wound and unwound it around his finger.

"It seems you know that Darqin, a little better than I imagined."

I turned to face him.

"Ansel, do I detect a note of jealousy?" I smiled.

He didn't smile back. "Should I be?"

"You're serious? His take on the two times we met is a delusion. I can assure you of that. All I did was try to be civil to him. I don't know how he twisted that into believing I offered him my attentions. Ansel, do you think I would even entertain any thoughts about that confused boy?"

"It seems he certainly entertains thoughts about you." He frowned.

I shuddered.

"Let me set you straight on the thoughts I do entertain." I pushed my fingers through his hair, brought his face to mine and pressed my mouth full upon his. He enfolded me in his arms and leaned into my kiss. His warmth set my heart on fire.

"Mmm, I believe I understand now," he breathed. "But just so I won't forget, would you mind repeating that thought?"

I did, passionately.

Chapter Thirty-five

A few mornings later, Ansel and I sat at the table together. The Healer and Gallen had not yet come down.

"Amáne, about Darqin ..."

"What about him? I thought I explained that the other night."

A corner of his mouth turned up. "I love the way you explained it."

He shifted to a serious tone, "But what I'm trying to say is, you need to keep your eye on him. Any attention he gets from you seems to give him the wrong idea. I've been watching him the last couple of days. I don't trust him. If he ever makes you uncomfortable, you tell me. I'll have a talk with him."

"Ansel, don't be silly. Thanks, but I can take care of myself. I'm sure, if anything, it's just a curiosity he has about me. He'll get over it. Then he'll settle in and be like the other recruits — just part of the team."

"You think I don't see some of the looks you get from the *team*?"

I sighed. "I'm just a trainer, Ansel. Like the Healer. Like you. No one is looking at me. Quit your worrying."

"Your naiveté is endearing to me, Amáne, but it could get you into trouble. You don't understand the way males think. Just be careful around him is all I ask."

"I said I can take care of myself. Stop lecturing me."

I knew he was sincere and only had my well-being in mind, but I couldn't keep my teeth from clenching. My emotions were on edge. The ban from flight progressively increased my dark mood. I gulped down the last of my tea and slammed the cup on the table. Without excusing myself, I sprang to my feet and stormed out of the kitchen.

"Amáne," Ansel called after me.

I ran as fast as I could across the courtyard, and through the field toward the far end of the barn. I grabbed a glaive from the weapons rack and worked fiercely on the pell. The exertion did me good. By the time my students showed up, my anger had dissipated. I shifted into a better mood to coach.

For our training workout, my group wore full armor. Besides getting accustomed to the weight, it also built their strength. Passed down through the years, the practice armor had seen a lot of wear. At the end of the session, one of the students broke a buckle on his breastplate. I dismissed everyone a little early, grabbed his breastplate and made for the barn.

My back to the door, I searched the small hardware drawers for the right size buckle.

"Alone at last."

I spun around at the sound of Darqin's voice.

"What do you need, Darqin?"

"I think I need you." He moved toward me.

I stepped back.

Ansel appeared in the doorway. "Is everything all right in here?" He looked at Darqin and then at me.

"Yes, Lord Ansel. I have it under control."

Ansel gave a reluctant shrug and walked away.

I turned my attention back to Darqin. "I'm not interested, Darqin. Now leave. Go take your break with the others."

He stepped closer. "No. I'd rather take my break with you."

He reached out to touch my face. I blocked his arm.

"Darqin, I'm warning you. Leave now."

"Or what Sir Amáne? You might slap my hand?"

I glared at him.

"All I want is a little of your attention," he said. "Now that can't be too much to ask."

He stepped toward me and grabbed my wrist.

I moved in, bent my elbow down in an arc toward his arm as I brought my hand toward my shoulder. It broke his hold easily. Stepping close, I swept my foot around and took his leg out from under him. He landed on his back with a thud.

I pointed out the door and said between my teeth, "Leave now, before I report what you just tried." *Why do I feel such pity for him that I'm going to let him go on this serious count?*

His face twisted with rage. He jumped to his feet and drew his sword. I didn't have a weapon with me — something I vowed I'd never do.

"I'm with you, Amáne." I felt Eshshah's strength flow through me.

Darqin lunged. I leapt out of his reach. My eyes swept the barn. I needed something to stave him off. The weapons were on the far side. He advanced and sliced at my head. I ducked.

"You won't insult me and get away with it, dragon rider. You're too stupid to figure out you'll never find another man that'll take you. And you think you're too good to accept me. You don't deserve to live."

He thrust his blade at me. I dodged, dove to the ground, rolled and leaped to my feet. Footsteps sounded at the doorway.

"Amáne, catch!" Ansel tossed me a sword. It flew in an arc toward me. I reached up and took hold of the hilt. Darqin lunged again. I parried, leaving my sword against the inside of his. Stepping in I raised my blade to vertical. Wrapping it around to the outside of his, I slid it down and jerked hard. In a matter of seconds I'd disarmed him. His blade clattered to the ground several feet away.

I pressed the point of my blade on his chest with just enough pressure to where it wouldn't break the skin, as long as he kept backing up. I followed until he came against a work bench. I could have run him through, but I spared him. I would not draw blood in an uneven fight with an unbalanced boy.

He put up his hands in surrender. His eyes bugged out in anger, mixed with fear.

Ansel leaned against the door jam, arms crossed.

Darqin shot a glance at him. "Don't let her kill me."

Ansel smiled, then looked at me. "I've seen you dispatch grown men in armor faster than that. What took you so long?"

"I could ask you the same question."

"My apologies. I was under the impression you had everything under control, rider."

"My error. Apparently I still haven't mastered my understanding of male behavior, my Lord."

"I concur."

I scowled at him.

He stepped in, grabbed Darqin by the scruff of his shirt and roughly escorted him out to face the Healer.

Chapter Thirty-six

I stood in the barn and watched as Ansel dragged Darqin away. Tears of frustration welled up. Once again my stupidity had gotten me into trouble. *Why can't I understand males and their way of thinking*?

My fists clenched. I wanted to scream. I stomped toward the rear of the barn, kicking Darqin's sword as hard as I could. It hurt. My rage increased. I passed the donkey's stall and the Healer's horse, Thunder. He snorted as I stormed by. I made my way to the very last stall, in the farthest corner of the large barn.

Turning my back to the wall, I slid down and sat in the hay. I tilted my head back and stared at the rafters above. My shoulders jerked with sobs.

I felt Eshshah's soft hum. "Eshshah, please, I don't want to be consoled. Can you just leave me alone to wallow — just for a bit? Thank you." I knew she wouldn't condone it for long.

My misery absorbed me. I didn't hear Ansel's approach until he stepped into the stall. He lowered himself beside me, stretching his long legs in front of him. Taking my hand, we sat in silence.

Ansel turned my hand over in his, intently examining my palm, and tracing my fingers. It was distracting. I couldn't fully concentrate on my sour mood.

I finally broke the silence. "That whole incident could have been avoided if I'd listened to you. You were right, I am naive. I didn't have it under control like I thought. I guess I just don't understand your kind."

"My kind? You make us sound like some sort of bizarre animal or something."

"You are. And, I'm ignorant. I have no idea how you males think."

"Allow me to explain something, Amáne. Besides your formidable position as a dragon rider, you're a beautiful girl with weapons skills any male would envy."

He ignored my confused reaction, and continued. "Most have never met anyone like you, and no one knows quite how to deal with you. Add to that your innocence, and truthfully, you drive men crazy."

"Is that a compliment or an insult?"

"Neither. I'm just giving you a lesson on the way *my kind* thinks about you."

"Why can't they just accept who I am — a trainer? Just a trainer. Not a female, or male, or anything other than a trainer. Is that so difficult?" My voice rose.

Ansel sighed, let go of my hand, and turned to me. "Is that difficult? Let me think. How do I answer that question?" He reached over and pushed back my disheveled hair. His other hand held my face. He tilted his head and pressed his lips against mine.

"Hmm. Yes, to answer your question, it is difficult. Very difficult," he whispered. Pulling me closer, he cradled me in front of him, and kissed me more fervently. He held me tight as my heart beat out of my chest. A warmth spread through me.

He pulled away to gaze at me. I became lost in his intense green eyes. They were on fire. A nervous twinge went through me as I tried to read his face. He leaned in, hesitated, then stopped. My lips burned for more. I felt he could read that in my eyes.

Ansel started to say something, but stopped. He shook his head and bit his lower lip. His eyes closed and he seemed to struggle with his thoughts. Opening them, a resigned look rose on his face. He kissed my forehead, gently moved me out of his way, and rose to his feet.

Extending his hand to help me up, he said, "Come on. Let's go before you get another lesson on *my kind* that you don't need to learn yet."

Leaving the stall hand in hand, I trembled. As we turned the corner, we practically ran into Gallen. He looked at Ansel, then at me, still flush from Ansel's kisses. A disapproving look flashed in his eyes.

In a controlled voice, Gallen said, "The Healer is looking for you, Amáne. You'd better get that straw out of your hair before she sees you. And I will have a word with you later."

I think I must have gone beyond red. My jaw dropped. I gasped. Before I could defend myself, Ansel spoke up.

"No need for alarm, Gallen. Your girl is safe with me. Her honor is my first priority."

Gallen's shoulders relaxed, "Thank you, Lord Ansel. You do understand my concern?"

"Completely. I'm no longer that same person you once knew."

I wondered what it was about Ansel that had concerned Gallen. I shook my head and headed out to find the Healer, picking the straw from my hair as I went.

Chapter Thirty-seven

I found the Healer in her library just as she signed off with Rider Calder.

"Are you all right?" she asked searching my face.

"Yes. But I feel like such a fool. I should have been able to read him better."

I slumped into a couch and put my head in my hands. The Healer sat next to me and pulled me to her.

"Amáne, you're not expected to know how to read people. That will come with time and experience. You're a beautiful young lady with exceptional skills. It throws a lot of people off, especially men."

"So I've been told."

"Then your best option is to start believing it."

I nodded.

"What will become of Darqin?" I asked.

"Dorjan is holding him until Calder arrives. Calder has the facilities to keep Darqin while his fate is decided. He's a three-day ride from here, on horseback. I just spoke with him. He's leaving shortly."

"Again, another waste of time because of me," I complained. "Somehow, I think I should have been able to do something to avoid that situation."

"Don't be ridiculous. Some things you can't control."

Several days later, the Healer found Ansel and me at target practice.

"I'll be heading to Dorjan's in the next hour. Calder is leaving to take Darqin back to Glinfoil," she said.

"I'd like to join you," Ansel said.

"Me too," I added.

"No. You're not going, Amáne," Ansel said in a stern voice.

"Yes. I have to."

"What reason could you possibly have?" Ansel asked.

"I have two reasons. One, I want to be a witness to his leaving — I want to see him ride out, hopefully punished and put away, so he'll never seek me out again. And, two, I want to try to forgive him. If I could remind myself what a miserable wreck he is, I think it would help."

Ansel's jaw dropped as he stared at me. The Healer tipped her head, eyebrows raised.

"I've learned a lot about forgiveness these last few months," I said.

Ansel continued to stare.

"Forgiving my father was the most liberating feeling I've ever experienced. I have a father now instead of a man I would have gone to my ancestors hating. Then there's you, Ansel. How many times have you forgiven me for my thoughtlessness and anger?"

"That doesn't even compare to this. It's as different as sun and moon. That man tried to kill you."

"But he didn't. I just need to try to forgive him."

With an exasperated look at his aunt, he said, "Healer, are you going to help me out, here?"

"Ansel, while I see your point," the Healer said, "I'm going to have to concede to Amáne. This is for her own resolution."

His jaw tightened. "Fine. But you'll not even get near him. Do you understand?"

"Thank you, Ansel. I have no desire to get near him." I slipped my arm in his.

♛

We stood out front at Dorjan's house. It was time for Calder to leave with his charge. Dorjan fetched Darqin and led him out. His hands were secured in front with leather manacles. Much more humane than the iron I'd worn on more than one occasion. Dorjan helped him onto a horse tied behind Calder's.

Ansel pulled me further away, a protective arm around my shoulders.

Darqin swung his gaze around to me. His eyes swept over Ansel and then back to me. I was taken aback by the hatred that burned in his eyes. His features twisted into an angry grimace. He spat in my direction.

"That was uncalled for, boy," Dorjan boomed.

Darqin shouted at me, "I swear you're gonna regret what you did to me, Sir Amáne. You and that ugly scaled creature of yours." He glared at Ansel. "And that —"

Calder swung his horse around and backhanded him.

Ansel ushered me into the house. He pulled me close and held me tightly. I buried my face in his chest.

"Do you still want to forgive him?" Ansel asked.

"I'm trying to."

He squeezed me tighter.

Chapter Thirty-eight

"I'm worried about Calder," the Healer said as she joined us in the kitchen. "It's a three-day ride to Glinfoil. He should have arrived last night at the latest. I've tried to contact him. He doesn't answer."

"Maybe Sovann and I should fly there and check," Ansel said.

"You may just have to if we don't hear from him by tonight. Gallen can go with you."

I sat up straight. "Wouldn't it be better if Eshshah and I went with them?"

They both whipped their heads in my direction. My hopes fell. "I just thought that ..."

"It would take a lot more than a delayed dragon rider to get you in the saddle, Amáne. Put it out of your mind," the Healer admonished.

I pounded the table. Gritting my teeth, I jumped to my feet and made my way to the library. *Maybe I can distract myself with some of the Healer's books*.

The communication disc buzzed as I stomped into the room. I grabbed the knob and watched as the glass shimmered into an image.

"Calder!" I said. Barely recognizable, his eye had swollen shut; an angry gash cut across his cheek; his split lip bleeding; blood stained his shirt. "What happened, Calder?" I yelled over my shoulder, "Healer, come in here, quick."

Calder waited until the Healer arrived, Ansel and Gallen on her heels. The Healer groaned when she saw the rider's condition.

"Darqin's gotten away," Calder said. "I let my guard down. I'd found a spot to stop for the night and decided to start a fire before I tied his feet. Made the mistake of turning my back on him. He found a branch and beat me good with it. If I didn't have Bade's venom running in my veins, I'd be a dead man. I'm sure he thought he'd finished me off. By the time I came to, he was long gone. Took the horses. I followed his trail for a while. He must have had some tracking experience. He did a pretty good job covering his footprints. Didn't look like he headed back to Dorsal. I followed him for a long time, then lost him. He's heading north. I'm sorry." His shoulders slumped with defeat.

"It's all right, Calder. I'm worried about you. Get yourself taken care of," the Healer said.

"I came to Glinfoil to contact you. I plan to replenish my supplies and leave soon to continue the search for Darqin."

"No," put in Ansel. "Right now, we need you there. You can't be going on a wild chase to find him. We'll put the word out to apprehend him when found. If he were headed in this direction, it'd be a different story. Amáne's safety would be at stake. You sound sure he's headed the opposite way. Get your injuries tended to. We want you healthy. Thank you, Calder. You did everything you could."

Calder nodded.

“Contact us tonight,” the Healer said.

We all saluted and signed off. I took my hand off the knob.

“Where do you think he’d go?” I asked. “I doubt he’d head back to Anbon.”

“No idea,” the Healer said shaking her head. “Hopefully somewhere he can think about turning himself in. But he doesn’t strike me as the remorseful type.”

Chapter Thirty-nine

Late one afternoon I wandered into the Healer's library after a particularly hard workout. It had became more difficult for me to fight off my wretchedness from being grounded. Eshshah suffered with me. My declining disposition was not lost on Ansel. My temper was volatile.

Dorjan and Ansel happened to be there poring over a map of the kingdom. I'd hoped to have the room to myself.

I plopped myself on a bench and removed my boots. The cool tile felt good on my hot, tired feet.

"So, Amáne," Dorjan said, "I haven't gotten a chance to ask you if you saw any two-headed dragons in Orchila?"

"You're funny, Dorjan." I didn't make any effort to look amused.

"No, I'm serious. Did you see any?"

"Sure, they were all over the skies," I said.

"Do you mean in all of your studies you've done, you never heard of Diacephal?"

"What are you talking about? Who's Diacephal?"

"He was a two-headed dragon that lived ages ago. Before Leyna, even before Ansel's great grandfather, King Eadrid."

I gave Ansel a look, silently asking *is this true*?

Ansel offered a slight nod. Since he was an expert in dragon lore, his confirmation of this incredible creature peaked my interest.

"You're serious, Dorjan? A two-headed dragon?"

"Absolutely. He was a white dragon."

"His scales so bright, they were nearly transparent," Ansel added.

Completely drawn into the story, my frustration melted. "I don't know why I never found any account of him in all of the manuscripts I studied. Where can I find more information on him — maybe some illustration?"

"Drawings are rare," Ansel said.

Not only did I forget my troubles, but my excitement rose. This would give me something else to occupy my mind.

"Eshshah," I said in thought transference, "what do your memories tell you of the two-headed dragon?"

"The two-headed dragon?"

"Yes, Diacephal. Dorjan and Ansel told me about him."

A low rumble of her laughter echoed in my head. "Amáne, I'm afraid Lord Ansel and Dorjan are having their fun with you."

"What!?" I said out loud.

I turned on the two men, who suddenly looked guilty.

"You horrible men!" I shouted.

They burst into laughter, which made me even more mad. The heat rose in my face. I picked up one of my boots and hurled it at Dorjan catching him hard on the chest.

He grunted. "We really had you going. A two-headed dragon? Really, Amáne?" His booming laughter filled the library.

"You really are that gullible," Ansel laughed.

I picked up my second boot and launched it at Ansel. He ducked. The boot crashed against the wall.

"Then you shouldn't be so proud of your success if I'm so easy to fool."

"I believe my wife will be expecting me home, soon," Dorjan said. "I'll be leaving now. Good luck Lord Ansel. You'd be wise to come up with something to appease her wrath." With that he slipped out of the room.

"Coward!" Ansel shouted after him.

Laughter has a tendency to quench an enraged fire. I could hear Dorjan still roaring as he left the house. Ansel snickered. I bit the inside of my cheek to keep my lips from twitching.

Trying to hold my angry edge, I put my hands on my hips and faced Ansel, "Yes you'd better figure out how to appease my wrath."

"I might just have something that will do the trick." He paused and met my eyes.

"Well?" I demanded.

"Well, how would you and Eshshah like to go with Sovann and me tonight on a small, easy, safe, simple quest?"

I gasped. *Am I dreaming?*

"What? A quest? With you and Sovann and Eshshah? Do you seriously mean it?" Then I froze. "Ansel, are you playing with me again? Because if you are ..."

"No, I'm serious. But I'm not talking about the kind of mission to which you're accustomed. It won't be life threatening. No danger, no breaking into castles, just a simple trip — hardly what you'd call a quest. Dorjan has to assemble a large supply of lightning balls. He needs more scales from Eben's late dragon, Salama. We'll fly to Nicobar, where Eben lives. He has a bag ready for us. Would that appease your wrath?"

I threw my arms around him. "It would absolutely appease my wrath. Ansel, you have no idea how this makes me feel."

"Oh, I think I do."

"I love you, Ansel." I kissed his lips three times.

"So that's what it takes to buy your love?"

I hit him in the chest. "Don't be ridiculous. When do we leave?"

"As soon as it gets dark, which will be soon. Go get ready."

I charged out of the library and headed to my chambers.

"Eshshah, we get to fly tonight!"

"I know, Amáne. At last!" Her excitement mirrored mine.

I threw on my breastplate and riding gear, grabbed my helmet and cloak and rushed back to the library for my boots. Ansel was still there rolling up the maps left scattered before Dorjan's hasty retreat.

He noted my attire. "Why the breastplate? We're just going for a simple ride to Eben's, not a skirmish."

"I wear my breastplate almost every time I fly. The Healer said it's a good habit to get into. You might do well to heed her advice."

Ansel shrugged.

Shaking my head at his dismissal, I picked up one of my boots and looked around for the second.

"Where's my other boot?"

"You mean the one you launched at me?" Before I could answer, he reached behind a table and came up with it, "This one?"

I grabbed for it, but he moved quickly. He lifted it above my head — just out of my reach.

"Ansel! Give it to me."

"Get it. It's right here," he taunted, holding it high.

I tried to snatch it from him, but his reach was beyond mine. When I jumped, he countered with a jump of his own. He hid it behind his back and dodged me when I lunged. I chased him around the room, but couldn't get any closer to my goal.

"Ansel!"

He was thoroughly amused.

"You seem to be having a fun day at my expense. Now give me my boot."

Ansel smiled and raised it over my head again.

My chase tactics didn't seem to be working. Changing my strategy, I stopped directly in front of him. I leaped up and wrapped my legs around his waist, nearly knocking him down. My goal was now within reach, but suddenly he lost interest in the game. He lowered his arm without resistance. I yanked my boot out of his hand. Before I could claim victory, he pulled me close. We locked eyes.

My heart pounded like thunder as he tilted his head and pressed his mouth against mine.

"You cheated," he breathed. "You took advantage of my weakness."

"Weakness? You don't have a weakness."

"Ah, but I do — my weakness is you."

Before I could respond, he kissed me once more.

"Hmm. If I would have known about your weakness," I said, "I might have gotten a flight out of you much sooner."

I smiled as I released my legs, pushed off from him, and landed lightly on the floor. My knees nearly gave in, my head reeled. I did enjoy his attentions, but even as my heart still pounded from his kisses, I couldn't wait to fly again with Eshshah. Barring me from flight proved more difficult than I would have imagined.

"I'm afraid, even with cheating, it's doubtful you could have flown earlier. Not everyone in the Council was fully convinced we should give you respite from your punishment so soon, and for such a small task."

"Truthfully, Ansel, you could have convinced them you needed us to fly to Nunn for some chicken eggs, and they would have allowed it." I laughed, ignoring his serious note.

"This is not a pleasure ride, Amáne." He hesitated. His shoulders slumped, "I might as well tell you now. My justification for requesting you on this flight is to save me a trip back here. We'll all go together to pick up Salama's scales. You and Eshshah will bring them back to Dorjan. Sovann and I must continue to Serislan."

"You sure know how to put a cloud in front of my sunshine, Ansel."

It was inevitable that his time here would come to an end, which made it all the more difficult to accept.

I chewed my bottom lip as I sat on a bench and pulled on my boots.

"No matter. I'm going to consider it a pleasure ride, anyway." I sighed. "At least until it's time to leave Eben's." I tried to smile, but a tear got in the way.

Ansel lowered himself next to me.

"Do you really have to leave so soon?" I asked.

"It feels like 'so soon,' but I've been here for several weeks. Longer than I should have. I have duties in Trivingar that need my attention. Leaving earlier wasn't possible. I worried about you after your sentencing. Now I know you'll be fine."

His eyes met mine. "My time here, seeing you every day has been like a dream. One day that dream will become a reality. I promise." His face brightened. "Until then, let's just enjoy the moment. The surprise isn't over."

"What do you mean?"

"Come on. It's time to ride."

Chapter Forty

While Ansel and I saddled Sovann and Eshshah in the courtyard, Gallen brought out Ansel's satchels. I caught a look on Gallen's face that puzzled me. As I tightened the girth around Eshshah, the Healer brought out a bag that wafted the most delicious aroma — the smell of roasted meat.

I eyed it curiously. The Healer just smiled.

"I thought we were going to eat travel cakes on the way," I said. "How are we supposed to manage a full meal while we're flying?"

"We'll just have to ask our dragons to fly slowly so I can toss you your share without too much mess."

"What are you up to? You all have a guilty look about you."

The three of them glanced at each other, then back at me. Complete innocence masked their faces. Gallen shook his head in feigned ignorance. I cocked an eyebrow and decided I'd better stay on my alert.

The Healer and Gallen both gave me hugs. My suspicious mind suggested they were a little too strong and held a bit longer than necessary. Gallen gave me a leg up. They stepped back and saluted us as Sovann and Eshshah launched off the ground.

I closed my eyes but couldn't hold back my scream of pure joy.

"Eshshah!" I yelled out loud.

She rumbled her delight. The four of us laughed our way over the water as we headed east.

"Ansel, why are we going east? Nicobar is northwest."

"We're just doing a short detour. I have something I need to take care of."

"What would that be? There's nothing in this direction."

I turned to him as Eshshah and Sovann flew closely abreast. My heart melted at the smile that turned his lips. Sovann peeled off and headed north. Eshshah followed.

"Answer me, Ansel," I shouted over the wind.

Eshshah caught up and we flew alongside them again. An excitement filled Ansel's face. Sovann banked sharply south. Again Eshshah followed. I could feel her tension.

"What are we doing, Eshshah? What's this all about?"

She rumbled.

Sovann and Eshshah spiraled higher until they caught a wind current and soared closer to each other than I'd ever imagined. Their wings overlapped.

Eshshah felt my surprise. "It's fine, Amáne. Sovann and I do this all the time."

Ansel and I were so close we could almost reach out and touch each other. It was thrilling.

"Ansel?"

Silence, but this time, I sensed Ansel could barely contain his emotions. I picked up on a nervous energy.

Ansel, nervous? I must be imagining things.

"If someone doesn't tell me what's going on, I'm going to get very mad or very scared. We keep switching directions, and we're heading the wrong way. Nicobar is north. Have you all gone mad?"

"Amáne."

"What Ansel?"

"May I ask you a question?"

"I hope it's for directions. You certainly don't know where you're going."

"No, it's not for directions."

"Then what is it? It looks like this day of having your fun with me is not over yet. And now you've included our dragons. Out with it!"

"Amáne."

I rolled my eyes and heaved a great sigh.

"What?"

"Will you marry me, Amáne?" he cried out with exultant joy.

I sat in stunned silence, forgetting to breathe. That was the last question I'd expected from him.

"Amáne?" Ansel's worried look brought me back.

I turned to him with tears in my eyes. I opened my mouth, but nothing would come out.

"Amáne, answer Lord Ansel," Eshshah said.

"I ... er ... Ansel ... I can't ... think of anything I'd rather do than to marry you. Yes! Yes! And yes once more." My body shook. I felt giddy.

Our dragons trumpeted with joy.

The contortions on poor Ansel's face made me burst out laughing. It registered from confusion to fear to utter relief, all in a matter of seconds.

"I thought my heart was going to stop," Ansel said. "It would have if you hadn't said yes. I suppose you owe me from all my teasing. You win."

"It wasn't on purpose, Ansel. I couldn't have done that to you. It's just that ... that you took me by complete surprise. I really couldn't breathe. What a brilliantly romantic notion. Proposal on dragonback."

Both dragons peeled into a sharp dive. I realized we were headed toward my favorite cove.

We landed softly on the sandy beach. I couldn't unbuckle quick enough. Ansel was first off, already at Eshshah's foreleg as I slid from the saddle. I jumped into his arms.

We kissed as my tears of happiness united with his.

"Wait right here," Ansel said.

He rushed back to Sovann. I couldn't see what he was up to as I heard him shuffling about on the other side of our dragons.

At last he came back around and took both my hands. He acted like a small boy as he said, "It's ready. Close your eyes."

Ansel led me a short distance across the sand.

"All right, you can open them, now."

"Ohhh," I whispered. He had laid out the most magnificent outdoor meal I'd ever seen. A quilt spread on the sand held the roasted meat the Healer had prepared along with cheese and fruit. There was even one of the Healer's candelabras lit and perched on a rock near the quilt.

At the edge of the spread, Ansel went to one knee. He pulled out a ring from a pouch that hung on his belt.

Taking my hands, he said, "Amáne, my love. Please accept this ring as a token of my troth. A solemn vow that my heart will always belong to you. Just as I'd known when you first told me your name."

"Yes, I accept," I said as he slid a most beautiful gold ring on my finger. The band started wide at the top, then narrowed at the bottom. An intricate design of connecting swirls wove its way around with a dark patina in the recesses. It was topped with a deep blue stone — a sapphire. My favorite. My life couldn't have gotten any better.

CHAPTER FORTY-ONE

"Look, a shooting star," I said to Ansel. "Did you know when you see one you're supposed to make a wish? You have to finish making it before it disappears, or it won't come true."

We lay on our backs on the quilt and gazed up at the myriad stars that decorated the sky. Ansel squeezed my hand and brought it to his lips.

"My wish has already come true," he said.

I thought the smile on my face would never go away ... ever.

We had just finished a delicious meal, even better than the feast served at Ansel's birthday ball nearly a year ago. Not wanting our moment to end, we lingered after we had packed away the left overs. The night breeze whispered and the waves lapped the shore. The new moon assured the best star gazing. Our dragons lay contented, nearby.

Ansel rolled onto his elbow and studied my face. He traced my eyebrow, then down my nose and rested his finger on my lips. He let out a reluctant sigh. "I'm afraid it's time for us to leave. Eben will be expecting us."

He kissed me tenderly. With one last lingering gaze, he rose to his feet and offered me his hand.

We folded the quilt, loaded it in a pack, then donned our helmets and riding cloaks. Ansel gave me a leg up to my saddle and we were airborne.

After a two-and-a-half hour flight, we spotted the rather large township of Nicobar. The outpost was located a small distance further to the south, in the low-lying hills. Unlike other outposts, located high up in cliff faces, Nicobar Outpost lay hidden in a small hill at ground level. Similar to the others, the cavern was undetectable. Dorjan had instructed our dragons where to find the hidden entrance.

We knew Eben had enough property for us to land almost at his front door, but we couldn't chance discovery. We decided to leave Sovann and Eshshah at the outpost and walk into Nicobar. It would allow us a bit more time to spend in each other's company. My head still reeled from our extraordinary evening.

Ansel and I found the road that headed into town. Before leaving the outpost, I'd strung my ring on a leather thong and tied it around my neck to hang under my tunic. I tucked my hair up into a cap and took up a masculine gait. A female walking with a man through town at that late hour would have brought too much attention.

The taverns did a lively business. Their light poured out from the doorways onto the road. The laughter and music from one establishment joined with the same from the next. The patrons from the more crowded pubs overflowed onto the street.

We kept to ourselves, and stayed on the less-traveled lanes. But we still drew attention, as we strode along toward Eben's, whose house lay on the other side of town.

"Hey little boy, shouldn't you be at home in bed, hangin' on to your mama's apron strings?"

"Come on in. We'll make a man outta ya here."

"Isn't that spear a little big for you? You'd need to cut it by half to wield it."

A couple of times, I slowed my gait, ready to respond to their rudeness.

"Keep walking," Ansel whispered out of the corner of his mouth. "We don't need any trouble."

I sucked in my breath and tried to tune them out. We were nearing Eben's when a tavern brawl tumbled onto the lane as we passed by. Three men locked in the fray crashed into me before I could dodge them. I went down hard. The trio suddenly joined forces and turned on me, blaming me for their altercation. Rolling onto my feet, I dodged a kick, then blocked a punch. With the butt end of my glaive, I trip one of them. Ansel effortlessly took care of the other two. We left them sprawled in the dirt, moaning, as we quickly slipped down the nearest alley.

"Are you all right?" Ansel asked.

"I'm fine. I think my pride is a little more wounded than my shoulder. I should have seen that coming. I guess my mind isn't where it should be right now."

I gazed up at him. We couldn't get caught embracing in the alleyway, so with a quick squeeze of my hand, he returned my smile and we continued to Eben's.

"Here we are," Ansel said as we arrived at the cottage gate. Eben lived on a dark lane on the outskirts of town, a quiet and private piece of property.

Ansel unlatched the gate and we headed up the walkway. Both of us froze. The door was ajar and light streamed out onto the walk. Angry voices sounded inside. Something wasn't right.

Ansel drew his sword slowly, avoiding any sound as he slid it from its sheath. My glaive at the ready, my heart pumped. Adrenaline flowed. I slowed my breathing and concentrated on the energy to fight. He pushed in the door and checked that the room was empty, then motioned for me to follow. A tussle echoed in a far room. Then thuds — the sound of fists on flesh.

Three men, as if from nowhere, leaped into the room, wielding crossbows. The bowstrings were drawn, bolts in place and aimed directly at us.

"Drop your weapons or we'll send your friend to his ancestors."

Ansel put down his sword. A soldier grabbed my glaive and yanked my dagger from my belt.

"Move!" he bellowed.

We were herded down a hallway into another room. A pair of the king's soldiers stood on either side of a chair in which a motionless Eben was tied. He was slumped over, bruised and bleeding.

Eben groaned. I breathed in relief that he still lived. He looked horrible. My anger rose at what these men had done to him. I moved closer to comfort him, but a soldier stepped in front.

Ignoring the man, I lowered my voice an octave to sound less feminine, "Eben, it's us." He would recognize my voice, even at this altered level.

"Shut up!" growled the soldier in front of me. He raised the butt end of Ansel's sword and brought it down on me. I blocked the brunt of the assault, but it still caught me on my cheekbone. Pain ricocheted in my head. Ansel gasped but was held in check by two of our captors. My sight blurred, but I stayed on my feet. Ansel's anxiety was a great motivating factor.

"Clap those irons on 'em and take 'em to the back room."

The younger soldier, not much older than I, took our hands behind our backs and in turn locked the manacles on our wrists. The heavy bands cut into my skin. He led us toward the door.

The man who appeared to be in charge held up his hand. "Hold it. Let me check something, yeah." He circled Ansel and me, eyeing us curiously.

"Amáne," Eshshah called, "we're on our way."

"Fly wide of the town, Eshshah, and land in the field next to the cottage. Take care of any soldiers out there, then wait for further word. We can't have you crashing into the house just yet. They might kill Ansel or Eben if you do."

I sensed Ansel was having a similar conversation with Sovann.

"Follow Ansel's instructions if they differ from mine," I added.

The head soldier drew his knife and turned to Ansel. My blood went cold. My mind raced. *I have to stop him!* I was ready to leap in front of the knife or knock Ansel down before the man struck. My efforts might be futile, but I couldn't just watch them kill him.

I stayed my action when it appeared the man was not about to use the knife against Ansel. He lowered it to Ansel's arm. Taking a hold of his right sleeve, he slashed the fabric. Sovann's linking mark made it known Ansel was a dragon rider. Next, he slashed my sleeve.

An evil sneer rose on the man's face. "What have we here? We've stumbled on a treasure, boys. King Galtero's gonna reward us big, ya hear? We came for one filthy dragonless rider and we'll go back with three," he laughed. "Or I shoulda said two-and-a-half, yeah." His eyes raked me up and down.

"You're too puny to be a dragon rider. An' your a might young, what?" He brought his face close to mine. His his vile breath nearly gagged me. I wanted to butt him with my head and break his nose. It would not have been the best decision with two cross bows trained on us.

"Hold this one, Bort. Tight."

The young soldier moved behind me. I could smell his fear. *Good.* Although at this point, I couldn't make use of his unease. With Ansel's life at stake, a hasty move would be too risky. I didn't struggle as he took my elbows and brought them closer together at my back. He put his arm through both of mine and held me tight.

Satisfied I was sufficiently restrained, the leader grabbed the top of my cap. I gave him my hardest glare. His eyes flickered as he hesitated in the space of a heartbeat, before he yanked it off. My hair tumbled in a tangled mass around my shoulders. The man's eyes went wide, as did his sneer.

Ansel exhaled a long slow breath. Out of the corner of my eye I could see, by his tense body, he was ready to move against the man antagonizing me. Chains or not.

"Eshshah, tell Ansel to hold off. Now is not the time." His jaw tightened as he got my message.

"Well boys," the soldier said, "our little treasure just became a big pot o' gold. What we got here is not just any little dragon rider, ya hear? It's the girl from the Prophecy. King Galtero's been scouring the kingdom for 'er. And we got 'er right here, yeah. Prepare for a life of luxury." He laughed so loud, Eben stirred from unconsciousness. The other four joined in the laughter.

"Bort, go get the captain an' tell 'im we'll need more men. The five of us ain't enough to transport these three to the king. Especially this one. I hear she's a might slippery, yeah. I'll make sure she ain't gettin' away."

He personally herded us to the back room.

Chapter Forty-Two

Ansel and I sat on the floor, back-to-back, chained to the leg of a heavy piece of furniture. We told our dragons to stand down until we had a course of action. Our situation, although dire, did not appear hopeless. At the moment, we knew Galtero wanted us alive — to be delivered to Castle Teravinea.

Eshshah and Sovann intercepted Bort en route to the captain. I snickered to myself as I pictured what the poor boy's face must have looked like when he ran into two full-sized dragons.

I assessed our situation. I'd been in worse predicaments. I shook my head at the turn of events. *What an evening. A marriage proposal one minute, chained prisoner to my betrothed the next. Not quite how I pictured our night to progress.*

"Maybe some time in the future," I whispered over my shoulder to Ansel, "when we're just sitting around, enjoying each other's company, with nothing else to do, you can explain to me how this quest was not life threatening."

Ansel groaned. "I'm so sorry, Amáne."

"I should have warned you," I said, "that most of my

undertakings involve capture and restraints. Next time you should think before inviting me along."

"Amáne," he warned, not appreciating my humor.

Truthfully, my light mood seemed inappropriate, considering the circumstances. Eben had been beaten; my eye had swelled shut; Ansel had descended into a sour disposition and the room stunk. Perhaps I'd finally lost my mind. Strangely, I wasn't afraid. Ansel and I were in this together. I didn't have to worry about him worrying about me. And even more appealing — this trip was his idea. However, this didn't mean that I'd resigned myself to defeat.

"Are you ready to leave now?" I asked.

"Amáne." He whispered loudly. "Stop joking. Have you gone mad? This is serious."

"I am serious. Are you ready to go?" As I finished my sentence, I whispered, "Aperio," and turned my dragon-scale key. Ansel's manacles slid from his wrists.

I'd always kept Aperio's key around my neck. This time, fortune was on my side. Fiona and I agreed it made more sense to have the key available closer to my hands. She devised a small pocket that she sewed inconspicuously inside the sleeves of all my clothing.

As I sat annoying Ansel, I'd worked the key from my sleeve and then into the keyhole to his restraints.

He took the key from my hand and whispered Aperio's name as he unlocked my irons.

I held my hand out for my key. "Sorry, Rider, you'll have to get your own."

Without a sound, we leaped to our feet. I caught him shaking his head, bewildered.

"That time in the future that you were talking about?" he said in a whisper, "... remind me to tell you all the reasons why I love you."

A corner of my mouth went up, "Deal."

I took in our surroundings. It appeared to be Eben's workshop. That would explain the sulfur-like smell in the room. Eben was fond of conducting experiments with chemical compounds, always looking for a stronger metal or a more effective weapon.

"So, now what, Ansel? We can't very well run out there empty handed. They have crossbows."

He bent over and revealed hidden sheaths in his boots, a sturdy throwing knife tucked in each one. I eyed the blades and then his face. With a smile, I shrugged as if to say, "They'll do." I was rather impressed. *I'm going to have to get Dorjan to put knife sheaths in my boots.*

A broken tapestry rod leaning on a bookcase caught my eye. I grabbed it and tested its balance. It was a far cry from my glaive, but I could make it work as a quarterstaff.

"I have an idea," Ansel said. He motioned toward the door. We moved silently in that direction. In a combination of pantomime and whispers, he revealed his plan. I nodded in understanding, then positioned myself to the right of the closed door. It would open on my side. Ansel retreated a bit further into the room.

After a nod to make sure I was ready, he called out, "Guard! There's something wrong with the girl. If you don't help her, she'll die."

The door flung open. The man had his sword drawn, but not at the ready. I thrust the heavy rod in front of him as he entered. He flew headlong and crashed to the floor. His sword clattered ahead of him.

Ansel made a split decision. Instead of sending him to his ancestors, he struck the butt of his knife against the side of the guard's head. The man lay motionless.

The commotion brought another guard rushing into the room, his blade poised for action. Ansel stood ready for him, holding the other guard's sword in a strike position. To my surprise, the man turned and threw a shot at me. I blocked it with the tapestry rod. He hesitated. I brought my makeshift weapon around and struck his sword hand. The guard grimaced in pain. His sword went flying. I followed though with my shoulder and he went down backwards. Ansel lowered the point of his sword to the man's throat. A mixture of fear and shock filled the guard's eyes as he waited for the death stroke. It never came.

"Take your friend and move him over there," Ansel said, pointing to the piece of furniture to which he and I had been chained.

The frightened man complied.

Ansel locked the manacles on the two guards. With one of Ansel's knives, I cut strips from my already-shredded sleeve. We stuffed their mouths with the fabric and tied another strip over.

Ansel and I shot a quick nod at each other assuring the other we were fine. He grabbed the second guard's sword and handed it to me. I hefted it to get its feel. It was not well made. It seemed Galtero spent little on his men or their weapons. Poor equipment for poorly trained soldiers. I doubted he compensated them any better than he equipped them. These two might be persuaded to fight on our side. We could offer substantial pay and could use more soldiers.

We both listened to make sure no one else approached. We heard nothing. With caution, Ansel stuck his head out the door and looked both ways. He leaned into the hallway and retrieved a crossbow. Handing it to me, he ducked out again and procured another. To our advantage, our two guards must have abandoned their crossbows in favor of their blades. Ansel and I sheathed the *borrowed* swords. He checked the hall once more, then signaled all clear. We rushed to find Eben.

"What's takin' Bort so long? He shoulda been back by now," a voice came from up ahead. "Go see if you can find him. At his pace, I'll be old and gray before I can spend my reward."

"Eshshah, there's another heading your way."

"We'll take care of him," Eshshah said.

Ansel and I made our way to the doorway of the room where the lead guard held Eben. The soldier was the last of the five who had come for the dragon rider. Eben, still tied to the chair, had at least gained consciousness. The guard sat on a bench nearby with his crossbow on his lap.

Turning back to me, Ansel made hand gestures indicating our next move. I signaled my understanding. Ansel counted, one, two, three on his fingers and we simultaneously leaped into the doorway.

"Surrender, and you live," Ansel shouted.

The guard sprang to his feet and raised his crossbow.

Ansel and I pulled the levers on our weapons. Each of our bolts found their mark. Unfortunately, the soldier released his shot before he hit the ground. His bolt also found its mark.

Pain exploded in my chest. My lungs emptied. The impact threw me backward and my head hit the floor. The room swam around me. My eyes widened as I struggled to take in a breath. Squeaking sounds were all I could utter.

Ansel spun about to find me thrashing on the floor.

"Amáne!" he screamed. He dropped to his knees beside me. Cradling me, he put his head in the crook of my neck.

"Amáne," he whispered. "No."

I felt Eshshah's concern, but unlike Ansel, she knew I would find my breath.

I'd had the wind knocked out of me before. I would recover shortly, but it didn't ease my panic. I saw the terror on Ansel's face as he searched me for a fatal blow. If it wasn't for my dragon-scale breastplate, the shaft would have gone right through me at that close range. Ansel would have found the wound easily. I wanted to assuage his agony, but I had no voice.

At last my lungs filled, painfully.

"I'm all right, Ansel." My words came out in a scratchy whisper. "Ansel ... I'm not dying ... look ... my breastplate ... it saved me."

I knew I'd cracked a rib. I couldn't take a deep breath, but it was something Eshshah could take care of as soon as I got to her. I kept it to myself.

"You'll smother the girl, Lord Ansel, if you don't back off and let her breathe," Eben said in a hoarse voice.

"Thank you, Eben," I said.

Ansel, still in shock, pulled back. He gave a short exhale.

"Amáne, I thought ..."

"I know."

Trying to relieve Ansel's anxiety, I added. "Do you think it'll leave a bruise?"

Ansel shook his head, but managed a lopsided smile. "I believe you've finally gone mad. But I'll never question you wearing your breastplate again."

I let him help me up. It took a moment to steady myself. My head throbbed. I reached back and felt the knot at the base of my skull. I swallowed my hiss of pain.

Before Ansel could read my face, I turned to Eben. I used Aperio's key to release his chains. He scrunched his eyes and grunted when he tried to get to his feet.

"Let me help you, Eben," I said. I prepared to place my hands on his shoulder, suspecting he had a broken collar bone.

"Amáne, let Eshshah and Sovann treat him," Ansel said.

"He's in too much pain to move him. I'll be careful. He needs just a bit of attention so we can take him to our dragons." I gave Ansel what I hoped was an reassuring look. "Please, Ansel?"

Ansel nodded, but stood close by to stop me if he felt it necessary. My hands heated as I began to will Eben's pain away. I reached the end of my strength before I felt I'd finished. But, I was learning my limits. My injuries had taken their toll. I didn't have enough energy left to do any more for Eben. Before I spent myself, I released my hands.

"Thank you, Amáne. I can breathe now," Eben whispered.

Which is more than I can say, I thought as I took in shallow breaths.

"Good control, Amáne," Eshshah said. "You're learning. I was about ready to tell you to let up. You need attention yourself."

I felt her strength flow into me. She knew I had nothing left to ease my own pain.

"Thank you, Eshshah."

My head cleared enough for me to stay on my feet. Without her help, I don't think I could have made it to where she and Sovann waited. I let Ansel half-carry Eben to our dragons as I struggled slowly behind.

When they finished healing Eben, Eshshah turned to me. She placed her nose on my chest and breathed as she hummed her healing tune. Then she treated my head.

At last I could take a deep breath. I closed my eyes and inhaled.

Ansel caught my great relief and scowled. "I've told you before, don't ever hide your pain from me again, Amáne." He looked hurt, almost angry.

"Yes, Ansel. I'm sorry."

Everything had been put back in order at Eben's. We'd contacted the Healer and relayed the events, then spent time with Eben, discussing our plans. He'd thanked us profusely for our aid. I shuddered to think what would have happened to him if we hadn't arrived when we did. I knew what nightmares awaited in that castle. And I knew the cruelty of which Galtero was capable. With Eben in his hands, our cause would have suffered along with Eben.

A deal had been struck with our four captive soldiers. They jumped in eagerly when Ansel presented them with the option to join our side. They had no loyalty to Galtero or anything for which he stood. I noted the respect they offered Ansel, even before they knew his identity. Then when Eben revealed Ansel's surname, all four soldiers fell to one knee before him. I nodded with pride.

Ansel and I stood facing each other, his arms around my waist, my hands resting on his chest. The satchel of Salama's scales, the original reason for our perilous trip, hung at my side. The time had come to part while we could still fly under cover of darkness.

Gazing into Ansel's deep green eyes, I said, "I think we made a good team tonight. I could get used to going on quests with you."

"If I had my way, you wouldn't go on any more quests."

"Don't say that. And besides, I don't always get restrained. Sometimes I get a ride in a wild river, and sometimes I get to make friends with dark things that lurk under the castle."

He gave me a pained expression. I laughed.

"You have to admit, it was quite an exciting night." I said.

"Now that it's over and I know you're all right."

"We should do this more often."

"Enough, Amáne."

"As you wish, but truthfully, Ansel, the most exciting part, was how this trip started." My hand went to my beautiful ring that hung around my neck. I stood on my toes and kissed him.

"It's hard to believe it's still the same outing," he said.

I nodded, then rested my forehead on his chest. He pulled me closer. Both of us became silent. Neither wanting to let the other go.

I turned my face up to his. With an effort to smile, I said, "So, you'll let me know if you need me to bring some chicken eggs from Nunn?"

"What?"

"I'm going back to my punishment — my ban from flight, and a house empty of you. I'm just trying to think up an excuse for Eshshah and me to go on a flight." I shrugged. "And see you again."

He ran his finger over my quivering lip. My effort to hold my tears failed.

"Deal. I believe I will be needing chicken eggs from Nunn."

He covered my mouth with his in a passionate kiss.

Chapter Forty-Three

Our flight back home went quickly, but a sadness surrounded Eshshah and me. Our separation from Sovann and Ansel became more difficult each time.

We received a hardy welcome when we landed in the courtyard. Both the Healer and Gallen shared the relief we were home safely, and the excitement of our betrothal. Although it was nearly morning, we sat for a long time at the table over cheese and hot mulled wine. I shared the details of our evening, including Ansel's proposal.

The days passed slowly as I returned to my duties at the Healer's. The weapons classes went well. We trained quite a capable company, here in Dorsal — elite soldiers whose hearts were fully into our cause.

Gallen worked with Eshshah and me on our aerial tactics. He had us use the smaller, lighter fighting saddle, which allowed more movement. The rider can stand and twist as necessary during battle.

The Healer spent a lot of time on the communication device. She and Ansel discussed battle strategies with the other dragon riders. They formulated the plan to gather the trainees and recruits from the various localities and advance them to the City of Teravinea. Our direction toward our goal was no longer a dream. We fell headlong into the task of taking the throne from Galtero.

Ansel and I stayed in contact as best we could. His duties took him to various camps set up to amass our army. Most of these encampments did not have a communication device. I lived on edge when Ansel traveled to these locations. It gave me a taste of what he must have gone through each time my whereabouts made me unavailable.

One evening I joined Gallen and the Healer in the library after a long relaxing soak.

"Amáne, we have an assignment for you."

My eyes lit up. My mouth spread in a wide grin.

The Healer gave a short laugh. "You're reacting without even hearing about what we're tasking you."

"No matter, Healer, anything will make us happy, just as long as we get to fly together. You could send us to Nunn for chicken eggs and we would jump at the chance."

She eyed me curiously, not knowing my joke with Ansel.

Eshshah rumbled a laugh.

"Never mind." I shook my head and smiled. "What is it you need us to do?"

"The time has come for us to stop working under the cover of darkness."

I raised an eyebrow.

"Ansel must reveal his identity to Teravinea. And we must let the kingdom know that dragons now live."

The importance of this moment sunk in instantly. "How?" I asked.

"We'll go on a campaign to the larger townships and cities,

especially the ones where the riders have been stationed. We'll introduce Ansel in the proper manner — as the son and rightful heir of King Emeric Drekinn. Eshshah and Sovann will fly in full daylight."

A ripple of excitement went through me. "At last."

I felt Eshshah as she joined in my elation.

The Healer continued, "With your permission, and Eshshah's, I'll ride with you. Upon our announcement, the heir to the throne lives, the barons, lords and mayors will have the opportunity to pledge their fealty to our lawful king, or decline and be marked as our enemy.

Our king, I repeated in my head. It had been a while since I'd thought of him as such. It made me nervous to think it. To me he was Ansel. My love. My best friend.

"This is a serious mission, Amáne."

"Healer, you don't need to tell me. Eshshah and I know full well the importance of this trip. And of course you have our permission to ride with us. When do we leave?"

"In two days' time. The members of the Rider's Council are preparing to notify the heads of their townships that they'll be receiving a royal visitor. Just which royalty or visitor is left up to their imagination. They have no idea. Best to keep them guessing."

Diplomatic affairs confused me. Thankfully, I had nothing to do with the arrangements.

The two days passed quickly. Ansel and I spoke several times via the communication disc. He smiled at my excitement. I noticed he couldn't hide his.

It was early morning when the Healer and I geared up for flight. The sun had just barely risen. The Healer and Gallen exchanged last-minute wishes in the courtyard. I gave them space in their private moment. Dorjan joined me as we checked the straps on Eshshah's tack. We made small talk as the two said their farewells. It had been a while since they'd been separated for any length of time.

I mounted and locked wrists with the Healer. She swung up behind me. Dorjan and Gallen saluted us as Eshshah took flight.

Chapter Forty-Four

Eshshah, the Healer and I flew straight to Trivingar. We didn't bother to stop at the Arevale Outpost. It was no longer necessary to hide our existence. Even though we flew too high for Eshshah to be recognized as a dragon, soaring over Teravinea in full daylight proved an unexpected release for Eshshah and me.

Trivingar came into sight in record time. Eshshah was just as anxious to get there. Our descent brought us low over the small township and countryside. The sight of us created quite a stir as we passed. People pointed, livestock scattered. We landed in the field beside the manor. Sovann and Ansel stood together awaiting our arrival.

Salutes and salutations over, Ansel embraced his aunt before he turned to me. He enveloped me in his arms and swung me around. I laughed. He muffled my laughter with his kiss.

"Ansel, we're flying in daylight and revealing our dragons. Can you believe this moment has finally arrived?"

"It's been a hard road, but thanks to you, my *Girl of the Prophecy*, and your glowing dragon, we've come this far."

Eshshah uttered a pleased rumble.

"Despite all my efforts to thwart it with my stupidity," I said.

"Don't forget how we first met," Ansel countered, "my own stupidity and some brilliant thwarting of my own."

"Let's not bring any of that up," broke in the Healer. "Don't you have some refreshments and a hot soak to offer an old lady after a long trip?"

"Old lady?" Ansel laughed. "You have a lot more years to add to your collection before I could consider you old."

We all laughed. Ansel helped me take off Eshshah's saddle. Attendants took our baggage and scurried off. I grabbed Eshshah's fangs and drew her face close, kissing her nose and thanking her in thought transference.

Ansel put his arms around the Healer and me and led us into his manor. He escorted us to our rooms.

Giving each of us a kiss on the forehead, he said, "I'll leave you two ladies to relax a bit. We'll meet in the dining hall in two hours for a midday meal before we make our first campaign visit."

I pushed the door open and entered my room. The tapestry Ansel had commissioned, the one depicting Eshshah and me at our cove, brought a smile to my face. The aromatic fragrance of herbs surrounded me in a sweet caress. I inhaled. A hot soak had been prepared for me.

The bathing room door opened. I turned to see Eulalia rushing toward me, arms out.

"Mistress Amáne, or should I call you Lady Amáne, now? Congratulations on your betrothal, let me see your ring. Lord Ansel just about had a conniption fit worrying if you would like it, it certainly is stunning, you'll make the most beautiful bride. I'm so pleased to see your pretty face again, especially after I heard you had gone missing, you don't know how scared we all were.

Lord Ansel worked himself into a state, he did, but we shall not go into that, let's get you into your soak, the water is piping hot, just the way you like it."

I took a deep breath after that, even though I hadn't said a word. "Thank you, Lali. I'm happy to see you, too." I gave her a warm hug, before slipping into the hot inviting tub.

Lali knew we would be riding out after we ate. She didn't fuss over me wearing my riding gear to meet Ansel for a meal. She usually scoffed at my male-like attire and insisted I put on a gown. I was thankful she held her tongue. It must have been difficult.

The Healer met me at my room and rushed me out the door to the dining hall. Ansel stood up as we entered. My heart did a little dance.

We discussed our plans as plates of meats and cheeses were set before us. The aroma was enticing, but I could do no more than pick at the fare. My excitement built with each moment. I had no idea what to expect. The sooner we started, the sooner I could get a feel for what it entailed.

Appointments were made to meet two lords that afternoon and probably three the next day as we worked our way south. Some stops would require more time than others. Our last stop would be Dorsal. Many of the townships we planned to visit still had the same lord or baron as when Ansel's father ruled. We were confident they would accept Ansel as the rightful heir and give their support.

Our first stop was Arevale, just on the other side of the border from Serislan. Avano and Lord Volkner met us in the field east of the lord's small castle. Avano spent time between Ansel's Trivingar Manor in Serislan and Arevale in Teravinea. He and the lord of Arevale were long-time friends.

Lord Volkner saluted us as we landed. Before Avano made the introductions, the lord threw a puzzled look at Ansel, and then shook his head as if he might have been seeing things.

"Lord Volkner," Avano said, "may I present Ansel Drekinn, rider of Sovann; the Healer, formerly Nara, rider of the late Torin; and Amáne of Teravinea, rider of Eshshah. Fellow Riders, I introduce to you, Lord Volkner."

I noticed Avano didn't use any title for Ansel.

"Drekinn?" the astonished lord said. "Then my old eyes did not deceive me. You are a relation to the late King Emeric."

"His son," Ansel stated with a tip of his head.

Without hesitation, the lord went to one knee. "My Lord. I'm speechless. We were told the son lost his life along with his parents."

"Rise, Lord Volkner," Ansel said. "I'm very much alive."

The lord rose slowly, painfully. His hair, white with time, was tied back in a short queue. His eyes sparkled as he gazed at Ansel.

"Ah, but I forget my manners," he said. "It has been long since I've had the honor of being in the presence of our incredible friends, the dragons. May I?"

Ansel and I nodded our consent to speak to our dragons.

Addressing Sovann, he said, "Sovann, mighty golden dragon, may your life be long and your talons ever sharp."

He looked up at my dragon, and said, "Eshshah, fiery red dragon, may your scales ignite the hearts of all dragon lovers as you have set fire to mine."

Both dragons responded with a nod, pleased at his compliments.

Ansel and I started to speak at the same time. I clamped my mouth shut and let Ansel translate Sovann and Eshshah's thanks. The Healer gave me a nod of approval.

My duty and that of the Healer's was to accompany Ansel as his personal guards. The fact the Healer was his aunt, or I his betrothed took rear saddle to our duties.

Lord Volkner ushered us into his castle and straight to his dining hall. It seemed that plans and negotiations here took place around food, just like they did at the Healer's. The lord offered Ansel his head chair at the large table. To my surprise, Ansel accepted it. Then I understood. It was his way of acknowledging Lord Volkner's acceptance as the royal heir. I nodded to myself as I took in my first lesson in the subtle art of diplomacy and protocol.

At the lord's request, Ansel told his story of his rescue by his aunt during the tragic death of his parents, King Emeric and Queen Fiala. How he'd been in hiding for the past nineteen years.

"I knew your father well. It was more than a fortnight's ride to the City of Teravinea. In my younger days, I made it several times. But, your father had the advantage of travel by dragon, which put us close. He visited often. Our forests and our hunting proved an attractive diversion for him."

Lord Volkner turned to the Healer. "Now I remember. You had the honor several times of transporting the good king here for his visits, on your beautiful gray Torin. It was said you and your mighty dragon perished that night. I am thankful you lived. My heart goes out to what you suffered with your loss, but I'm filled with gratitude you saved the young prince. Now we have hope that Teravinea may be restored to the grandeur it enjoyed under the rule of the House of Drekinn."

A sense of pride welled up in me. I loved the form of respect this elderly lord showed toward Ansel, and the love he held for his kingdom.

When Ansel petitioned his support, Lord Volkner replied, "I will give you what I can, my Lord, but I'm afraid to say my coffers aren't what they were when your father lived. They have been reduced greatly under Galtero's rule."

"Thank you, Lord Volkner, but your money is not what is needed. We need men, and women, to back our cause. We need to raise an army."

"Women?"

"If they so choose to assist in whatever way they can. I'm not opposed to women taking up the sword. At one time, I understand, our women were quite capable."

"You know your history. I'm pleased to see that. I do have a sizable contingent of men well-trained here at the castle. For the purposes of defending Arevale from foreign invaders, of course." He gave a *you-know-what-I-mean* nod. "I can increase my contingent without much attention from Galtero's spies. I'll quietly open the call to females as well."

"That would be greatly appreciated. We have the means to pay your soldiers well."

Details were finalized and we took our leave of the good Lord Volkner. I had to quell my desire to give him a big hug.

Thus our days passed as we made our way south. Most stops were very successful. The majority of lords and barons accepted Ansel Drekinn as the rightful heir to the throne. They laid their swords down in front of Ansel, the hilt facing him. Some showed less enthusiasm, but still offered pledges of support and oaths of fealty. Most remembered the prosperity Teravinea once enjoyed under the Royal Family of Drekinn. The people felt the oppression of Galtero's rule and their depleted resources.

Several nights were spent in castles or manors at the invitation of the lords. My favorite nights were spent in the outposts along the way. The three of us were able to relax and be ourselves. The Healer and I could figuratively take our hands off the hilts of our swords. Ansel and I abandoned our professional relationship and enjoyed each other's company.

We left an outpost early one day to head for Nicobar, Eben's locale. Our dragons spiraled down and landed in the clearing next to Eben's home. He saluted us and without any delay, leaped onto Sovann's foreleg, locked wrists with Ansel and swung up behind him. Sovann didn't have a double saddle, but the flight would be short. Eben looked well at ease riding without being strapped in.

We arrived at Lord Faetor's rather large manor house. A dull fortress-like construction that lacked in style and beauty.

"Lord Faetor completed his home only two years ago," Eben announced. "I'm not impressed with his architect. The building mars the beauty of our surroundings. He's not a native Teravinean. He came across the Teravinea Channel from a kingdom far to the west. Maybe the manor reflects the austerity of his home country. I've met him only once before, and personally, I don't care for the man. His staff was not very receptive when I sent him word of your arrival. I'm not sure what he's been told."

In all of the other stops, either an official delegation or some form of welcome had been arranged. Many included colorful flags, some even displayed a festival air. The lord of Nicobar sent only two representatives out to receive us in an empty field. They neither saluted us nor greeted our dragons. I glanced sideways at the Healer. She didn't look pleased. I made it a point to be more vigilant.

The attendants led us to the door of an anteroom. They left us there and walked away without a word. Several people lined up awaiting an audience with Lord Faetor. The room was devoid of furniture. Only a few tapestries graced the walls.

We stood in silence. I didn't know what to make of the situation. My anger rose. I had a mind to storm through the doors and lash out at this Lord Faetor. I did not appreciate his rudeness. Of course I knew better. I suppressed my desire. Especially when I noted Ansel appeared outwardly unbothered, though I did notice a slight tightness in his jaw. Eben assumed a mask of boredom, but his eyes betrayed annoyance.

I began to pace the room. After my third pass by the Healer, she reached out and grabbed my arm. At a stern look from her, I forced a casual stance.

After we waited at least three-quarters of an hour, a manor guard opened the door for us to enter the lord's audience room. The room looked like a throne room. Tall columns lined the walls, each topped with ornate gold capitals. *Who does this man think he is?*

We proceeded down a carpet the length of the long room. The lord perched on a high-back chair that sat on a dais — an imperial look on his fleshy countenance. His rotund body made even larger by the yardage of fabric used in his clothing. It was almost comical how his feet didn't touch the floor. I wondered if he thought his callers wouldn't notice. Personal attendants or advisors stood on either side.

Two large dogs lay by his feet. They barked as we approached. At a hand signal from Lord Faetor they quieted, but their teeth remained bared. Menacing rumbling continued in their throats.

There were no chairs or any form of comfort for us. We stood before him as he looked down upon us.

"Lord Faetor," Eben began. "I present to you Ansel Drekinn, rider of Sovann; the Healer, formerly known as Nara, rider of the late Torin; Amáne of Teravinea, rider of Eshshah. Fellow riders, meet Lord Faetor."

The Healer and I, being dragon riders, stood on equal ranking with the lord. Protocol held we bow to each other. The Healer and I did so. The lord did not return the bow, but eyed us suspiciously. A false smile turned his mouth. It didn't reach his eyes.

Ansel remained upright. "Lord Faetor, thank you for receiving us."

The lord frowned at Ansel. "What brings you to Nicobar? And by what right do you come before me armed?" Two guards stepped out from behind the columns. We already knew of their presence. Others still hid in the shadows.

What an ill-mannered man. It amazed me how Ansel could remain so calm and seemingly unperturbed. I tried to keep in mind Faetor was not from Teravinea. He may not know the name Drekinn or be familiar with dragon protocol — excuses I didn't accept.

Instead of answering Faetor's question, Ansel began, "The Kingdom of Teravinea throughout the centuries had been known as a fair and peaceful, yet powerful kingdom. We had the dragons and their riders to thank for our prosperity."

I understood Ansel was trying to get a feel for which direction the lord leaned in regards to the kingdom. *Did he support Galtero*?

"There are no dragons in Teravinea. I've been told they may have never existed."

"If you had been available to receive us, you would have seen there is no truth in what you've been told," Ansel said in a controlled voice.

Faetor cocked an eyebrow. He turned and shouted at an attendant at the other end of the room. "Send for the steward!"

A door opened to our right. My hand tightened on my glaive. I saw the Healer and Eben move their sword hands at the ready. It was a subtle move, barely noticeable, outwardly non threatening.

A man entered and quickly moved to the lord's side. Faetor had no idea of the sensitivity of our hearing. He whispered to the man to verify how we arrived. The man confirmed our arrival by dragon. Surprise registered on Faetor's face.

The lord addressed Ansel, "I stand corrected. My assistant has informed me there are two large dragons in my field. I should like to see your beasts before you leave." He narrowed his eyes, "Is my livestock safe out there? I hold you responsible if they ravish my prize herds."

I cringed inwardly at his use of the word *beasts* and the outright insult that they would dare touch his herds. Eshshah and I used open thought transference so she could be a part of this meeting. "Eshshah, I'm sorry for his disrespect. I hardly believe I'm still in Teravinea."

"I'll excuse it on ignorance, Amáne. Don't let it disturb you."

Ansel's jaw tightened. "Lord Faetor, may I recommend you borrow some manuscripts from Eben to learn the nature of dragons. They are not beasts, nor do they ravage livestock."

Faetor nodded. "Perhaps I'll do some research on the creatures, Ansel Drekinn. I may even think about acquiring one of my own."

I bit my lip before anything would come out of my mouth.

"Now, again I demand to know the purpose of your visit."

"While you are obtaining information on dragons, perhaps you can also ask Eben for a history of Teravinea. You'll find the

Royal Dynasty of Drekinn fills most of the pages. That family ruled this kingdom for nearly a millennium."

The lord straightened in his chair. His advisors on either side eyed Ansel with interest.

"Drekinn? Your line?"

"My direct line."

"You're telling me ..."

"My father was King Emeric Drekinn. He ruled Teravinea until he was killed."

"King Galtero came to the throne to take up the vacancy." Faetor filled in.

"That's not how I would word it, but yes, Galtero seized the throne."

"And, I am to believe you are who you claim to be, why?"

Ansel showed him his ring. "You need only to check Nicobar's archives to match the seal to King Emeric."

Faetor shrugged his acceptance of Ansel's ancestry. The look on his face and the shift of his eyes revealed something untrustworthy. As to what it regarded, I could only guess.

"I offer you an apology, Lord Ansel. I am not from Teravinea. I agree, I should learn the history of this place I now consider my home. Please accept my invitation to join me for the midday meal. I have an excellent kitchen staff. They will be serving soon. It will be an honor if *you* would partake. Your help can eat with the servants."

I stiffened.

The lord continued, "We can discuss the purpose of your visit over my chef's specialty, spit-roasted boar."

I was repulsed by the way he licked his lips. Certainly this pig-of-a-man had missed few meals. He placed more emphasis on the roasted boar than sincerity in his apology.

"My companions are not my help, Lord Faetor. The four of us will accept your invitation." Ansel swept his hand to include the Healer, Eben and me. He was quick to remedy the situation in a way the lord could not oppose.

Faetor's eyes flashed displeasure.

"Very well." Faetor gestured at his steward, who took several steps backward before he turned and hurried out of the room.

Lord Faetor slid off his large throne-like chair. I politely looked away as I fought the vision in my head of a child trying to come down from an adult-size seat. I commended myself on my control, the urge to laugh nearly won.

Chapter Forty-Five

We were ushered along a lengthy hallway. Large marble sculptures of great warriors stood on either side. They reached the height of nearly three men. Massive double doors opened to the great dining hall. The Healer and Ansel were directed to sit on one side of a long table, Eben and I across from them. Lord Faetor already sat at the head of the table in an ornately-decorated chair, slightly elevated above ours. It contrasted the plain chairs in which we sat.

This man used every opportunity to show dominance. I thought to myself, it must have something to do with his small stature. Maybe he had a need to compensate for it. I'd never met anyone like him. His dogs stood by, doing as good a job trying to intimidate as did Lord Faetor.

The table lay spread with golden plates and bowls, filled with cheeses and exotic fruits. More than we could possibly eat. Another of Faetor's attempts to show superiority. The aromas made my mouth water. I hadn't realized how hungry I'd become.

A young serving girl entered with a large tray of sliced meat on a bed of potatoes. Although I expected the boar's head to be on the platter, the presentation was still splendid. Apple wedges lay in an arrangement around half of the tray.

The girl, with hesitant steps, approached Faetor first with the meat. I wondered at that, since protocol would have dictated she offer Ansel the first serving. Faetor knew the rank of his guest and should have informed his staff.

Lord Faetor caught the server's eye and made a facial gesture. She tipped her head slightly in a nod. *What's going on here?* My senses heightened as I tried to discern the silent conversation.

Without being obvious, I paid close attention to the girl. She served Faetor several slices of meat and potatoes from one side of the platter, then moved to serve Ansel. She offered portions from the side of the plate garnished with the apples. The same with the Healer and Eben. When she came to me, again she chose from the apple side. I had an opportunity to look more closely at the tray — the separation of the two portions of meat. The girl's trembling hand caught my eye. As soon as she served me, she rushed out of the room with the platter.

Realization hit me like a Valaira. Without waiting for Ansel or the Lord to begin the meal, I reached in front of me and knocked my goblet of wine over onto Ansel's plate. The dark wine splashed onto his light blue tunic. A horrible thought of him bleeding flashed through my mind as the blood-red vintage spread down his front. Ansel jumped to his feet as the wine cascaded off the table. He shot me a puzzled look.

"I'm so sorry, Lord Ansel. You know how clumsy I am. I can't believe I just ruined your meal. Here, let me help you."

I leaned over the table and grabbed Ansel's plate. "You certainly can't eat this, now. The kitchen staff can bring you another." I gave Eben and the Healer a look that I was certain they understood. *Don't touch your food.* They were already fully vigilant.

"Lord Faetor, I think your dogs would enjoy my ineptitude. Maybe they'll even stop growling at me. Here boys." I bent over and put Ansel's plate on the floor for them.

The dogs padded excitedly toward me.

"Stop! Gor, Set, come," Faetor shouted at his dogs. They slunk back to his side with eyes still on the meat.

I feigned a puzzled look.

"They don't eat scraps off the table," he said.

"I saw you giving them portions from your plate. What's wrong with this meat? It was served from the same platter. Oh wait, yours came from one side and ours from the other."

"Guards!" Faetor jumped from his seat and ran to hide behind a column.

Several armed men rushed out from the dark recesses of the room. They came at Eben and me on our side of the table. Others charged the Healer and Ansel. I readied my glaive, the riders drew their swords. Gor and Set snarled and bounded toward the fray. They inadvertently helped our cause as they jumped and snapped at anyone in their reach, including the guards that tried to get to us. Eben and I made quick work of the men on our side. I jumped on the table before the dogs reached me. The last guard went down under Ansel's sword. I ran the length of the table, maneuvering around the bowls and utensils, and jumped off the end. We sprinted out of the dining hall, Faetor still screaming orders. In his panic, he'd switched to his native tongue.

The four of us bolted down the hallway toward the entry. The Healer and Eben stayed near Ansel. I brought up the rear. Gor and Set were gaining on me. I halted and wheeled around. One leaped at me. A swipe of my blade and he dropped.

The fat lord labored down the corridor, after his dogs. He

released a wail when he saw his pet go down. The second dog stopped when he reached his companion lying in a pool of blood. Faetor grabbed a spear that hung on the wall. He screamed at the remaining dog. I couldn't understand if he was telling him to attack or fall back. Meanwhile, Faetor trudged up the hallway as fast as his portly body could move. I wondered what he planned to do with the spear. He obviously had no idea how to wield it. I had the inclination to wait for him just to find out.

I heard a clash of metal in the direction the other three had run. They'd already turned a corner. I couldn't see who'd engaged them.

"Eshshah." I called on her strength.

"I'm with you, Amáne."

I felt Eshshah's strength fill me. Wedging myself between one of the large warrior sculptures and the wall, I braced myself and shoved it over. It crashed to the ground, blocking Faetor's path. Pieces of marble exploded from the fallen figure. Dust rose into the air. Faetor was too fat to climb over, or go around it.

"Amáne?" Ansel called, after the crash.

"I'm fine."

I rushed around the corner to join my companions fighting in the entryway. My help wasn't necessary. They'd dispatched several of the guards and the rest ran away screaming in terror. I smiled at the reason for their sudden retreat. Eshshah stood outside the doorway. Her large head lowered as she peered in. A deep rumble echoed from her throat.

"Thank you Eshshah," I said.

Ansel hastened toward me with concern. He touched my cheek. His finger came away bloody.

I wiped my face with the back of my hand. "It's just a scratch from the marble shards. Eshshah helped me knock over a statue."

"That would explain why you look like a ghost," Eben said.

I looked down to see the marble dust that covered my clothes and skin.

"Let's get out of here," Ansel said. "We'll mark this overweight lord as one of Galtero's own."

Chapter Forty-Six

Ansel and I stood close in the Healer's courtyard, preparing to say goodbye once again. He'd spent a couple days with us at the end of our trip. Our final meeting with the Lord Mayor of Dorsal went well. As I thought all along, Dorsal would give its full support to Ansel.

Now that he had openly initiated his campaign, Ansel would be occupied all over the kingdom. He had to go back to Trivingar to settle his silk business and manor house. Then, he planned to spend time at each of the military encampments. He'd be inspecting the troops and overseeing drills, filling his position as leader and future king. I would resume my punishment. Grounded, until the Council, the Healer or Ansel deemed it necessary for me to take to the saddle.

"It's getting more and more difficult to leave you," Ansel said "The longer I'm around you, the longer I want to stay."

"I feel the same. Promise me you'll be careful, Ansel. I wish there were communication discs in those camps. It's going to be awful not knowing where you are or if you're safe."

He tilted his head and eyed me sideways. "I know the feeling."

I winced. How many times had I put him through the

same agony?

"You have to promise me you'll be careful, too," Ansel said.

"What, so I won't slip while mucking out the stalls? Or in case I prick my finger when picking rose hips? Or maybe one of my students will scratch me with a waster. I'm grounded, remember?"

Ansel shook his head and smiled. "Don't be so forlorn. You and Eshshah will be needed more, now. You'll be flying errands and transporting dragon riders and messages to such an extent you'll wish to be grounded."

"I'd never wish that." I brightened at the prospect Eshshah's and my punishment would be set aside. If only it had been for a reason other than war. But that reality couldn't be changed.

Ansel slipped his hand behind my neck. His fingers tangled in my hair as he pulled my face to his. I inhaled his spicy dragon scent as we kissed.

Too soon, we parted, saluted and locked eyes once more. He turned and mounted. Sovann and Eshshah offered their last affections to each other. Sovann gathered himself and leaped into the air. The wind from his great wings blew my hair and my clothes as I watched them take to the air.

True to Ansel's prediction, Eshshah and I flew errands. We delivered supplies, including Dorjan's lightning balls; maps; medicines; orders. We made several trips, but not one of the locations were we fortunate enough to find Ansel and Sovann.

Occasionally, we received word from him when he was near enough to an outpost to contact us. I breathed in relief each time I spoke with him, no matter how brief the conversation. At times he looked so tired, my heart broke.

One afternoon, the Healer called me in from practice. "We need you and Eshshah to go to Anbon, the mountain refugee camp.

Bern is there now and has some critical information that has fallen into our hands. You will pick it up and deliver it to an encampment in central Teravinea. Expect to be gone for a few days. Bern mentioned they may need you to run some messages once you get to his camp. If you get close to an outpost, please contact me."

"Anbon? Of course, Healer. We'll leave straight away."

I hesitated. My face twisted in a question I was afraid to ask.

The Healer read my concern. "No, Darqin never showed up at Anbon."

I nodded, relieved I didn't have to see him, yet troubled about his disappearance and his intentions.

After a two-and-a-half hour flight, Eshshah spiraled down into the mountain camp. The children gathered on the edge of a field where she would land, excited to see Eshshah once again. As soon as I slipped out of the saddle, I signaled to the mothers it was safe to let the little ones approach. The group raced to her and saluted her in their various childish ways. Truly a refreshing sight.

Rushing directly to the cave Bern had set up as his headquarters, I literally ran into a man who'd just turned the corner. He reached out to steady me.

"Father! What are you doing here?" I wrapped my arms around him. He embraced me tightly.

"I was just coming out to greet you. I had a delivery for Bern — the information you came for."

He searched my face. "Amáne, I can't look at you without seeing your mother." A sadness crept into his eyes. It quickly faded as he hugged me once more and said, "Congratulations on your betrothal. Lord Ansel is a lucky man."

"Thank you, Father. How did you know?"

"Lord Ansel asked me for permission to marry my daughter,

of course."

"That sounds like Ansel ... Lord Ansel. Thank you for giving him permission," I said with a smile.

"I wish your mother could be here for you."

"Father, there's so much I need to ask you, but we have no time. I'm to pick up the satchel and leave immediately."

He turned and escorted me into the cavern.

"I know, my sweet. I have a lot to tell you. I've been keeping a journal for you. Things I want you to know."

"I would love to read your journal, but I want to hear it from you as well."

"Yes, of course, my love, but just in case, I'm writing it down at every chance I have."

A twinge of fear rippled through me. "What do you mean, 'just in case'? Father, are you in danger?"

"It seems Galtero's chief advisor has been taking counsel from a younger man. Whatever he is putting into the advisor's ear has him eyeing me with a bit of suspicion."

I gasped. "Then leave the castle. Meet me in Dorsal. Please."

"No need for you to be concerned. I'll be fine. There's still more I need to do."

"But ..." I paused and turned to him. "Are you the one involved with getting the elite soldiers inside the castle walls?"

"Ah, you've heard. Yes. It's a brilliant plan suggested by Bern. Galtero's extravagant lifestyle will be his undoing. He has a penchant for fine silks and rich fare. Lobster is his latest passion. Serislan is known for both lobster and silk. King Tynan of Serislan has sent some of his finest soldiers trained in explosives. They are also well-trained in the merchant trade. As long as they continue to satisfy his greed, Galtero welcomes them under his roof. His enemy is gathering right under his nose. The fool."

Duer met my eyes. "If ... I mean, when I accomplish my goal, I promise I'll head straight for Dorsal. I'll be in contact with Bern. Don't worry about me. I'm making restitution for my part in helping Galtero attain the throne. Our cause needs me for just a bit longer."

"You've more than made up for that mistake, Father. I need you, now."

Taking a deep breath, he said in a hoarse voice, "Stay safe, my daughter. Stay strong." He kissed my forehead and hurried out. I noted the pain in his eyes. His bootsteps echoed as he strode away.

Wiping my tears on my sleeve, I faced Bern. We saluted each other.

"Amáne, my good wishes for you and Lord Ansel." He gave me a fatherly hug.

"I really must have been the last to know," I said, attempting a smile. "Thank you, Bern."

He handed me a satchel and gave me directions to the encampment where it was to be delivered. Before I turned to leave, Bern put his hand on my shoulder.

"It'll be all right, Amáne. Your father's a brave man, and too smart to get caught."

I nodded, but couldn't say anything for fear my voice would crack.

Once Eshshah and I took flight, I let my tears flow. Eshshah hummed to comfort me.

We flew for less than an hour, following the directions Bern gave us.

As we approached the encampment, Eshshah perked up. "Sovann."

"What?"

"Sovann and Lord Ansel are here."

My heartbeat quickened; my breathing accelerated.

Eshshah picked up her pace. The military camp spread out below us. Countless tents of various shapes covered the top of a hill. They were set up in concentric circles around a large tent. Several pennants waved above the central pavilion, a large banner stood before it. A golden dragon on a field of deep purple — the royal banner of the Drekinn, the Dragon Kings of Teravinea.

Sovann met up with us in the air as we approached. He and Eshshah flew high, then soared as they spiraled their descent. Sovann glided close below us. Eshshah could have reached down with her forelegs and touched him if she chose. Sovann turned his head up toward Eshshah, who bent her face to his. Mid-flight they touched noses.

We landed in an open clearing. I had to keep in mind I was on a delivery mission and must remain professional. There would be no demonstrative encounter with my betrothed.

Setting my face with a neutral expression, I approached the guard at the entrance to the command tent and informed him I had a delivery for Lord Ansel. The man evidently mistook me for a messenger boy. He held out his hand for the package.

I patted the satchel at my hip and said, "I'm to deliver it personally. Please tell someone in charge Rider Amáne is here."

The young soldier turned red. "I'm sorry sir ... I mean ma'am ... er Rider Amáne. I didn't recognize you, I mean I never met you, but I —" He gave up, offered a sharp salute and stepped aside.

"Thank you," I said. He saluted again.

The inside of the pavilion seemed even larger than it looked from the outside. Men leaned over maps spread on the tables that lined the walls. My eyes scanned the area. There was no one there I recognized. Then I spotted Ansel at the far end, his back to me.

I took only a few steps inside and stopped, unwilling to interrupt. Struggling, I gained control of my racing heart. Someone nudged Ansel and motioned in my direction.

Frustration showed briefly on his face until he saw me. Our eyes met. His eyes softened as he moved toward me. I was taken aback by how tired he looked. An angry gash slashed across his cheek. I pressed my lips together to keep my groan from resonating. My hand started to reach for his face to heal his injury. But this was not the time or the place. I faced my commander, pulled myself to my full height and saluted him. He saluted in return.

"What brings you here, rider?" A note of concern sounded in his voice. "Is there bad news?"

"No, my Lord. I hope it's good news. The Healer sent me to Anbon. Bern gained possession of some intelligence that's critical to our cause." I reached in my satchel and handed Ansel the folded parchment. His hand brushed my skin as he took it. A shiver ran through me. I lowered my eyes before I lost control.

Ansel unfolded the document. "This could be the advantage we've been looking for." He locked eyes with me. Hunger reflected in his intense gaze. "Thank you Rider Amáne. You'll find refreshment three tents down to your left. I'll join you when I get a moment."

Turning on his heels, he proceeded quickly back to the table where I'd found him. He carried himself with such authority.

My heart ached with longing as I watched his retreat. As if he felt my gaze upon him, he turned around, caught my eye and kissed the air in my direction. I smiled, nodded and threw a kiss back.

Chapter Forty-Seven

I found the mess area. They certainly didn't go hungry in this camp. Several large pots of stew simmered over the fires just outside the tent. Even if I wasn't hungry, I would have had some anyway. The aromas were that enticing. The tent, with the front side open to the outdoors had three rows of tables. Benches stood on either side. Two young soldiers conversed at the first table. At the far end of the second table, I spotted a familiar figure.

"Avano!"

I rushed to where he sat. He stood and we both saluted. This attracted the attention of the two soldiers, who realized I was a dragon rider. They rose and saluted. I nodded in return just as Avano wrapped his arms around me and lifted me off the ground. He planted a kiss between my eyebrows.

I happened to look over at the soldiers who gaped at Avano and me.

I laughed realizing I hadn't removed my helmet. As soon as Avano put me back on my feet, I pulled it off. My hair spilled out. Their stares turned into the familiar male ogle to which I'd become accustomed. Ignoring them, I turned my full attention to Avano.

"I gave my salutations to Eshshah," he said. "She told me you'd gone to seek out Lord Ansel. I thought maybe you and he might be having a little *conversation*." He wiggled his eyebrows and winked. I punched his arm. "So I left you two alone and figured I'd see you out here."

"There was no *alone* in that tent and no *conversation*," I said, as I seated myself opposite him.

"What a pity. I'm sorry to hear that."

I rolled my eyes.

"Oh, and let me congratulate you on your betrothal. I'm truly happy for you and Lord Ansel."

"Thank you, Avano. It's so good to see you again. It's been too long." I studied his face. "You look nearly as tired as Ansel ... Lord Ansel. What have you two been doing?"

"We've been busy on patrols. This is a strategic location. Galtero's men would like to hold this hill. We have to keep a close watch. A small band of spies tried to penetrate the perimeter this morning. They retreated into the woodline where Sovann couldn't follow. We had to dismount and chase them down."

"Is that what happened to his cheek?"

"Yeah. He got in too close and stopped the edge of a shield with his face."

I scowled at Avano. "I thought you were supposed to be looking after him."

"I had my eye on him. I was ready to step in if needed. He was doing fine on his own. It's just a scratch."

"It's a gash, Avano." A little more heat than I intended echoed in my voice.

Avano jerked back in mock fear, then smiled at my concern. "Then you should convince him to take a little break and you can heal it for him."

Concern rose in Avano's voice. "Truthfully, I'm glad you're here, Amáne. You came none too soon. Lord Ansel needs someone to talk some sense into him; he needs to step back and take a breath; allow one of us to assist more. We're all quite capable. There's a large meadow west of here. Your dragons could hunt. Why don't you suggest a private ride with him, and head there?"

The two young soldiers at the other table leapt to their feet and saluted. I turned in the direction of their gaze. My heartbeat accelerated. Avano and I jumped up and saluted Ansel.

Our eyes met. I hesitated, but maintained my professional bearing. My inclination would have been to rush up and throw my arms around him. I wasn't sure that action would be acceptable. My tentativeness was nullified as Ansel reached me in three long strides. He pulled me into a warm embrace and buried his face in my neck. He inhaled deeply, savoring the spicy scent of my hair. Without delay, he tilted my head back and kissed me. His kiss revealed an urgency that I shared.

Avano cleared his throat. "I wonder if the Healer still expects me to chaperone."

Ansel and I pulled apart. We laughed at Avano. It was good to see Ansel laugh. His tired appearance lifted a bit.

The three of us seated ourselves. A cook rushed to the table and placed three bowls of steaming stew in front of us, then saluted. We dove into our meals. No one said a word for several minutes. The contents of our bowls were consumed so quickly, the steam still rose from the empty vessels.

Avano nudged my foot under the table. When I looked up, he tilted his head and his eyes toward Ansel. A silent *go ahead and ask him.*

"Ansel, I thought maybe you could get away for just a while. We can fly to a nearby meadow. Our dragons could hunt and we can spend some time together."

Ansel glanced at Avano, then at me. We shrugged our innocence.

Avano interjected, "I'm sorry my Lord, but the truth is, fatigue is dangerous. Important decisions could mean lives, or even the kingdom. And we need your full strength to lead."

Ansel pursed his lips. "Ah, so it is a conspiracy." He said it in such a way, we knew he didn't mean it as a serious accusation.

He raised his hands in surrender. "As you wish. It appears I've been outnumbered. Avano, this must be your doing. I'll leave the command to you. See to it the reports are prepared for the Healer."

Avano grimaced. I smiled in triumph.

After only a few minutes flight, we spotted the meadow Avano had mentioned. A rather large clearing that sat next to a slow-moving stream. I smiled at the relaxing view. We unsaddled our dragons so they would not be encumbered while they hunted.

Ansel and I held hands as we proudly watched our beautiful companions fly off together. We turned to each other and forgot the world in a long kiss.

I touched Ansel's cheek. "Let me take care of that for you."

"It's just a scratch, Amáne."

"I believe I'm understanding your kind more and more. I think you must all think alike. It's not just a scratch." I smiled up at him. "Besides, it'll leave a big scar and I don't want my betrothed showing up at the archway with a less-than-perfect appearance." I pulled his face down to mine and kissed him. "Please, let me heal it Ansel."

"I don't want you to tire yourself."

"I won't. I promise."

He sighed. "If you must."

I tugged him to where we had left the saddles. Mine made the perfect back rest. He winced as he lowered himself to the ground and leaned back against my saddle.

I knelt next to him. "Are you hurt somewhere else?"

"Truthfully, I think there's not one place on my body that doesn't hurt." He allowed a tired smile.

"Oh, Ansel. What good would it be to win the crown and be too broken to wear it? You need to take better care of yourself. It's your duty. And Sovann should be looking after you."

"It's not for his lack of attention, he's offered. I haven't the time to spend on such things."

"Then allow someone else to help you. You can't do it all yourself. Your riders are more than willing to assume their responsibility. You have to remember, they were doing this before you were born."

He nodded. There was no denying my point.

"Let me see what I can do for you," I said as I pushed his hair back.

I placed my hands on his face and closed my eyes. Humming Eshshah's tune I willed his injury toward healing. The heat radiated from my hands. My concentration centered on both healing him and staying aware of the intensity and the drain on my body. I found if I took it slowly, my strength was not severely affected.

Ansel began to relax under my touch. His cheek was well on its way to healing. If I could help his muscles loosen and relieve his tension, that would be a plus. My hands heated as I placed them on his chest. His body sank back. I became mindful of my waning strength. Before it reached an undesirable level, I eased up. My hands were hot, but not blistered as when I previously overexerted myself. A soft snore escaped Ansel's lips.

Pleased with the results, I leaned against the saddle and watched him sleep. I surveyed his face, the curve of his nose, his full lips. It brought to mind the times he had watched me sleep. At last I understood his fixation. It proved to be a pleasant diversion while he rested.

Eventually, my eyes became heavy. I dozed beside him, my head resting on his shoulder. I awoke after only a short nap and resumed my study of his face as he slept.

Our dragons returned fully sated. Ansel startled awake, a disoriented look crossed his face.

"I must have dozed off," he said.

"Dozed? You were snoring."

"I'm sorry, Amáne."

"There's no need for you to be sorry. You needed the rest. It's part of healing."

He looked sideways at me. "Did you have anything to do with putting me to sleep? You and your powers?"

I laughed. "I merely healed your cheek and tried to help you relax. You look so much better than when I found you at the command tent. And speaking of the command tent, we should be heading back before Avano sends out a search party."

As we saddled Eshshah and Sovann, Ansel asked, "When does the Healer expect you back?"

"She said we would probably be gone for a few days. Do you have an assignment for us?"

"I have my cartographer copying the map and plans you

brought. I need you to leave tomorrow at daybreak to take the copy to Braonán. Sovann can give Eshshah his location. The Nunn Outpost is not far from there. I'll have a report, and Braonán should have one as well. Contact the Healer and read her the reports. You should be back here before nightfall tomorrow."

"Yes, Ansel. Thank you."

"Don't thank me. If I could, I'd send you to the northernmost part of Serislan until this war is over."

I threw my head back in exasperation and rolled my eyes. I didn't want to ruin our time we'd spent with each other, so I pressed my lips together and remained silent. *Why can't he accept the fact that it's Eshshah's and my duty to help him win the throne*?

We saddled up. Ansel gave me a boost, then leaped on Sovann and we flew back to camp.

CHAPTER FORTY-EIGHT

The next morning I arose before light. My restlessness would allow no more sleep, so I headed to the mess tent. Avano already sat at a table, sipping hot mulled wine. I took the seat in front of him. The cook put a bowl of hot porridge before me.

Avano raised his eyes from his cup, "Whatever magic you worked on Lord Ansel yesterday proved very effective."

"I don't do magic," I snapped.

He ignored my sharp response and continued, "He's made a sensible decision to move on to Braonán's location soon. Braonán will have had time to study the map you're delivering today. They can discuss it at length and in person. It's been some time since Lord Ansel visited there, and it's good for morale when the troops see their high commander. Our prince is a very fine leader. He has much of his father in him."

I allowed a small, yet sad smile.

"You'll probably be asked to repeat todays' flight and accompany him to Braonán's."

"Eshshah and I will gladly make that trip a hundred times if it means we can fly with him and Sovann. Moreover, the longer we can break from our punishment, the easier I'll be to get along with."

"Ah, that explains it. After today's flight, I hope to see a more pleasant Amáne."

"I haven't been that horrible, have I?"

"No, you haven't." Avano smiled. "I caught the tension you've been under, but you've played it well. Truthfully, grounding is one of the more severe punishments I could think of. Although it doesn't hold close to a loss." A shadow crossed his eyes as he, no doubt, recalled his late dragon, Cira.

Before I could respond, Ansel entered the tent. Avano and I stood and saluted. Ansel strode to my side, took my face and kissed my forehead, then brushed my lips with his.

As we sat, he said to me, "I hope your night went well. I apologize for not having a tent set up for you. If there were women in this camp, I would have put you up with them. I can't believe you convinced me you'd stay in one of the officers' pavilions."

"I see her persuasive powers haven't waned," Avano said.

I rolled my eyes at him, then turned to Ansel. "It wasn't necessary to have a private tent. I was perfectly fine with the officers, although it did get a little noisy with all the snorers."

"Hey," Avano said, "you fit right in."

"I don't snore."

"Maybe not, but you sure thrash around a lot, and you talk, too."

My eyes went wide. I felt my cheeks color. I'd been told before that I talk in my sleep.

Ansel put his hand over mine. "I hope my assignment wasn't to blame for your nightmares."

"Of course not. I have plenty of fodder for my nightmares. Delivering a map doesn't rank among them. Eshshah and I are looking forward to flying."

We finished our morning meal and returned to the command pavilion. Ansel handed me a satchel with the copy of the map and critical information. He included a report for the Healer.

Both men walked me to Eshshah to help saddle her. Avano finished tightening the girth, then turned and saluted me. He strode back to camp after a wink in my direction.

"Safe flight. I'll watch for your return tonight," Ansel said before he kissed me goodbye.

He stepped back and gave me a leg up. We saluted as Eshshah launched off the ground with a powerful leap. Her wings whipped the air around Ansel. I closed my eyes and inhaled with joy.

Our mission went well. Eshshah and I thoroughly enjoyed ourselves. We delivered the satchel to Braonán and headed straight for the Nunn Outpost to dispatch the reports to the Healer.

Eshshah let Sovann know when we were on our return approach. We found Ansel already in the field waiting. He rushed over and gave me a hand down.

"What are you laughing at, Ansel?"

"I'm not laughing, I'm just enjoying the look on your face."

I tilted my head. "What look on my face?"

"The fiery look you get when you ride. You're practically glowing." He kissed me, then a serious look replaced his amused one. "Amáne, I am truly sorry."

"Sorry about what, Ansel?" My eyebrows raised.

"I see the toll your punishment has taken on you and Eshshah. I can't imagine what it would be like to be banished from flight. Don't consider this as playing lightly with your sentence — it is a serious charge, but I can't bear to see you suffer like this. I'd like you and Eshshah to fly with us to Braonán's camp in the next day or two, and I'll see if I can at least offer you an additional mission like today, so you and Eshshah can get some more flying time before you have to go back to Dorsal. Truthfully, it would be a great help to me."

Chapter Forty-Nine

Ansel and I stayed up late talking before we said good night. After assuring him once again the officers' tent suited me fine, I let myself in and settled into my cot.

"Amáne, are you awake?"

"No, go away." I turned over and pulled the quilt over my head.

"Amáne?"

I threw the covers back and rolled over. "Ansel? I thought I was dreaming. What's wrong?"

"Nothing. I hope. I couldn't sleep. Something's bothering me. I don't know what it is. I thought I'd ask you to accompany me on a patrol. Dawn is another hour away, but I couldn't wait."

"Of course."

I extracted myself from my bed covers and pulled on my boots while Ansel waited. I'd gone to bed still dressed in my tights and tunic.

Groggy from my interrupted sleep, I stumbled out of the tent. A water basin stood just outside. I scooped a handful of cold water and splashed it on my face. We proceeded to the field and grabbed the saddles off their stands.

I glanced over at Ansel as he finished buckling Sovann's breast shield and threw on a fighting saddle. Eshshah wore her breast shield, but we used the travel saddle we'd arrived with.

"Ansel, that boot peg strap is cracking."

"I know, I'll have to get it looked at sometime."

"You can't use that. It's not safe. Isn't there another saddle around here?"

"This is the only single one, here. It'll be fine."

"But, Ansel ... "

"Don't worry about it. I'll get it repaired today, I promise. We're just going on a short round."

I scowled, but didn't press the issue.

We took flight, and despite my concern with Ansel's anxiety, and with the condition of his saddle, I couldn't help the breath of euphoria that filled me at takeoff. I caught Ansel eyeing me, a smile on his face as well. My heart swelled with love.

We flew fairly low, our eyes scouring the dark predawn valley for any sign of something amiss. Our flight began in small circles above camp, increasing in wider and wider bands. After about a quarter of an hour of this pattern, Ansel signaled for us to head in.

"Amáne, over there," Eshshah said. Ansel looked in the same direction. No doubt he'd gotten a similar prompt from Sovann. Just beyond a ridge was a dark mass. I blinked and could make out what looked like a shadow moving along the ground. As we came closer, my stomach tightened. Armed enemy troops moved steadily below us. They headed toward the encampment.

"Sovann and I'll go rouse the camp," Ansel said. "You two stay up here and keep an eye on their progress. Fly high. Don't let them spot you."

With that, Sovann banked a hard turn and headed back to headquarters. Eshshah and I spiraled higher. Adrenaline pumped through my body as we waited for Ansel.

Eshshah followed Sovann in open thought transference. He and Ansel flew low over the camp. Sovann trumpeted a warning. Ansel shouted out a call to arms. Tents flew open as soldiers rushed out and fell into formation. Ansel jumped off of Sovann to give directions to Avano, then leaped into the saddle and they headed back.

He and Sovann met Eshshah and me as we circled high. "We have to hold them until our troops arrive, Amáne."

I nodded.

Eshshah and Sovann folded their wings and dove from the sky. I leaned until my back nearly touched the rear of my saddle. The ground rushed up toward us at a frightening speed. At nearly ground level our dragons pulled their dive. We appeared out of the darkness as if from nowhere, to face the front line of soldiers — their eyes grew wide in shock.

Sovann belched out a large flame and took down a good portion of the front line. Eshshah swerved the other way and flamed the right leading edge. The soldiers looked about to panic and retreat. A shout from their midst commanded them to pull to order. Arrows flew in our direction. They fired blindly into the dark, but a few came quite close. One grazed my arm. I didn't have any weapons, but my sword and dagger. They would be of no help in this battle. I wished for a shield, but wishing was pointless. All I could do was stay low against Eshshah and offer my support and what little strength I could. She dove, dodged and flamed at every pass. Our advantage was the darkness, but the light of dawn began to show its face.

Ansel had his bow. He made use of it to pick off the soldiers further back, while Sovann took care of those in front. We continued our assault as the sun rose.

At last our troops arrived. The horse soldiers were first on the scene. They engaged the enemy with a fierceness that made me proud. Ansel and I took on the battle further behind the line, to avoid flaming our own men. Our foot soldiers reached the fray and dove into the battle. We pushed the opposing troops back. Advantage tilted our way.

Sovann and Ansel circled nearby while Sovann replenished his combustion capacity. My eye caught several of Galtero's men throwing a cover off a piece of equipment. My heart stopped. I'd seen that weapon before.

"Ansel!" I shouted, but too late.

I watched in horror as a harpoon hurled directly at him and Sovann. Eshshah threw a sharp warning. Sovann swerved. Everything seemed to happen at once. The evasive maneuver, I thought, had saved them. Before I could take a breath of relief, I cried out in anguish. The projectile sliced through Ansel's thigh as it flew past them. Ansel howled in pain.

The boot strap I'd warned him about could not hold the force of Sovann's sudden action. It snapped. Ansel was thrown from the saddle. He hung upside down by the strap that secured his right boot. I heard the sickening crack of bone. His leg bent in an unnatural angle. The remaining strap held him for only seconds before it reached its limit. I watched helplessly as Ansel tumbled from the sky. Of all we'd been through, I had never known the terror I felt at that moment. My mouth went dry. My scream stuck in my throat. A collective moan reached my ears as our troops witnessed their prince fall.

Eshshah gave me a warning as she dodged a harpoon. I looked back in time to see Sovann dive and snatch Ansel out of the air, just a short distance from the ground. His body hung limp from Sovann's talons. Drained of all emotion, I clung to my saddle in shock.

"Amáne, snap out of it. We cannot do anything for Lord Ansel at this moment. He lives. Sovann says he lives. He'll take Lord Ansel back to camp. There will not be a camp if we can't stop this wave."

I closed my eyes and shook myself to clear my head. A swift look about showed me the tide had turned. It was now our side falling back, as if our men had given up hope. They had witnessed their beloved leader carried off as though dead.

We could not allow defeat. Eshshah flew low above our troops.

I shouted at them, "He lives. Prince Ansel lives. Long live Drekinn."

Eshshah turned and began a relentless assault against our foe. She belched flames and bellowed a frightful roar at the enemy. Her attack destroyed the harpoon cannon. She left it in ashes, along with those manning the hateful object.

We made several passes. She flamed as I brandished my sword.

"For the crown! Long live Drekinn!" I yelled to encourage our troops.

The advantage shifted once again. Our men took heart. They joined in my chant, "Long live Drekinn," as they pressed back against Galtero's men.

The enemy broke rank. Confusion reigned. They scrambled in retreat. Victory assured, our soldiers full of hope, I felt the time was right to leave them to do clean-up.

Eshshah and I headed back to headquarters. My fear for Ansel returned to the forefront. We'd barely touched the ground when I unbuckled and slid out of the saddle. I leaped down and raced to the hospital tent, Eshshah close behind, picking her way through the rows between the tents. Sovann had his head thrust in the open side of the enclosure, blocking my view.

Eshshah groaned. "Amáne, it does not look hopeful. Sovann says he may be losing him. He can't pull him back."

I rushed around Sovann and nearly fainted at the sight. So much blood! The vision I'd had when I spilled the wine on Ansel flashed in my head.

The camp medics huddled around him wringing their hands. They'd tried in vain to save their lord.

"No!" I screamed. I shoved them out of the way, drew my dagger and cut through the bloody wrappings around his thigh. I gasped. The bone protruded through the gash created by the harpoon. *This is bad.* I placed my hands on Ansel's gaping wound as Eshshah's healing powers joined with Sovann's. Ansel's muscles strained in spasms. I yelled at the helpless men to hold his ankle and pull for traction. I had to get the bones realigned — to mend enough so I could turn my attention to stop the bleeding. Had it not been for Sovann, he would have bled out already. One look at Ansel's face and my heart sank. It was deathly pale.

"Eshshah, move in. You need to be at his leg."

She put her head further in the tent and rested her nose next to my hands. She began her humming. I closed my eyes tight and hummed along with Eshshah. My hands began to heat. I concentrated harder. Sweat streamed down my face. I could feel the bones begin to fuse.

"Amáne," Sovann said, "his heart is fading."

"Then you better try harder, Sovann! Don't you dare give up!"

Blisters formed on my palms as I threw my whole self into the healing. The bone was well on its way to healing when Sovann let out a sound that stopped my heart. Eshshah joined in with her keening wail. Her lament for the dead.

"No!" I screamed again.

I swung my eyes to Ansel's face. His lips were blue. His chest did not rise. His spirit had left him. Anger flickered hot in my chest. *How could you do this to me?*

"Ansel Drekinn, you will not go to your ancestors! I won't let you. You can't abandon me now. You can't. You can't." My wail joined that of our dragons.

In hysterics, I beat upon his chest. I pounded my fists over his heart with all the energy that was left in me. Arms wrapped around me, trying to pull me from Ansel. I swatted them away. Men flew backward at the force of my blows.

"Enough, Amáne," Eshshah entreated.

I didn't listen, but kept up my relentless efforts to start Ansel's heart. I didn't know how pounding him with my fists was going to help, but in a blind fury, I continued.

"Hold," Eshshah said. "I hear a faint beat. Amáne, you've called him back. Stop before you break his ribs and send him more pain."

Ansel gasped in a great breath. His eyes opened wide. I stared in shock as life returned to his face. He grimaced and lost consciousness. But, he lived.

I laughed and cried at the same time. The medics rejoiced. Sovann's trumpet of joy filled the camp.

I turned my attentions back to Ansel's leg and the angry laceration. I verified our treatment had repaired the bone before I pulled the torn skin together. Eshshah, once again, joined me as I held my hands against Ansel's thigh and concentrated my failing strength to heal him.

"Amáne, stop. Sovann and I can finish."

Her warning came late. In my frenzy to save him, I had not paid attention to my healing powers and how they drained me. My head spun. I felt myself fall across Ansel as all went black. Eshshah's words were the last I heard.

CHAPTER FIFTY

Gentle fingers softly stroked through my hair, soothing away my nightmarish dreams. I smiled. "Mother?"

"No, my love. It's not your mother."

The smile remained on my face as I opened my eyes to meet Ansel's green eyes. Lines of worry surrounded them.

"Ansel, what are you doing up? You should be resting and healing." He sat on a stool next to my cot.

"I've had plenty of rest. Sovann and Eshshah made sure of it. All of yesterday and through the night, they kept vigil. They gave me enough treatments to heal the Canyons of Tramoren. How are you feeling?"

I sat up slowly, testing my strength.

"I feel rested. Our dragons must have poured their attentions on me, as well. Poor things, with both of their riders down."

"Amáne —"

"Ansel, please don't scold me. I was terrified. I thought you'd gone to your ancestors. I am learning my limits, but seeing you ..." I swallowed. "It was too much to bear."

He pressed his lips together, and nodded. "Do you feel well enough to walk with me?"

"Thanks to Eshshah and Sovann, yes."

I sat up with care and pulled on my boots, pleased I felt very little fatigue. Ansel took up a walking stick, and winced as he rose from the stool.

"Let me help you with —" My mouth snapped shut as he threw me a piercing glance. "I mean, maybe you're due for Eshshah and Sovann to give you another treatment. Your body went through too much trauma to be completely healed so soon. You have to take it slowly."

"And I could say the same to you. Let's head to the field. They're coming back from hunting, now."

We made our way to the clearing where our dragons would land.

"What is it Ansel? You look like you have something you need to tell me."

His brows knit as he took several breaths. Letting the last one out slowly, he finally spoke. "Sovann said my heart stopped."

I nodded. The memory of my fear shot through me.

"Amáne, I've heard your accounts of how you visited the Other Side, the Shadows. I believe I found myself there — with my ancestors."

I stopped mid-stride and put my hand on his arm. "Ansel," I whispered. Only with great effort did my knees not buckle.

"I saw my parents," he said.

My hand involuntarily tightened on his arm.

"I knew they were my parents even though I'd lost them when I was but three days old. I used to study paintings of them. Even if I hadn't, I still would have known them."

"What did they say to you?" My voice trembled.

"My mother said to persevere, even in the face of great

loss. She told me I must not lose hope, because in the end, my misfortunes will make me stronger."

I gasped. "That's nearly what my mother said to me. And then again, Senolis, the Ancient One from the Valley of Dragons, repeated a similar line."

I paused. "What loss do you think she meant? The crown? But that can't be. The Prophecy says that *fire and water will take to air, to crown Drekinn, the rightful heir.* Fire and Water is Eshshah and me. You will win the crown, Ansel. Of that I'm sure."

"Prophecies are not written in stone, Amáne. And I don't know of what loss she spoke."

He gazed at me, his face difficult to read. I felt he had a sentiment on the subject that he didn't wish to share. Something gnawed at me, but I wrapped it up and pushed it to a far corner of my heart.

"Ansel, we can't agonize over something so ambiguous that we can only guess at its interpretation. There are too many affairs more pressing. I know it's hard, but try to put it out of your mind. I believe it will be one of those foretellings that are uncovered only after they've occurred." I reached my hand to his face and smiled in encouragement.

Our dragons flew in, saving me from Ansel's intense stare.

"Excuse me, I have something I must say to Sovann," I said turning away from Ansel.

I approached the beautiful gold dragon. He stood noticeably larger than Eshshah. I opened up my arms to invite his face to mine. As was my custom with Eshshah, I grabbed his fangs on either side of his mouth and pulled him close to me. Resting my forehead on his nose, I said in thought transference, "Sovann, great golden dragon, I beg your forgiveness. I should not have spoken to you so harshly when we were trying to save your rider. I'm ashamed of my disrespect. There was no excuse for it."

"Nonsense, Amáne. There was every excuse for it. Without your passion, I fear we would have lost Ansel. You pushed me further than I thought possible. I drew from a power I didn't know existed."

"Love will do that," I said.

"Your apology, though appreciated, is not necessary. I owe you my thanks for saving my rider."

I kissed his nose and released his fangs.

Ansel joined me in front of Sovann. He reached up and scratched his dragon between his eyes.

Sovann must have conveyed the necessity for another healing treatment. Ansel shrugged and nodded. Eshshah came forward and both dragons poured their attention onto Ansel's leg. He released an audible sigh.

Then putting his arm around me, he directed us back into camp, "Tomorrow we fly to Braonán's encampment. But first we'll visit the Nunn Outpost. I need to speak with the Healer."

Chapter Fifty-One

We enjoyed a pleasant flight to the Nunn Outpost. I caught Ansel deep in thought throughout the ride. I wished I could ease his worry, although, I wasn't sure what exactly it entailed.

We dismounted in the entryway. I whispered, "Sitara," to illuminate the light shields. Eshshah and Sovann treated Ansel's leg again. He grabbed his walking stick and we made our way to the library. His healing had gone well with both dragons pouring their attention on him. My guess was that he'll only need a couple more days before he can abandon the crutch.

I threw a longing look at the door to the bathing room.

"You deserve a hot soak, Amáne. After we contact the Healer, you should treat yourself. We can spare a bit of time. I'll take the opportunity to search the library for maps we haven't already seen."

"You're too good to me, Ansel."

Ansel and I entered the library and moved directly to the communication device. He put his hand on the brass knob and whispered, "Gyan," and then, "Nara."

The glass shimmered. The Healer's face appeared. We exchanged greetings and salutes.

"Ansel, I didn't expect to see you," the Healer said. She narrowed her eyes at him. "Is everything all right?"

He cleared his throat. "It is now. I needed to tell you face to face."

The Healer raised an eyebrow. Gallen stepped in next to her with a questioning look.

Ansel relayed the story of his harrowing experience. Gallen and the Healer's concern increased as his narrative unfolded. When Ansel told them his heart stopped, the Healer paled.

"It's only because of Amáne's perseverance, and her healing power, along with Eshshah and Sovann, that I stand before you now. Otherwise, it would be as was agreed, Aunt Nara. You're my next of kin. The crown would have gone to you. And, as Sovann approved, you would be his rider. "

The four of us remained silent for a long moment. The Healer's eyes rested on me.

I didn't have to tell her, I had overextended myself once again. Before she could reprimand me, I said, "Healer, I'm learning my capabilities and my boundaries. The thought of what could have happened to Ansel was too horrendous. I had to give all I could."

"Amáne, I blame myself for not making time to help you. Yours is a case that demands research. As far as I know, there were no other riders that held this gift. I do possess a small amount of healing powers, but not near to your magnitude. I'll assign myself that task as soon as I can — for your safety."

Her eyes held mine as she said, "I thank you once again for your sacrifice and your sense of duty."

I nodded.

She turned back to Ansel, "I take it there's more to your story?"

He took a deep breath before answering. "Yes. I thought you should know, I visited the Shadows, and saw my parents."

The blood drained from the Healer's face. Gallen's eyes went wide.

Ansel shared what his mother told him about persevering even in the face of great loss. The Healer nodded slowly.

"What do you think she meant?" the Healer asked.

Out of the corner of my eye, I caught Ansel's quick glance in my direction before he answered.

"I don't know." He pressed his lips together.

The Healer nodded again. "Messages from the Other Side are, at best, vague. You would do well to not waste your effort in trying to interpret her words. I'm sure her intention was not to upset you but to encourage. Take it as such."

Gallen stepped in to change the subject. "Lord Ansel, have you had the chance to look over the map and plans Amáne delivered?"

"Yes. It was a stroke of fortune we got our hands on this information. Galtero knows Gorria Hills Pass is the best route for our army to reach Castle Teravinea. According to the map and battle plans Duer provided, they're mustering for an ambush. I'm sure Amáne filled you in on this when she contacted you two days ago."

"She did. We're waiting for our copy when Amáne comes home. It would help to see the details in the map."

"We're heading to Braonán's camp after we leave here," Ansel said. "He has the plans as well. I don't doubt he's already come up with some options. I'll have Amáne make one more trip back to Avano before I send her home with reports."

"Very well. We'll expect her home tomorrow evening."

Ansel and the Healer exchanged a bit more news before we signed off.

As soon as the Healer's image faded from the glass, I gave Ansel a quick wave and rushed out to the bathing room.

CHAPTER FIFTY-TWO

I carried my boots and padded back to the library after my short but enjoyable soak. The door slid open silently. Ansel sat at a table with a leather-bound book in front of him. He paid no attention to the book, but stared at the opposite wall as if in a trance. A frown creased his forehead.

"Ansel? Did I catch you dreaming off?"

His head jerked at the sound of my voice.

I slid in beside him and put my hand on his arm. "I'm sorry. I didn't mean to startle you. You must have been a long ways off. What's bothering you? I mean besides the obvious. We are in the face of war. But, is there something else?"

Ansel managed a slow far-away smile. He pushed a lock of my wet hair aside and kissed my forehead. "It's time for us to leave."

I didn't press him. He would tell me when he's ready, although I couldn't help being confused as to why he chose not to share.

We walked in silence to the entry cavern where our dragons waited. Eshshah lowered her head so I could kiss her nose. I turned around to find Ansel behind me, still with his troubled expression.

He gathered me in his arms and buried his face in my hair.

"Amáne?"

"What is it, Ansel?"

"I love you."

"I love you, too." There was more he needed to say. *Doesn't he know I want to help him resolve whatever is eating at him?*

His eyes surveyed my face, then he kissed my lips before giving me a boost up to the saddle.

During our flight to Braonán's encampment I caught Ansel's gaze on me more than a few times. It was not the loving look to which I was accustomed, but one filled with anxiety. A sense of alarm rose in my chest.

"Eshshah, is he questioning his decision to marry me? I know he loves me, but maybe our union wouldn't be the best for the kingdom."

"Amáne, don't think that way," Eshshah admonished. "I'm sure the pressure of his duties and the preparations for war are the cause of his anxious mood."

"You're probably right. I shouldn't be so self-centered as to think it has something to do with me. I just wish whatever it is, he would tell me. It hurts that he's keeping his worry to himself."

We landed in a clearing near the camp. After removing my dragon's saddle, I took my leave of Eshshah. Ansel grabbed his crutch and we proceeded to the command tent to find Braonán. We met him heading in our direction.

"My Lord," Braonán said in his booming voice as he saluted the two of us. "Amáne." He threw a puzzled look at Ansel. "A walking stick?"

"I had a bit of an accident two days ago. Thanks to Amáne,

Eshshah and Sovann, I live another day to fight."

Braonán's eyebrows nearly touched. "After all our work, we prefer to have you in one piece when you've won the crown."

He jerked his head toward the camp's center. "Come, we've got a barrel of DragonScale Ale. I'll put a spigot in it, and you can fill me in over a pint or two."

We entered the command pavilion. Braonán called for food and drink to be brought. Soon the aroma of the camp stew, along with cheese and bread reminded me how hungry flying made me.

Braonán listened intently to Ansel's story. I added my perspective at certain points. Ansel didn't include the fact he'd seen his parents in the Shadows. I omitted it as well. At the end of the narrative, Braonàn shook his head slowly. He swung his eyes to me.

"Thank you, Amáne." There was a note of deep emotion in his voice.

I bit my lip and nodded.

Braonán cleared his throat as he rose from his chair and retrieved the battle map I'd delivered a few days ago. With his thick arm, he shoved our empty bowls to the side and spread the map on the table. Eshshah joined me in open thought transference.

"We've been successful with our raids on Galtero's supply trains." Braonán said. "His army is receiving far less provisions from the usual routes than they need to sustain their forces. Our ally, King Tynan of Serislan, has sent us a squad of elite soldiers. They've infiltrated Castle Teravinea, posing as merchants. They're supplying lobster, silk and meat to replenish Galtero's personal stores. Galtero knows he can hold the castle indefinitely should we try a siege. The Gorria Pass is the last major supply route they still hold." He pointed to that spot on the map. "If we can take it, his army will suffer greatly.

"According to Duer's information, they are mustering about twenty thousand troops in these hills. They'll wait for us in ambush. At our closest estimate, our troops number approximately twelve thousand."

"Do we even stand a chance, Braonán?" asked Ansel.

"Ansel, Lord Ansel, you must not lose hope," I interrupted, "I've read plenty of accounts where the size of the forces were just as unmatched, yet it was the smaller army who saw victory. And an even more decisive advantage," I added, "we have our dragons."

Ansel studied the map intently. "We'll put a feint retreat into effect."

"My thoughts, exactly, my Lord," Braonán said.

"It will allow us to choose the site of the battle," Ansel said. "Rather than the narrow pass in which they expect us to fight, we'll set up to the west." He swept his hand over the area. "The road bends here. Even at the high ground they occupy, they cannot see beyond this part of the road."

"Excellent, Lord Ansel. We'll deploy an advance unit to engage the enemy briefly, then retreat. This will draw them into our own ambush, set up here."

"Eshshah and I can be on this northeast side," I interjected. "And it would be to our advantage if Lord Ansel and Sovann could be on the southeast. We can attack Galtero's rearguard, and then direct our assault where needed."

Braonán nodded at me. "You have an eye for strategy." He smiled in approval.

Ansel pursed his lips, but said nothing.

"Our reconnaissance team will set traps here," Braonán added. "It takes two men to rescue one injured. That could help our odds."

For the next hour or so, we refined our plans. When our discussion neared its end, Braonán caught me stifling a yawn.

"Amáne, the women's quarters are five tents down in that direction. I've had a cot set up for you, if that's agreeable."

"I could sleep on a bed of rocks right now, Braonán. Thank you."

Both men stood up when I did. Braonán and I exchanged salutes.

"I'll walk with you, Amáne," Ansel said. "Braonán, I'll be back shortly."

We made our way to the field to say good night to our dragons. Eshshah and Sovann gave Ansel another healing treatment before we headed back into camp.

Ansel and I stopped in front of my tent. He turned to me and pulled me close. His crutch fell. We ignored it.

I reached up and touched his furrowed brow. "I wish I could smooth this crease, Ansel."

He took my hand and kissed my palm, but gave no hint he would share his concern. His fingers ran through my hair as he brushed his lips against mine. I closed my eyes. No one existed, but Ansel and I.

A sharp voice came from behind me. "Don't even begin to entertain any thought of sneaking into the women's tent, soldier. Or, you'll have —"

The words cut short as Ansel looked over my shoulder. I spun around to find a large woman, her hands planted on her hips, her mouth open, her eyes wide. She recovered and dropped to a deep curtsy, bowing until her head nearly touched the ground.

"Your Grace. I didn't see it was you. Please forgive me," she said.

"Rise, Hildred. It's good to see you're protecting those in your charge." A note of humor rang in Ansel's voice. It made me glad to hear it.

"My Lady, Rider Amáne." She lowered herself again as she addressed me.

"Hildred," I gasped, "there's no need to —" Ansel squeezed my arm.

"You may as well get used to this," he whispered.

The woman remained in her bowed position. Ansel nudged me and tipped his head in her direction.

"Oh. I'm sorry. Please rise, Hildred, I ... I ..."

"Hildred, no need to worry yourself," Ansel broke in. "I have no intention of entering. I'm just escorting my betrothed safely into your care."

"Of course, Your Grace. Thank you, Your Grace. Rest assured."

Chapter Fifty-Three

I had hoped to lay a while longer in my cot, when I heard, "Amáne? Are you awake?"

"Yes, Eshshah. Why even ask, when you know already?"

"You should get up."

"The sun isn't even up, the day has barely broken."

"Sovann says Ansel could use your company."

I popped up to a sitting position, then moaned as the blood rushed from my head. "Ansel? Is he all right?"

"Yes, but he's had a fitful night."

"He's so stubborn. I wish he would tell me what's been bothering him."

"You two can be so contrary. One just as headstrong as the other," she said.

I pulled a tunic over my nightshirt, and tugged on my tights and my boots. Stopping at the basin, I splashed cold water on my face, ran my fingers through my disheveled hair and tied it back with a leather thong. I headed out to find Ansel.

He sat on the ground leaning against Sovann's foreleg. I kissed Eshshah good morning, greeted Sovann and lowered myself beside Ansel. He took my hand and held it tightly in both of his. We sat in silence.

"Ansel," I finally whispered. "Please tell me what's wrong."

"Nothing's *wrong*, my love."

"Then what has you walking as if you live in a different world? Why do I catch you staring at me so sadly? Did I say or do something that has you doubting me?"

He groaned. "No. I have no doubts about you. Please don't ever think that. I love you more than a flower loves the sun."

He drew me close and kissed me.

When he pulled back I gazed into his green eyes. They radiated with love. But, behind that, deeply hidden, I read fear. My stomach clenched.

Before I could say anything, he leaped to his feet and offered his hand to help me up. "Would you and Eshshah like to join us for a short flight?"

"Do you even need to ask?"

We saddled our dragons and spiraled up out of camp. The valley spread out below us, long shadows played along the ground as the sun rose. The view took my breath away. I looked over at Ansel and cheered to myself when I caught his elation. For a few moments, his anxiety melted in the flight. We flew only for a short time. I think Ansel just needed to fly to clear his head. He and I surveyed the surrounding area to make sure the camp's position was secure.

The rest of the day passed quickly as I waited for reports to be drawn up for me to carry to Avano and to the Healer. I killed some time sparring with Braonán. It had been a few days since I'd done any serious practice. The exertion did me good. Afterwards, we pored over the map and discussed the Gorria Pass.

The time arrived for Eshshah and me to head back to Dorsal. I gathered my satchels containing the materials I was to deliver. Bidding farewell to Braonán, I headed with Ansel to where Eshshah waited. I decided not to mention his mood again or ask him what bothered him. I had to accept that there were possibly some things he could not, or would not, share with me. It hurt. But what hurt more was that he suffered alone.

Ansel checked the girth on Eshshah's saddle. Then climbed on Eshshah's foreleg to test the belts in the seat. He seemed to tug at them a little more fervently than necessary. A curse slipped out of his mouth.

"Ansel!"

"Forgive me, Amáne." He looked truly embarrassed. "I just wish I had a way to know you've arrived safely. I would prefer that Gallen come up with a more transportable communication device."

He jumped down and took me in his arms. He kissed my forehead, both cheeks and then my lips.

"Be safe," he said.

"You, too."

CHAPTER FIFTY-FOUR

"The Dorsal unit leaves in two days' time," the Healer said. Eshshah and I had flown in the day before. We leaned over the map spread out on a table in the Healer's library. She continued, "Dorjan and Kail will ride with the company. They'll head up to join Calder and his unit," she rested her finger on Glinfoil. "Then continue toward the Gorria Pass."

The Healer traced the route they would take, moving north on the western edge of our kingdom, then veering east toward the City of Teravinea. "It'll take more than a fortnight before they arrive on the western side of the Gorria Hills."

"Calder and Dorjan will not accompany their units all the way to the Gorria Hills," Gallen said. "They'll break and swing over to Avano's location, here. Kail will lead the troops the rest of the way."

The Healer turned to me, "With yours and Eshshah's permission, Gallen and I will need transport to Avano's. You'll need to make two trips. We have to be there within a week."

"Of course, Healer."

The entire township of Dorsal came together outside the southwest walls. Mothers gathered to send off their sons and husbands, and a handful of daughters, with emotional farewells. Pride showed in their faces. Their family members would fight under the Drekinn banner of the golden dragon, to return Teravinea to its former glory. Yet a fear showed in their eyes — knowledge that some may not return.

The Lord Mayor proudly led the farewell ceremony for our Dorsal troops. We were sending only about two-hundred men, but they were highly trained by the Healer, Gallen and Dorjan.

"Amáne," Fiona called. I turned and greeted my friend as she dragged her new husband, Kail through the crowd. Their recent wedding would be the talk of Dorsal for many years to come. They wanted to pledge their troth before Kail went off to battle. It had been quickly planned, but did not lack in the grandeur of any wedding that took months of planning. Fiona certainly had the knack for social events.

Fiona's arm was locked tightly in Kail's. Her eyes were red, but she held a resigned smile. She gave me a hug with her free arm, stepped back and said, "I'm charging you with keeping an eye on my husband."

Kail rolled his eyes.

"Fiona, I'll do my best to make sure he comes home safely." I knew exactly how she felt — and she knew I did. We took comfort in each other. Of course we both were aware his homecoming was not up to me.

Dorjan called to mount up. With last kisses and hugs the soldiers took to their saddles. They rode out of town amidst farewells, tears and cheers. The banner of the royal golden dragon on a field of purple waved at the lead. We followed them up the road and past the harbor, to the edge of our township.

Fiona and I held on to each other until we could see them no more. Her twin sisters Rio and Mila found us in the throng and attached themselves on either side. The four of us walked arm-in-arm back to where Eshshah waited in the nearly-empty festival field.

Eshshah had become a popular member of our township, now that we had been revealed. As usual, the children were the most comfortable with her. She lay contented as they scampered around her. A few climbed her foreleg or played near her tail until their mothers admonished them to leave her alone. She never tired of them. The little ones saluted me as we approached.

Once a dragon rider granted permission to speak to their dragon, it was generally understood that permission remained.

Without hesitation, the twins approached my magnificent dragon.

"Mighty fiery Eshshah," Rio and Mila began almost simultaneously, "pride of Dorsal, we love you. With your ancient powers, please put in a good word for us to any dragon egg nearby. We so want to become dragon riders when we come of age. Thank you." They finished with a crisp salute.

I felt Eshshah's amusement at their salutation. She nodded appreciatively.

Fiona's greeting was more traditional.

We kept each other company for a bit longer before we bid farewell.

CHAPTER FIFTY-FIVE

The days flew by and the Healer and I found ourselves packed and standing in the courtyard as dawn brightened the eastern sky. Eshshah wore the double saddle, her breastplate secured. Gallen gave me a boost up. I locked wrists with the Healer and she swung up behind me.

With a powerful thrust of her hind legs, Eshshah leaped into the air and executed her first downsroke. We spiraled up above the Healer's expansive property and headed north for Avano's encampment.

In less than three hours, we arrived. I felt Eshshah's disappointment before she voiced it in thought transference.

"Sovann and Lord Ansel are not here."

The military camp looked quite different from when I last saw it. Most of the troops had marched out. Practically deserted, only a fraction of the tents were left standing to accommodate the twenty seven dragon riders that would convene here, along with the soldiers that would accompany them.

Avano met us as we landed. He saluted the three of us and offered a hand down. I stayed only a short time to help unload the Healer's gear, then Eshshah and I headed back to Dorsal to get Gallen.

Our second approach, Eshshah conveyed the same

disappointed announcement. Ansel and Sovann still hadn't arrived.

Gallen helped me remove Eshshah's saddle. I toted the rest of my belongings to my tent before joining the Healer in the main pavilion. For the first time since my insubordination hearing, I faced the other dragon riders. No one showed any ill will, but gave me a warm reception. All knew my punishment had been set aside for a time.

By evening all the riders had arrived at the encampment. All but Ansel. Braonán was the last to see him. He said Ansel had wanted to visit with the troops already entrenched near Gorria. He would more than likely show up at our location by the end of the day. Outwardly, he maintained an unperturbed attitude, but I detected an uncomfortable edge.

Once again the maps were spread out. We pored over them as a group. The Healer traced the road to the Gorria Hills. "It's a two-day march from our position. Our forces will halt about a league before this bend in the road. We will not be visible to Galtero's men. When all is set, we'll launch our plan. We can reach the bend in one hour or less. Amáne, you and Lord Ansel will meet us where we make camp each night."

Nighttime fell and still no sign of Ansel. I paced outside my tent for what seemed like hours. Finally, I decided I needed to turn in. I had to will myself to sleep, with Eshshah's help.

I found myself running in the corridors beneath Castle Teravinea. The smoke that swirled around me made it difficult to see. My father ran with me, ushering me through the maze-like turns. Pursuers' bootfalls echoed behind us. We were in search of Ansel, trapped somewhere below the castle. Just when I thought we'd found him, he'd disappear, only to shout for help from another cell.

"Ansel," I called desperately, but received only a faint answer.

My father and I reached a gate that led outside the castle. The light of day hurt my eyes. I looked up to see Sovann and Ansel above. The sun at their back. *How did they suddenly show up outside the castle*?

Even as they flew, I knew something was wrong. Sovann did not pump his wings. They hung limp. He and Ansel fell from the sky, but at an unrealistically slow speed. None-the-less, I knew the impact would crush Sovann's ribs. It would be a fatal crash. I could do nothing to stop it.

"Eshshah!" I cried. But for some reason, her reaction came just as slow. She couldn't fly, but trudged toward me on foot, at a pace I could have matched at a walk.

At my wits' end, I tuned to my father for help. My eyes went wide, my breath stopped. A man with dark hair rushed up behind him. With a long black sword, he sliced my father's throat. Blood spattered over me. I screamed.

I bolted upright in my cot, sweat drenched my clothes.

"Amáne, shhh. You're dreaming."

My eyes flew open. "Ansel!" I threw my arms around his neck and held him fiercely. "They killed my father. His blood was everywhere. Sovann ..." I clamped my mouth shut before I revealed the part about Sovann. Ansel's mother's words came back to me. *Is it to be Sovann that is his great loss*? I kept it to myself.

"You were having a nightmare. It's all right." He smoothed my hair.

"Eshshah," I said in thought transference, "why didn't you tell me Ansel and Sovann were in camp?"

"Lord Ansel gave orders not to disturb you."

Making an effort to even my breathing, I pulled Ansel closer.

When my body stopped trembling, I loosened my grip around his neck, and pulled his face to mine. We locked in a long kiss.

I pulled back and searched his face. My voice still shaky, I said, "Where have you been?"

"Get your boots on. Let's not disturb these people any more than we already have."

I looked around with an apologetic smile at the sleep-filled eyes from the other cots. It was still a couple hours before daylight. The Healer looked at both us of us, breathed a sigh of relief and turned over.

We walked hand-in-hand to the deserted command pavilion, found a bench and sat close. I looked up to him in a silent request to fill me in.

"I've been visiting the troops. I can't very well fly close to the hills during the daytime. We're fortunate the moon is waning. I planned to only visit those near the Gorria Pass, but then decided I should pay a visit to the other encampments further west. They will not be involved in this battle."

"I guess I should have thought about that," I said.

"Our army seems to have grown considerably. We've gathered support as we've marched toward the City of Teravinea. Many are farmer's sons and daughters, but their loyalty is astounding. The love my father generated shows. I just hope I can fill his position without disappointment."

"Ansel, I'm sure you already have." I pushed his hair back and kissed his cheek.

Chapter Fifty-Six

I spent the morning assisting the troops move gear and equipage to wagons and pack horses. They'll leave before noon and march until daylight ends, then set up camp. Another day's march would bring them within a league of the bend in the road. My stomach turned as I looked at my fellow dragon riders. *Who will meet their ancestors in this coming battle*?

Ansel and I stood by our dragons and watched as the dragon riders and several swordsmen and pikemen headed out. The royal standard flowed proudly at the front of the column. We would meet them when they make camp at nightfall.

Shortly after, we took to the air. We flew high, where we couldn't be seen. Only the dragon riders would know us for what we were. We followed their progress from our height, and found nothing amiss.

Evening fell and we met up with the riders. No tents had been set up. Camp fires were kept at a minimum and hidden. At the onset of dawn they would move again. The mood was somber. Most riders chose to recline alone and spread their bedrolls at a distance from each other. A few spoke quietly. The Healer, Braonán and Ansel studied a map.

The next day, before the sun shone its rays, we broke camp. The unit marched out. Ansel and I remained at the deserted campsite. He leaned against Sovann and brooded. I took out my honing stone and ran it along the edge of my sword. When I tired of that, I unsheathed my dagger and did the same. Then my glaive. More than likely none of my blades will be used, but I had to have something to do. The few times I looked up, I caught Ansel staring at me.

Putting aside my weapons I moved to where Ansel sat and slid down next to him. His hand slipped into mine. We stayed in silence for a while before he suddenly leaped to his feet.

"This waiting, doing nothing, is driving me mad. Let's go up and keep an eye out."

We saddled up. At Ansel's word, our dragons leaped off the ground. They spiraled high, up where the air was frigid. Most of our day we spent gliding and circling. Our dragons never tired of soaring. We kept track of the troop of dragon riders as they made their way toward the Gorria Pass.

At last the darkness allowed us to land at the final encampment. It was the largest camp yet, as several other units had joined in this one location. Tents spread far over the grassy clearing. The order was silence. For this many soldiers in one place, the quiet seemed a bit unsettling. Camp fires were also not allowed. Cold rations for everyone that night.

Ansel and I left our dragons at the edge of the encampment as we made our way to the far end, where the riders would be set up.

We arrived at the small sector designated for the dragon riders. The atmosphere was tense, but there was much more activity than the night before. The riders whispered and even laughed quietly together as they oiled and sharpened their already well-conditioned blades, or waxed their bow strings and told battle tales. These seasoned men had seen their share of war in the many years they'd lived.

Avano came up beside me as I stood surveying the activities. "How are you doing, Amáne? Are you scared?"

"I've been in a couple of battles, but they were spontaneous. This is the first where I knew I would be in battle the next day. I'm not sure which is more frightful."

Avano nodded. "I haven't been in as many large engagements as most of the riders, but I still remember the night before my first one. It was before I linked with Cira. I was a foot soldier. Instead of taking example from the seasoned veterans, we younger men decided to follow the old adage 'Eat, drink and be merry, for tomorrow we die.' We all hated life at the early morning call to arms. Standing in formation on the battlefield that morning, I remember hearing my heart pound and my breath roaring in my head, and not much else."

"Are you scared, Avano?"

He took a moment before he answered. "I would say, rather, I have a strong desire to live. I know eventually my ancestors will call to me — maybe even in tomorrow's battle — and I won't be able to deny them. That's reality. But, if I have my say, I would prefer to stay among the living."

The Healer and Ansel approached.

"Amáne, it's time," the Healer said. "Are you clear on where you and Eshshah are to wait the night?"

"Yes, Healer. To the north and east of the hills. Eshshah knows the location. We will wait for Sovann to give Eshshah the order to take flight in the morning."

At the distance Eshshah and I would be from Sovann, I would

be too far away to be able to hear him. But, Eshshah could. He and Ansel would wait south and east of the hills, closer to the advance unit of dragon riders as they marched toward the pass. Collectively, the riders would convey to Sovann in thought transference when they were on the move. We had practiced it. If the riders put all their efforts into transmitting the message, Sovann would be able to hear them.

Once we got word, Eshshah and I were to wait a small space of time before we join in the battle. We were to rush the enemy from behind as they engaged our troops. Our dragons would attack the rearguard.

The Healer turned to Ansel and Avano. "If you'll excuse us, I have some things I need to say to Amáne."

She put an arm around me and led me to the edge of camp. Turning to me she held my hands in hers. After a pause, she said, "A night before a battle sometimes brings out declarations that should be voiced. I know you already know this, but I need to tell you that I am so proud of you. As harsh as you may have found me at times, it was always because I loved you and wanted you to succeed. You have by far exceeded my expectations. I know I'm not your mother, nor do I ever hope to take her place. If I'd been fortunate enough to have had a daughter, I would hope she was just like you."

"Thank you, Healer," I managed to choke out.

"This isn't just pre-battle talk, Amáne. I truly mean what I say, and I apologize for not saying it sooner and more often."

I nodded. "My mother was wise to leave me in your hands." I wrapped my arms around her and hugged her tight. She stroked my hair and kissed my forehead.

I went through camp and hugged or saluted, or both, all of the riders. Many gave encouraging words, no doubt remembering their first battle. My nerves were on edge. I couldn't wait to be airborne. At least then it would just be Eshshah and me. I could have my pre-quest jitters with only my dragon as witness.

At last, I faced Ansel. We were to leave together, but soon after take off, we'd fly in opposite directions.

He pulled me close to his side as we headed toward our dragons. I made an effort to match his long stride.

"Let me check your equipment for you," Ansel said.

"I've already checked it."

He went over it anyway. Inspecting every inch of my fighting saddle; my boot straps; the boot pegs; the girth strap and buckles and Eshshah's breast shield, until he was satisfied all was in good order. I had seen him go over his own equipment earlier. After his mishap, he'd learned not to play so lightly with the condition of his gear.

Afterward, he helped me saddle Eshshah. I lent a hand in saddling Sovann.

Our satchels and weapons hung in their places on our saddles. We made one final examination before we faced each other.

"I want you to make sure you put on every piece of your dragonscale armor."

"I will, Ansel."

"Even your rarebraces. Remember the arrow in your arm at the Dorsal Outpost."

"Yes, I remember. I'll put it all on."

"Make sure your shield is at hand. You can expect archers."

I nodded.

"Keep your eyes open for harpoon cannons and destroy them first thing."

“Ansel, I know. I’ll be careful, and I ask you to do the same.”

He tightened his arms around me. The intensity of his kiss scared me almost as much as the battle looming ahead.

CHAPTER FIFTY-SEVEN

As soon as Eshshah and I spiraled up and headed north, anxiety washed over me. My breath came in gasps; my body shook; my heart threatened to leave my chest. With Eshshah's help I regained control. Inhaling deeply until my lungs filled, I paused before letting my breath out slowly.

We flew a long way north before banking east to fly around the Gorria Hills. It would have been nearly impossible to spot us, but we took no chances.

Eshshah found the field where we were to await the call to battle. Even at the late hour we'd landed, the night dragged on much longer than I thought possible. I lay beside Eshshah trying to will myself to sleep. My nerves jerked my body awake every time sleep approached.

"Eshshah, how am I suppose to get any rest tonight? I can't do it. What is it going to be like tomorrow? I can't bear the thought that many of ours will meet with their ancestors before the day ends. I know that's foolish thinking. We're heading into battle. Of course we'll have losses. I could be one of them. What kind of dragon rider am I when I lie here cowering? I'm supposed to be brave. Then why am I shaking and dreading sunrise?"

"Amáne, I don't believe there is one soldier alive that doesn't have concern for a coming battle. Even the seasoned ones, no matter how brave, would have to question what the morrow brings. I, myself, am anxious. I won't deny that. But, let's at least get some rest. We'll need our full strength or we will be worthless. Our victory is what we must concentrate on."

Eshshah began to hum her relaxing tune, and at last sleep overcame me.

It seemed like I had just closed my eyes when my dragon roused me before dawn. For a fleeting instant I wondered why I'd woken up in a field with Eshshah at my back. The answer registered immediately. After several deep breaths, I rose from my blanket and shook off my dread. I methodically began to don my dragonscale armor.

I pulled on my dragonscale boots that would protect my shins, then strapped on the cuisses for my thighs and the poleyn for my knees. I wished I'd had someone to help with the pauldrons that buckled on my shoulders over my breastplate. The rest of my arm pieces were difficult by myself, but I managed to secure them. I eased my hands into my dragonscale gauntlets. Every piece had been made with Eshshah's scales. Dorjan had attached them on a backing of leather, then covered them with another layer of leather. The result was a suit of armor that allowed complete mobility. It was light, yet nearly indestructible. I'd had several opportunities to prove its effectiveness. The last item I pulled on was my dragonscale helmet, my hair tucked inside. I lowered the eye shields and turned toward Eshshah.

She had slept in her saddle and breastplate. I checked all the straps and buckles and tightened the girth I had loosened the night before. Moving to her head, I grabbed her fangs and leaned my forehead on her nose. We held that position for a bit as we both hummed to each other. I sang my favorite ballad, *The Battle of Sregor's Field.*

"Sovann says it's time to mount up, Amáne. He says Ansel sends his love."

"Please tell him I send mine."

I pulled myself into the saddle and bent to buckle the straps at the boot pegs. I tested their strength and adjusted the tension a couple times before they were secure to my satisfaction. Grabbing my bow from where it hung on the saddle I strung it and placed it back in its spot. My small riding shield hung to my left. I unhooked it and slipped my hand into the leather straps.

Closing my eyes, I took in another deep breath.

I could hear the shouts and battle cries of Galtero's army in the distance as they charged down the hillside. Victory in their voices. The twang of countless bows reached my ears. The battle had begun.

Eshshah got the word from Sovann and launched into the air. I mentally prepared myself for the fight. My adrenaline flowed.

We burst over the hill and took the attacking force from behind as they headed down toward our troops. There were more enemy than I'd imagined. Eshshah spewed out flames at the rearguard of the charging army. Those that turned saw as their last vision, my terrifying dragon as she shrieked her war cry and shot an inferno into their midst.

When we pulled up to begin our next pass, I could see our advance unit, which included the dragon riders. They had turned from Galtero's army to execute the feint retreat, running back the way they had come. Arrows rained down on them. A couple stumbled. I couldn't tell who. Others grabbed for them and dragged them along until they found their feet. Eshshah and I turned back to our task.

A sudden clash of metal told me the counter attack had begun. The din of battle became our background accompaniment as Eshshah dipped and dodged above the enemy, flames shooting out at each pass.

Black smoke rose from the other slope where Sovann and Ansel fought. The flashes of flame spewed from Sovann's jaws as they dove into the fray.

The smell of burnt flesh assaulted me. My eyes burned, my throat closed.

Galtero's troops made an effort to stay in tight formation. It proved to our advantage. Our dragons succeeded in taking out quite a number of men in one pass. Even still, their sheer numbers were staggering. Eshshah continued her blazing attack, but I couldn't shake my uncertainty. *Will we see victory?*

"Hope is on our side, Amáne." Eshshah's calm assurance washed over me.

Our forces fell upon Galtero's men. In our enemy's surprise and confusion, their front line faltered. Our soldiers pushed through, creating more disorder before Galtero's troops could pull themselves together and push back.

I gasped as I caught a movement at the bottom of the hill. What I had thought were bushes at last glance, turned out to be a concealed harpoon cannon. The soldiers manning it had thrown off the screen and jammed a harpoon down the muzzle — another held a flame to the fuse.

"Eshshah, warn Sovann!" I yelled as Eshshah dove for the piece of artillery. "Tell him cannons are hidden under bushes at their flanks."

My dragon needed time before she could flame again. We didn't have that time. As we dropped from the sky, Eshshah darted back and forth in an erratic pattern. The soldiers manning the cannon were forced to shift their aim.

Even at the distance and speed with which we closed in, we made for an easy target. At point-blank range, I fervently hoped we would reach the weapon before it went off. The sparks from the fuse neared the barrel.

Eshshah gave me warning of her plan. I grabbed the saddle handle and braced myself, but wasn't prepared for the force of her maneuver. With a powerful backthrust of her wings, she shot her hind legs forward. My body flew back, my head followed. She smashed her legs into the cannon. My head whipped forward. Stars exploded behind my eyelids. My sight went momentarily black. I bit back my scream.

It took me a moment to recover. The pain burned in my neck. I managed to pull my attention to below me as Eshshah shot up into the sky. Her attack had shoved the cannon onto its side. The fuse went off and the harpoon sliced a trench in the ground, cutting through our enemy. Eshshah recovered her flaming abilities and dove down to finish off the weapon, along with its operators.

"I'm sorry, Amáne," Eshshah said. "Are you all right? I didn't intend that to be so abrupt."

"Aside from a splitting headache, I'll be fine."

"Sovann said Lord Ansel is concerned. He saw my maneuver."

"Please tell him not to worry about me. Just take care. Those weapons are on his side as well."

We recognized several more harpoon cannons camouflaged with branches. Soldiers were in various stages of frantically uncovering and loading. Eshshah dispatched them, and the men who armed them. Across the battlefield, Ansel and Sovann fought to eliminate those they found.

The sun moved across the sky. We continued blazing the rearguard, punishing them with dragon fire. In the intervals when Eshshah could not spew fire, she flew low over the enemy and blasted out her chilling shriek. This worked in confusing Galtero's men. I drew my bow and picked off the nobles who rode below. When there was no danger to our own men, I lobbed Dorjan's lightning balls.

Our strategy and our dragons at last allowed us to push back the opposition. We broke their lines as they became disorganized. Their mounted infantry stopped advancing. The men on the horses were terrified of our dragons and panicked. The war horses, even though trained for battle, bolted. They had never practiced with dragons diving on them.

Our forces pressed in. The enemy rear shoved forward to escape Sovann and Eshshah's path. The horsemen were squeezed in between. The desperation of their situation was readily apparent as they struggled to turn and fall back.

I watched in horror as the mounted soldiers hacked down their own men to clear a path of retreat. The massacre turned my stomach.

Confusion reigned in the enemy forces. Their general signaled a retreat, but too late to pull back in an orderly manner. Many turned and ran in a frantic wave. A great number laid down their weapons in defeat.

Eshshah and I flew over the battlefield toward small pockets of fighting — those that had not heard the order to retreat. Eshshah's cry sent fear into their hearts. They halted their fight and surrendered their weapons before our troops.

Never in my worst dreams did I expect to see such a sight as we toured over the battlefield. The whole plain was covered by those struck down, our side as well as Galtero's, although the losses were asymmetrical. Theirs, by far outnumbered ours tenfold.

I fought back my tears, and made a great effort to keep the contents of my stomach intact.

"Lord Ansel wants us to retreat to the rear," Eshshah said, "to return to the encampment. The battle is over. He said we will be needed there. He and Sovann are pursuing the horsemen. They'll scour the hills to make sure there are no enemy forces in hiding."

"Does he think we can be of no help in scouring the hills? What does he mean by asking us to report back to camp?"

"He was not asking, Amáne. It was an order."

I stilled my tongue, but that did not help still my angry thoughts.

Chapter Fifty-Eight

We arrived as the wounded were being brought back to camp. My anger abated as I saw that we would be of more help here.

The Healer rode in from the battlefield on a large war horse. She jumped off before the horse had stopped and rushed to tend the injuries that started to fill the hospital pavilion. Eshshah and I ran to assist.

Relief washed over me when I saw Kail. He gave me an awkward salute as he half-carried one of his brothers into the tent. I helped him find a place to lower him onto the ground. Blood flowed freely from a wound in his brother's side. He tried to decline my help, knowing there were others wounded more seriously than he. Disregarding his request, I placed my hands over his injuries, concentrating to at least stop the bleeding and allow him some release from the pain.

Surveying my surroundings, I saw several rows of battle-torn soldiers in cots and on blankets on the floor. Their groans and sobs filled my ears. Bern lay in a cot down the line. He looked in a bad way with a gash from his temple to his jaw and his arm in a crude sling — his breathing uneven. I moved quickly to his side and pushed his hair back. He grimaced.

Holding my hands over the laceration on his face, I closed my eyes and hummed Eshshah's healing tune. Bern's breathing relaxed. I eased up to conserve my strength. He at least, looked relieved. There were so many wounded, it was difficult for me to take it all in.

Eshshah worked several rows down on other soldiers. Her incredible healing powers and her strength allowed her to treat the wounded more quickly and in greater numbers than I.

The Healer came up behind me. Worry showed in her eyes. "Have you seen Avano?"

"No. Surely he's here somewhere?"

"He's the last of the riders to be accounted for. We've lost Andhun, rider of the late Qamra. May he rest with his ancestors."

I didn't know Andhun well, but the loss of even a single dragon rider was devastating. I repeated the Healer's words.

"Bern and Calder are the only ones that needed serious attention. The rest came through with only minor scrapes," she said.

"You're sure Avano isn't among these?"

"I'm sure. I'm sorry to have to ask. But do you feel up to the task of searching the battlefield?"

"Absolutely, Healer." I turned to Eshshah and said, "I'm going to leave you with the Healer. She needs you here. I'll be back shortly."

"Be careful, Amáne," Eshshah and the Healer said at the same time.

I borrowed a fresh horse and wagon and headed back toward the battlefield. The wagon, in case Avano was too injured to ride a horse. I refused to think of any other use. Fear had me by the throat. I needed to find him alive. Aside from Gallen, who was a father figure to me, Avano had become my favorite of the riders, although I loved them all.

My concern was so great that I hadn't thought about the task for which I'd made myself available. Reining in the horse, I leaped off the seat and stood motionless at the edge of the carnage. I took in the macabre sight around me. The stench, the blood; moans and raspy final breaths of the dying. Carrion birds circled overhead. Some had landed and already partook in their feasting. Fighting my nausea, I brought my arm up and buried my nose in the crook of my elbow. I used my sleeve to filter at least part of the smell of death that rose around me. One foot before the other, I forced myself to move through the field. *I must find Avano.*

Without warning, a hand gripped my ankle. I gasped and drew my sword as I looked down at a young man, my enemy. Pity washed over me. The soldier lay at the edge of the Shadows, ready to pass to his ancestors — his skin deathly gray. His leg lay apart from him, about an arm's length. Blood flowed from where it had been severed. I nearly vomited. Although so near death, the man's grip was strong. His mouth moved in unintelligible words.

My fear left me. I sheathed my blade and dropped to my knees near his head. It was difficult to understand his plea. Leaning closer, I took his hands in mine and bent to listen.

"Carlotta," he murmured.

"I'm not Carlotta," I said.

"Carlotta of Tramoren. My betrothed."

My throat closed.

"For her ... my heart," he said.

"She is your heart?" *What is he trying to tell me?*

"Letter," he said in a hoarse whisper.

"You have a letter for her?"

His lips turned up in a weak smile. He pulled my hands to his chest and tapped his armor. I carefully unbuckled the sides and removed his pauldrons from his shoulders to raise his breastplate. I took the letter, folded it and tucked it down the front of my shirt under my armor.

"I'll try to get this to her, I promise."

The young man's hand squeezed mine. Death reflected in his eyes as he whispered, "Thank you." Then he breathed his last.

"Amáne!" Ansel screamed.

The twang of a bow sounded. Two swishes and thuds echoed behind me. I spun around and dove out of the way. A halberd buried itself in the chest of Carlotta's betrothed — the very spot I had just occupied. A large man dropped after it, two of Ansel's arrows protruding from his neck.

Before I could recover from my shock, Ansel reached me and yanked me from the dirt. His hands squeezed my arms as he lifted me. My boots left the ground.

"What are you doing on the battlefield alone? Who gave you permission to be here?" Ansel said, his eyes filled with fear and anger.

"The Healer. I'm looking for Avano. You're hurting me, Ansel." My anger sprung up in reaction to his.

His eyes softened as he lowered me. He wrapped his arms around me and buried his face in my neck.

"Forgive me, Amáne. Stories are told of warriors who lost their lives on the battlefield after the battle was won. Sent to their ancestors by enemy they presumed dead."

I pushed away from him. "Or by their betrothed who snapped their necks in their haste to save them."

"I'm sorry." He pulled me back and took my face in his hands. "He almost ... I can't bear the thought of losing you."

"I know, Ansel." I exhaled slowly. My gaze fell upon the

large man who would have ended my life — with Ansel as witness. "Thank you. It was ignorant of me to drop my guard like that. I hope this is as close as you get to losing me." I trembled.

Ansel leaned down and kissed me. He held me closer.

Like a Valaira, realization hit me. A fear rose in my chest. His mother's words. She told him to persevere, even in the face of great loss. *He interprets that great loss to be me! And it just nearly came to fruition.* Suddenly my urgency matched his. I tightened my arms around him as a wave of shock took over my body.

"Ansel, now I understand what you've been hiding from me. But we mustn't think this way. Fear will do us no good."

Regardless of what I just said, I couldn't stop my tremors. The events of this day wrapped around me. Not just the horrors of the battle, but the tragedy of the young soldier, someone's betrothed. It came too close to home.

I took a deep jagged breath and met Ansel's eyes. "You will not lose me. I promise." I hoped I sounded more confident than I felt.

We clung to each other desperately.

A familiar voice sounded over my shoulder. "My ancestors can take me now. Truly, this is a vision even I couldn't dream up. Passion in the battlefield amidst the gore and the flies. It's rather disturbing."

I whirled around. "Avano! I knew you, of all people would be one to walk away from a battle. Your ancestors still want nothing to do with you."

Avano stood leaning on a spear, blood oozed from a wound on his thigh where his cuisse was missing — a strip of cloth tied above. A laceration over his eye left a dried streak of blood down his face.

"I came looking for you," I said.

His eyebrows raised. "Then you have a strange way of searching. How exactly does that work — seeking me while locking lips with Lord Ansel? I'll have to try that with you next time I'm in search of something."

"Avano," I said, "you are incorrigible."

Ansel and I ushered the rider off the field and helped him into the back of the wagon. I climbed in with him and treated his wounds just enough to start his healing and ease his pain. Avano sighed in relief. Eshshah and Sovann would complete his treatment.

Ansel shook the reins and we started back to camp.

Avano glanced over his shoulder and studied Ansel, then turned his eyes to me. I scowled under his scrutiny.

"What was that all about?" Avano asked. "If I didn't know better, I would think you two suffered from battle madness."

With a resigned exhale, Ansel explained to him about his mother's foretelling and his interpretation.

Avano gave a deep sigh and nodded. "No one has full control of their destiny. The threads that are our lives are interwoven in a way we'll probably never understand. You two share a love and a bond that's rare. But, don't let your fear of loss rule your life. No one gets out of here alive, anyway. We'll all meet with our ancestors sooner or later."

CHAPTER FIFTY-NINE

A week had passed since the battle of Gorria Pass. Our dead were buried, wounds were healed. We met with little resistance as we marched toward the City of Teravinea.

As Eshshah and I flew east, our view opened to a green valley spread below us. It sloped up to the walls of Castle Teravinea in the distance. Once abundant with vineyards, the land now stood barren. Galtero had confiscated all the properties immediately surrounding the castle and had let the grapevines go to ground.

The location for our battle camp had been chosen to the west of the fortress. It faced the main gate to the walled city. Row after row with tents of all colors and sizes were set up about a league from the walls — within sight of Castle Teravinea. The banner of the golden dragon on a field of purple waved before the command pavilion. Our encampment spread far as our army amassed.

No doubt Galtero sat behind his walls gloating, thinking our plan was to lay siege to the castle. Several siege engines in our camp helped convey that possibility. What he didn't know was that we had a specialized team inside his walls — experts in the field of explosives, sent by King Tynan. With their handiwork, walls would topple, without so much as a siege engine moving.

Through contact with my father, the date was established when we would breach the walls. The time dragged on as we waited.

One day as Gallen worked with Eshshah and me on aerial battle strategy, an idea came to me.

"Gallen, remember when you taught Eshshah and me the rope dismount?"

He nodded.

"Instead of using a rope for one rider to descend from a dragon, why not a longer line in which multiple personnel can be suspended and transported?"

Gallen showed an interest, so I continued. "Several loops could be spaced evenly along a rope tied to the saddle. Soldiers would use them as foot and wrist holds. With it, a dragon could move a small team. It could be used to insert or extract fighters into or out of a situation, like a stealth attack or a rescue."

Intrigued by my idea, Gallen worked with Dorjan to see if we could put it to use. Dorjan constructed a prototype and arranged several drills to introduce my device. After testing and reconfiguring the line, they decided it would prove worthwhile.

We found Eshshah could safely transport eight others and myself. Sovann, being larger, could manage twelve, plus Ansel. The rescue rig became a standard item on our fighting saddles.

Early one afternoon, the riders convened in the command pavilion. We gathered around the large battle table, complete with a replica of Castle Teravinea built in miniature. Small conical shapes were placed in the area that represented our encampment.

"At my signal, tomorrow," Ansel said, "the explosives team will blow these outside walls and this inner wall." He used a long stick to indicate the locations. "Our troops will enter at the breach.

With our dragons, we should be able to take the castle by the end of day. Calder will lead a small team in search of Galtero."

Ansel straightened and scanned the riders around him. "Some of you know I sent a messenger this morning to Galtero. She carried an invitation for him to meet with me on neutral ground. I'm giving him the opportunity to surrender. He sees our numbers. He knows most of the kingdom supports me. My offer to him would be safe passage out of Teravinea to live in exile."

Groans and protests traveled around the table.

"Riders, I'm not that naive to expect he'll comply with my stipulations. But if I can avoid the massive loss of life in the upcoming battle, I will be willing to take that chance. I expect him to decline, but I had to try."

The dragon riders went silent. My heart went out to Ansel.

"The girl should return by early evening with Galtero's response."

I had, in fact, spoken with the messenger that morning before she left. Her name was Berani. I advised her not to reveal she was female and coached her to carry off a more masculine walk and voice. Certain they would take her sword until she finished her mission and left the castle, I gave her one of my belts that held a concealed knife. She was an accomplished warrior. I knew she wouldn't hesitate to use it, but I still cautioned her to remain watchful.

Evening came and Berani had not returned. I worried for her safety. I knew about the twisted nature of Galtero. The memory of his arena of death still invaded even my waking moments.

I stood by myself near the edge of camp and faced the castle. The expanse of empty field stretched in ominous shadow to the fortress.

Ansel came up beside me and put his arm around my shoulder.

"You're just as worried about that girl as I," he said. "She volunteered first. Perhaps I should have chosen a man."

"Ansel. You know better than that," I admonished. "Besides, I made sure myself she would pass for a male. She should not be discovered as otherwise." *Even still, I hope she comes back soon.*

In the distance several horns blew from the castle walls, drawing our attention. The sky had not yet darkened. We raised our eyes and watched an object silhouetted against the blue – something catapulted from the castle. The strange shape grew larger as it flew toward us.

Whatever it was landed about halfway between us and the castle. Keeping our eye on the walls in case they fired again, Ansel and I moved quickly to the dark shape on the ground.

We were still several strides away when my blood went cold, my stomach clenched. I couldn't stop the scream that came from my mouth. A headless body lay before us.

Ansel pulled me close and turned my face to his chest, so I couldn't see. I shoved away and ran toward the body. My belt, that I had lent to Berani, verified my fear. This was the tyrant's answer to Ansel's message.

I stood trembling near the fallen messenger and shouted at the castle as I shook my fist. "You will pay for this, Galtero, and for all your crimes. I will personally bury my glaive in your black heart."

Eshshah flew to the field and touched me with her nose. She breathed her calming breath on me, then approached the lifeless body. Gently cradling the girl in her front talons, she took flight and tenderly carried Berani back to our camp.

Ansel guided me away from the site, looking as devastated as I felt. It was enough horror to lose people in battle. Such a barbaric act, when we were attempting a peaceful parley, was unthinkable.

CHAPTER SIXTY

The day of the defining battle dawned. At last the word came to mount up. Eshshah and I were to accompany Sovann and Ansel and cover the breached walls to assist our troops entry. Ansel would direct the battle from above.

We soared over the castle. The enemy soldiers had become accustomed to our surveillance flights. They were not alarmed at our approach but called taunts and curses. Some headed to the harpoon cannons on the battlements, but they only made half-hearted attempts. No one so much as struck a flint for the fuse.

Our enemy didn't realize this was the beginning of our attack. They had become complacent with our presence for so many weeks.

Instead of our usual path that took us near the walls before veering off, we flew directly over the city wall. Sovann shrieked a war cry as Ansel unfurled his pennant and signaled our men inside.

Sovann and Eshshah shot straight up and away. A loud explosion reverberated below. I looked down as the front outer wall of the city tumbled into rubble. Screams and shouts filled the air. The city watch at the entry gate were swallowed in the dust and destruction. Pandemonium broke in the battlements. A second eruption shook the ground as an inner wall crumbled.

Our troops fell into action. They clamored over the wreckage. The breach opened wide to accept our army.

I gasped at the unexpected sight below. A horde of ferocious-looking warriors poured from the outbuildings of the castle and fell upon our men. *Where had they come from*? More of these fierce men rushed from the barracks wielding giant axes. They charged into the battle with harsh cries. Our soldiers were too close to them for us to make use of our dragon's flames.

Ansel and I flew higher to get a better view.

"Over there!" Eshshah cried.

We turned our heads toward the sea. An armada of sleek black ships slid from their hiding place behind the protection of the cliffs north of the castle. Their flag hoisted high on their masts, a white shark on a midnight blue background. *Why hadn't we bothered to fly that far north on our patrols*?

Dozens of these war ships were already moored in the harbor east of the castle. I knew they had not been there the night before. Row boats filled with the savage-looking men pulled to shore. They spilled out of the boats, swarming like insects into the castle and around it. From our vantage point, it appeared the gates had been left open for them to enter the castle grounds.

Ansel signaled for Eshshah and me to follow him toward the ships. We began our onslaught, diving and flaming. It took several passes to incapacitate just one ship. There had to be nearly a hundred of them. Eshshah and Sovann could only slow the enemy approach. We overcame a number of the black vessels, watching as the sea swallowed them. But more sailed toward shore. Two dragons were not enough to stave them off.

"Amáne, go warn Braonán. He needs to send the second wave," Ansel called. "Sovann and I'll stay to try and slow their approach."

Eshshah banked a sharp turn and we headed back to headquarters. We flew low over the command pavilion where Braonán would be. Eshshah trumpeted an alarm as I called out. He rushed out of the tent and headed to where we landed.

"There's a fleet of ships on the other side of the castle," I said from my saddle. "They're fighting in support of Galtero. I don't recognize their colors. It's a white shark on a background of blue,"

"Norlaners. Mercenaries," Braonán said almost to himself. A troubled look reflected in his eyes. "They're some of the fiercest warriors known."

Braonán turned and called to his second in command. He gave orders to rally the next wave to the castle.

Sweeping his eyes up to me, he said, "Amáne, you have to go in and extract the Serislan team."

I gave him a puzzled look. I value every life, but I had to ask, "Why would twelve Serislan soldiers rate such importance? Couldn't Eshshah and I be of more benefit elsewhere?"

"Because one member of the specialized team is King Tynan's nephew, and heir to the Serislan throne."

"Ryant?" I asked in disbelief.

"You know him?"

"Yes." It took a moment to find my breath. *Ryant had asked for my hand in marriage when we revealed Ansel's identity to King Tynan.* "Why would he be here?"

"He insisted that he owe Teravinea a service."

I closed my eyes. He and his brother were held in the same slave ship as I. Eshshah and Gallen had saved us. *Is he trying to reciprocate for his rescue*?

"There are twelve of them," I said. "Eshshah can only safely lift eight plus me."

"Then the others will have to fend for themselves. King Tynan's heir must be rescued." Braonán's voice was sharp.

"Yes, Braonán. How am I to find them?"

"They were to first destroy the front gates, then the front interior wall. After that, they would head to the battlements over the river gate. You should come upon them there. Don't look for soldiers. They will be dressed as rich merchants in fine clothes."

Without another word, I removed the rescue rig from its place behind me, and secured it to a ring at the front of my saddle. I saluted Braonán.

Eshshah leaped into the air. We charged back to the castle.

Eshshah circled high as we tried to locate Ryant and his unit. I could see Ansel and Sovann in the distance, flaming the black war ships. Eshshah sent word to Sovann of our mission.

"Amáne, down there," Eshshah said.

Below me a group of men, fitting the description Braonán gave me, fought valiantly. They headed backward up the stairs that rose from the castle grounds to the battlements high above. The stairs were narrow, without any kind of railing. The small band of Serislanians ascended slowly, fending off a group of warriors pressing upon them. My heart sank when I saw with whom they fought — Norlaners.

Two of Ryant's men dragged one of their wounded up the stairs, a dark stain soaked the front of his shirt.

Eshshah screeched her terrifying war cry. She dove in and swiped her tail at the Norlaners, flinging several over the edge of the stairs to the stonework below. More rushed up to take their place.

They demonstrated their fierceness by slashing the air at Eshshah with their large axes. I did, however, note a slight hesitation at the sight of my dragon.

I threw the rescue rig down as Eshshah lowered toward the battlements. Realizing it would not be possible to lift out the wounded Serislanian with the rig, I said, "Eshshah would you be able to land on the wall?"

"I can do it, Amáne."

She maneuvered so she could get hold of the ledge of the wall-walk with her hind legs. Her talons scraped the stone as they found purchase. She grabbed the parapet wall in front of her with her front talons, using her wings and tail to balance. I snatched my bow from the saddle and hooked a full quiver to my belt. As soon as I jumped from the saddle, I froze. The injured soldier was Prince Ryant.

"Hurry, bring him here. He'll ride," I shouted at his men.

I paused to look at Ryant, his face pale. Sweat beaded on his forehead, his shirt wet with his blood. *I hope I'm in time.*

Ryant's eyes flickered open and a recognition crossed his face. I ordered those carrying him to get him up into the saddle. He raised his hand in a weak protest. I ignored it.

We were running out of time. The Norlaners were fighting their way up the stairs. Ryant's squad would not be able to hold them off much longer.

The men looked from Ryant to me. The life of their lord took priority. They did as I directed.

His men hoisted Ryant up to the saddle. I secured the boot straps and used another emergency belt around his waist to ensure his safety.

"Eshshah, I'll wait here. You take the men. Can you manage all twelve of them? It's much more than you've trained for."

"I can. I must. But, Amáne, I can't leave you here."

"Go, Eshshah. I'll manage until you return."

She reluctantly consented.

Eshshah lifted slowly off the battlement. I pulled the extraction line taught and ordered each man to grab a loop in their hand and put their foot in the next loop. She rose higher off the wall as each Serislanian secured himself. Our rescue rig was made for only eight. They had to double up on three spots. Several of the soldiers protested and insisted they be left behind so I could escape. I refused.

"Grab that line, now!" There was no time to argue, the Norlaners were gaining the stairs.

I took up my bow and began to pick off the axe-wielding warriors as Eshshah continued to stroke her powerful wings. She slowly gained altitude. The Serislanian team clung on.

Eshshah strained to lift the laden rescue line. I melded with her to offer what little strength I could. Once she had them airborne, I sighed in relief. Her wing strokes were less labored as she headed toward headquarters.

"Amáne, take care. I'll be back for you straightaway," she said as she flew off.

I continued to dispatch the Norlan warriors. My quiver emptied, but more swarmed up the stairs. I let out a curse when I realized I'd left my glaive on my saddle. Without hesitation, I drew my sword from its scabbard.

The large warriors were forced to ascend the narrow stairs single file. Although it may have prolonged my life a bit, my sword would be no match for their axes. *What was I thinking*? Even with Eshshah's venom running in my veins — which gave me my extra strength — holding them off would be nearly impossible. And my dragon could spare no extra strength for me at this moment.

A Norlaner mercenary cleared the stairs and leaped onto the battlement. He swung his blade. I dove and rolled, but had miscalculated. My roll took me over the edge of the wall-walk. Twisting I grabbed blindly at the ledge. My fingers found a grip. Hanging by one hand, I looked up into the sneering face of the mercenary. Death lit his eyes as he stood above. He peered down at me as a cat would eye a trapped mouse.

The Norlaner lifted his axe slowly, savoring my fear. I held my breath for the blow. A shadow passed overhead.

"Hang on, Amáne," Sovann swooped in. His tail whipped around taking out the warrior on the wall. He flamed those on the stairs.

I pulled myself back up to the wall walk, afraid to think of what almost happened. Sovann and Ansel hovered above. Ansel threw down his line. I grabbed the first loop as Sovann lifted me into the air.

Glancing down as I hung on, I thought I saw a group of Galtero's men ushering a man into a doorway. He looked a lot like my father. I shook it off. *It couldn't be him.*

We hadn't gone far when Eshshah informed me she was heading back our way. Her load had been safely dropped off.

Because of the rush of the wind, it was easier for me, and much more preferable, to communicate through the dragons. "Sovann, we'll do an aerial mount."

"Lord Ansel would rather haul you up so we can land and you can transfer to Eshshah from the ground."

"There's no time for that."

"Very well, Amáne, we'll do the aerial mount," Sovann relayed.

This was a maneuver we had practiced quite often since the

battle of Gorria Pass.

I hung from the rig while Eshshah soared in the same direction below, rising closer as we flew. Sovann and Eshshah kept at an even pace. Eshshah closed the gap until I was level with my saddle. I grabbed a ring attached to the saddle. Placing my free foot in the boot peg, I released the line, then swung my leg over and buckled in.

Our dragons adjusted to fly abreast. I saluted Ansel. His jaw was tight, but he nodded in relief.

We surveyed the battle from above and determined we were needed desperately back at the front wall.

Norlaners continued to pour out of the castle, punishing our troops in wild disregard. Our only consolation was that we hadn't waited another day to attack. All of the sleek black ships would have unloaded their warriors by then. Their numbers would have been devastating. As it was, our victory retained only a thread of hope.

When I thought it could get no darker for us, I cringed in terror. A putrid scent preceded the appearance of a host of Galtero's despicable lizards, with their riders. Flightless dragon-like creatures, about the size of horses, were Galtero's attempt to breed dragons. Though not nearly as large as Eshshah, they made up for it with their voracity.

The lizards rushed over the demolished walls and plowed into our troops. Bodies flew as they tore into our front line. I screamed as one of the beasts snapped its jaws on Bern, shook him like a rag doll and threw his lifeless body aside.

Eshshah attacked. She closed her talons on the monster lizard, lifting it into the air, rider and all. Mid-flight, she bit through its neck and dropped it onto the enemy below. Sovann did likewise as he fought the lizards off of our troops.

I heard my name echo in the back of my mind.

"Amáne, Charna Yash-churka has come to help," Eshshah said.

I looked below to see the large black lizard that was linked to me. He charged one of Galtero's monsters. Charna set upon the vile beast with a fierceness that startled me. But there were too many for us to defeat.

"Amáne, over there!" Eshshah directed my attention to the northeast horizon. A black cloud loomed in the distance, growing larger as it headed toward us. *What horror is Galtero sending our way, now?*

At the speed the dark mass approached, we could never outrun it, as tired as Eshshah was. Regardless, we would not abandon our troops. I didn't want to lose hope, but a thought pierced my heart that we were doomed.

Our forces were overwhelmed. More lizards rushed out. The Norlaner mercenaries continued to swarm through the castle grounds and out onto the battlefield. They cut down anyone in their path as they moved to flank us. Anger blazed through me. *I will not lose hope.*

I pulled out my glaive as Eshshah dove. She screeched her deafening cry. I brandished my weapon and yelled, "Rally for Drekinn and the crown!" Eshshah spewed an inferno through the enemy center.

In the next breath, a cool breeze of hope flowed from Eshshah.

"Amáne," Eshshah cried. "It's the Ancient Ones, from the Valley of Dragons!"

Chapter Sixty-One

The dragons from the Valley filled the sky. Hundreds of them blotted out the sun. Screams of terror rose from the battlefield.

Our troops panicked. Ansel rallied our soldiers to stand their ground. When they realized the horde came to support us, they cheered and fought with new life.

"Amáne," Eshshah said, "Sitara and Dinesh are leading the dragons. They told me Senolis, the Ancient One, sent them with his blessing."

I closed my eyes and whispered, "Thank you."

The storm of dragons hovered as Sovann and Ansel paused before Sitara and Dinesh to give battle direction. After a few moments, flights of them banked off and headed where needed.

I watched their ferocious attack as they dove upon the large lizards, scooping them from the ground, as Eshshah had done. They dropped them to their deaths in the midst of Galtero's troops.

Another flight fell upon the Norlaner mercenaries. The wild dragons belched their inferno on our enemy, leaving nothing but black ash. Eshshah and I renewed our fervor. Unbearable heat assaulted me as Eshshah plunged in and added her flame to the frenzy below. The smell of burnt flesh made me gag. The Norlaners broke and fled, but didn't stand a chance as the dragons pursued.

Thick smoke rose from the harbor where the sleek black Norlaner ships had been moored. The few mercenaries that managed to escape the inferno below would find their vessels aflame, in boiling waters, with nowhere to seek safety.

The battle turned quickly. The enemy sorely beaten, we took the castle in a short time. Small pockets of fighting could still be seen. One pass by a dragon to snatch an enemy from the ground sent those nearby scattering.

A cheer exploded from our ranks as we witnessed the Drekinn banner of the golden dragon raised over the ramparts. Dragons trumpeted in victory.

That evening I assisted the Healer in the hospital pavilion. The Ancient Ones possessed healing powers and offered their much-appreciated help. They worked beside Eshshah and Sovann treating the wounded. Several had decided to stay on and not return to the Valley. Eshshah told me they had felt an attraction to humans after hearing stories from Sitara and Dinesh, the two who had at one time been linked to riders of Teravinea. Meeting me had increased their desire to seek human companionship.

I checked in on Prince Ryant, who was recovering well. Eshshah had treated his injuries.

He gave me the dragon salute and said, "Thank you, Rider Amáne. And thanks to your beautiful Eshshah. Once again, Serislan owes you two for my life."

"You owe us nothing. Thank you for your bravery in aiding our victory."

He paused, and with a resigned smile added, "I'd like to offer you my congratulations on your betrothal to Prince Ansel. I should have seen the connection he had with you. It was brilliant thinking on his part in saving you from an arranged marriage. You truly deserve such a fine man as he."

I felt a bit awkward and wondered how he even found out. But I was relieved he seemed to have no hard feelings. "Thank you, Prince Ryant. I'm sure you'll soon find a young lady worthy of your attentions."

I excused myself with a curtsy and went back to treating the wounded.

The more I practiced my healing gift, the more I learned about it. My abilities increased. Though my hands burned — sometimes quite painfully as I placed them over a wound — I could conserve the energy I expended. A healing still drained me, but I began to understand when I needed to walk away and restore my strength.

We worked into the night. Ansel entered the pavilion just before dawn. Fatigue showed on his face, as I'm sure it did on mine.

"Will you walk with me, Amáne?" Ansel said.

"Of course," I said. I took his hand and followed him outside.

He led me to a spot where we could at least imagine we were alone.

"I'm pulled in every direction," he said, "but I wanted a few moments with you."

Ansel wrapped his arms around me and drew me in close. He covered my mouth with his warm lips. Our kiss became a release from all we had been through. I locked my fingers behind his neck and pressed in closer. Nothing else mattered but my betrothed. For just that one moment, it was only Ansel and I.

We pulled apart. I felt his heart beat as fast as mine.

As we stood facing each other, a shadow crossed Ansel's face

— his brows furrowed, "I marvel at the twist of fate that brought us this victory."

"What do you mean?"

"You and Eshshah were punished quite severely for an act that, in the end, ensured our triumph."

"And I'd do it again if it would guarantee victory."

"You'd better not." He gave me a sidelong glance before he kissed me again.

Ansel shook his head in wonder, "We've succeeded, my *Girl of the Prophecy*."

"Congratulations my King." I smiled up at him.

He touched my cheek and allowed a slight smile. "We're close, but we're not there yet, my love." His face saddened. "We have victory, but I have yet to be crowned. We've suffered great loss to get to this point."

"I know. We've lost Bern." My voice came out in a jagged whisper. "They're still searching for Eben."

Ansel heaved a great sigh.

"We still have to find Galtero," he said. "I have a squad hunting him. We will find him. It's our first priority."

"No doubt he's cowering somewhere in the castle," I said.

"Or has already made his escape."

"Ansel, has there been any word on my father?"

He pursed his lips. My heart stopped.

"There is word he was captured. It has been verified. I'm sorry, Amáne."

My knees nearly gave out. I held tightly to Ansel.

"I saw him! It was him. Ansel I could have done something."

"There was nothing you could have done."

"We need to find him."

"I've dispatched a search team," Ansel said.

"Let me help."

"They've left already. You're in no condition to join a search party, Amáne. Look at you. You can hardly stay on your feet. You're doing too many healings when you're so battle-weary. Please get some rest. We'll discuss where you'll best be needed when you wake."

I couldn't argue. Ansel was right. I allowed him to walk me to my quarters. I bid him good night — good morning would have been more appropriate. I entered the tent and dropped into my cot. But my fatigue prevented sleep from taking me. I lay with my eyes wide open. Tears flowed as the horrid events of the day flashed before me. I couldn't see myself ever being able to sleep again.

"Amáne," Eshshah said, "would you care to join me?"

I pulled the covers off my cot and trudged to the other side of camp where Eshshah lay. Spreading them near her neck, I settled in close to her warmth. She hummed a calming tune and soon I drifted into a dreamless sleep.

"Rider Amáne?"

I startled awake. Squinting at the light, I realized most of the morning had passed. A soldier stood before me, an apologetic look on his face. He saluted. I blinked and shook my head still heavy from sleep.

"Yes, what is it?"

"I'm so sorry to wake you, rider." He turned a concerned eye toward Eshshah. "Permission to speak to your dragon."

I nodded

"My greetings to you mighty Eshshah," the soldier said.

She dipped her head in response.

"I've been looking for you," the man said as he turned to me.

"I should have thought earlier that I'd find you with your dragon."

I sat up and ran my fingers through my hair, nodding for him to continue.

"I have a message to deliver to you. A courier arrived with a note for your eyes alone. He insisted he be the one to deliver it, but I wouldn't allow it. I asked, but he refused to divulge from where he came."

The soldier thrust out a sealed parchment and stood stiffly, even after I took it from his hand.

"Thank you." I hesitated, then added, "Dismissed."

He saluted once again, turned on his heel and marched away.

I examined the parchment and the insignia impressed in black wax. The seal looked familiar. I'd seen it on several pieces of correspondence in the command pavilion. My hand trembled as I stared at it. Taking a deep breath, I broke the seal and read its contents.

My Dearest Amáne, I write this note in haste. My position has been discovered. I was arrested yesterday for treason against Galtero. Fortune looked my way. I have escaped. Please, I need your assistance. Can you meet me at the river gate? I'll be hiding there. With all my love, Your Father

I couldn't believe it. He was safe. My heart raced. My eyes filled. "Father," I said out loud, "wait for me. We're on our way."

I grabbed Eshshah's saddle, ready to throw it on her, until she stopped me.

"Amáne, we can't just leave. Have you forgotten our position? Have you forgotten your punishment? You must get permission before we go. Quickly, find Lord Ansel, show him the note. I can't allow you additional insubordinate behavior."

"Eshshah, I love you." I held her fangs and kissed her nose. "I lost myself for a moment. Thank you."

I closed my eyes at the thought of what would have been a

grave mistake. Another charge against me could mean death. With the parchment in hand I rushed to find Ansel.

Sovann told me his rider was in the command pavilion. I charged into the tent, not even bothering to acknowledge the salute the guard gave me.

Ansel turned quickly from his conversation with Braonán, the Healer and some of his commanders. Concern showed in his eyes. His face looked haggard. It seemed he didn't take his own advice. Pity filled my heart for him. I'll have to insist he take a rest once I return with my father.

Without waiting I blurted out, "Ansel, I mean Lord Ansel, please excuse my interruption, but I have a note from Duer. He's escaped. I must go to pick him up. Look." I practically shoved the parchment at him.

Ansel took it from my hand. He examined the seal carefully. The Healer and Braonán came up beside him and studied the insignia. I shifted from foot to foot. *Why are they taking so long*? I bit my lip before I would say anything I would regret. Feigning patience, I stopped my fidgeting.

"It is his seal," Ansel said.

The Healer and Braonán agreed.

I couldn't hold back. I had to move this along before I exploded. "Permission requested to fly with Eshshah to pick him up. Please." My voice didn't come out as controlled as I hoped.

"Amáne, we're in the middle of something we need to finish. It shouldn't take more than a couple more hours. Wait for me and Sovann and I will fly with you."

I gasped and then pressed my lips together. *A couple hours? I can't wait that long. Could Duer wait that long*?

Instead of what I wanted to say, I took a slow, deep breath and prepared to argue my point logically.

"Lord Ansel, there has probably been some amount of time since my father wrote this plea." I tried to choose my words carefully. "The longer I, uh, we keep him waiting, the more dangerous it becomes. He has done so much for our cause for all these years. It would seem best to rescue him sooner rather than delay. Eshshah and I can leave now, with your permission, and can be back at camp before you have finished here."

"Do you recognize his hand?" Ansel asked.

"I've never seen his writing. Does it compare to the reports you've received from him?"

"It does look similar," the Healer said. "But we can't be sure if it was coerced. We have to be certain it is not a trap."

"May I ask if there is any way to be certain? While we discuss and debate, is he waiting with his life in our hands?" I couldn't believe my voice remained steady.

Ansel scowled and bit his lip. I hated to put this pressure on him, but it was my father we were talking about.

Turning to one of his commanders, Ansel asked, "Is the river gate secured yet?"

"Yes, my Lord. Our reports show there is no enemy activity on that side."

What if Ansel insists I wait for him? The delay could prove fatal to Duer. *Do I dare risk it and go anyway*?

"Amáne," Eshshah warned, "I will not take you without permission."

"I'm sorry, Eshshah. It was just a fleeting thought."

She rumbled her disapproval. Shame washed over me.

It felt like a long moment passed before Ansel said, "You do have a point, Amáne. There's not a way we can be absolutely sure. On the other hand we can't put his life in any more danger than it has already been for the last several years. We do owe him a great service, but you cannot go alone. I'm sorry, you'll have to wait for me."

Before I could protest, Rider Quinian stepped forward. "Begging your pardon, my Lord. With your permission, I will accompany Rider Amáne. Nye, from the Valley of Dragons will carry me. He and I could use some flying time together. We need to get to know each other."

Quinian was one of the older dragon riders. He was a quiet man. I didn't know him well. Nye had recently chosen him as a companion.

I smiled at him in thanks for coming to my aid. My hopes soared as I turned to Ansel.

He hesitated, then took a deep breath. "Thank you, Quinian. I'll give you permission for this task."

Ansel clenched, then released his jaw. Addressing both of us, he said, "You will keep a sharp eye for any foul play. You will land quickly, retrieve Duer even more quickly, and head back to camp without delay. Let Sovann know when you've returned."

I let go the breath I didn't realize I'd been holding. I wanted to jump up, laugh and hug him, but instead I saluted him. "Thank you, Lord Ansel. We'll be back very soon."

Before he had any time to reconsider, I spun around and hastened out of the tent, hoping Quinian would follow without delay. I ran back to where Eshshah waited.

As I threw on a saddle and tightened her girth, I nearly shouted out loud, "Eshshah, I have been blessed. Our mission to win the crown has succeeded. I have two wonderful men in my life. I will catch up with my father for all the time we've been separated. I will marry my love and heir to the crown of Teravinea. And I have you, my faithful friend. I'm the most fortunate girl in all of Teravinea."

Eshshah hummed in agreement as I sang a song of thanks.

Chapter Sixty-two

Quinian, Nye, Eshshah and I spiraled up and headed toward the castle.

"Thank you, Quinian," I said over the rush of wind. "I really appreciate you coming with us. I don't know what I would have done if I had to make my father wait another two hours."

"It's truly my pleasure, Amane. There's no way to explain what it's like to fly again. I can never replace Alcyone but I'm certain Nye and I will become close friends for a long time."

Nye hummed in pleasure.

The river gate was just ahead. It was the same gate from which I had escaped after my horrifying experience in the arena of death, when Galtero pitted me against his lizards.

The memory assaulted my joy. Anger burned in my throat. As soon as we returned to camp, I planned to volunteer for the manhunt. I recalled my vow to put a spear through Galtero's black heart, and I was determined to see it fulfilled. With effort, I pushed back my loathing. *This is a joyful mission. Don't let that cursed tyrant spoil it now.*

We descended as we approached the river gate. I saw my father standing outside the wall. Joy filled my heart.

"Who is that behind him? Why does my father not smile at us?" I asked.

My attention was so riveted on Duer and whoever accompanied him, I jumped at Quinian's shout of alarm.

My head jerked around as a harpoon careened past us. It plunged into Nye's chest. He let out an ear-splitting shriek as he threw his head back. His legs flailing in the air, I watched in shock as he tumbled backwards. Quinian was crushed under his bulk as they hit the ground.

In the space of the same breath, a rope meshwork catapulted toward Eshshah and me.

"Eshshah!" I screamed.

She veered, but not fast enough. The whirling net caught her wing. The weights spun around entangling her feet, her other wing and me. We plummeted from the sky.

Eshshah crash-landed in a heap before my father. The loud crunch of her bones was deafening. She lay still. I couldn't feel her presence as I tried to recover from the impact. My face had smashed into her neck. Blood gushed from my nose.

A chill went up my spine as I looked toward my father. Now I saw he was tied to a stake, mouth gagged, his eyes wide with terror. He shook his head in a belated warning.

In the next instant, the person behind him brought his sword around and slit my father's throat. His blood spattered the ground at his feet.

A scream burst from the depths of my heart. I struggled to get clear of the ropes that bound me.

My eyes flew to the river gate as the metal portal screeched open. A man in a full suit of black armor rode out on a large dark war horse. A phalanx of soldiers formed around him, bows and swords at the ready.

I recoiled at the sound of an oily voice. "Thank you, Darqin."

Galtero.

"What a winning idea you had, my boy, luring our little dragon rider here. And such a brilliant ending to her traitorous father."

Darqin. The twisted boy from Anbon who had tried to kill me for refusing his attentions. He stepped from his hiding place behind my father.

"Ha! It was well worth it to see your face, Sir Amáne," Darqin said, a wild look in his eyes. "I told you you'd be sorry. Oh, I am enjoying this moment."

"And it'll be your last!" I screamed.

Before I finished my sentence I freed my hands from the net, yanked a knife from its saddle sheath and hurled it at Darqin. It pierced his throat. Mid-laugh, his eyes went wide in surprise. He gurgled his last.

"You're spoiling my fun," Galtero said. His slick voice turned my stomach. "I had such delightful visions of what that boy could do with you."

His voice changed to almost a growl, filled with hatred. "But I won't miss another chance to finish you off. Your dragon is dead. Join her." He turned to the archers beside him. "Fire at will."

My riding shield was on my arm before the first arrows reached me. I blocked them as I freed myself from the net. Grabbing my glaive, I leaped from the saddle.

My dragon. My father. Quinian. Nye.

Red fury overcame me. I went berserk.

With no regard that I faced at least twenty archers plus the swordsmen, I rushed at them. The visor was up on Galtero's helmet. A demented laugh escaped from my throat at the look of incredulity on his face. He backed his horse to a safer distance.

I set upon the soldiers, slashing and thrusting my weapon. The closest went down without effort. A look at my blood-crazed eyes sent several to turn tail and retreat. I cut through the archers, hardly aware of my violence.

The swordsmen tried to stop me, but were just as easy to bring down as the lazy archers. The bodies piled before me.

I blinked as my head began to clear. My actions sickened me.

Two men were left in front of me. Terror froze their faces. They'd dropped their swords. I gulped in a deep breath as I became aware of the destruction around me. The blood of my enemy, mixed with my own from the strikes I couldn't evade.

My eyes rose to Galtero. I gathered the pieces of my broken mind, empty of Eshshah. I remembered my vow. Coward that he was, Galtero wheeled his horse around and bolted toward safety.

I pulled my arm back. With all my strength I hurled my glaive as I screamed, "Coward!"

The blade pierced his armor as he retreated. The shaft protruded from his slumped form as the horse carried him away. I hoped it reached his black heart.

My dragon. I spun around and sped toward Eshshah. She lay crumpled in the dirt. The net entangled her.

"Eshshah!" I screamed.

I cut away at the ropes. My dagger slashed at the buckles that held her breastplate. My ear on her chest picked up no sound. I pushed my hands onto her broken body near her heart. Squeezing my eyes shut, I hummed her healing tune. When I felt nothing, my mind still empty of her presence, I tried harder and hummed louder.

My hands heated. A glowing light flowed around them. The heat increased. My palms blistered; my eyes blurred as my interior fire escalated. Still nothing from my precious dragon.

She's gone. Stop trying, I told myself.

"No! I won't believe it," I answered.

I ignored the pain as I cried out her name and pushed myself like never before. *My Eshshah*. The smell of my burning flesh did not hold me back. My hair began to singe. Little wisps of smoke came off my clothing. Pain wracked my body, my sight darkened, but I couldn't bring myself to admit she was gone. Jaws clenched, I exerted myself with one final thrust. An excruciating flash shot through me as I found myself hurled into the Shadows.

Chapter Sixty-three

I floated above my dragon who lay motionless on the ground — my body deathly still beside her. Quinian and Nye lay at a distance.

Sovann careened toward us. Ansel leaped from the saddle before his dragon had tucked his wings. Further behind them, two more dragons with riders flew to join them at the tragic scene.

Ansel knelt beside my body and pulled it onto his lap. He caressed my smoking hair and kissed my face. He held me close, frantically calling my name. His body shook with grief.

Sovann approached Eshshah and nudged her head. The two other dragons, Sitara and Dinesh, moved in beside Sovann and nuzzled my lifeless dragon.

The Healer and Gallen approached slowly. They clung to each other as they looked on in shock.

I watched from above with little emotion — just as an observer. My lack of sentiment made me believe this was not the Shadows I had experienced before. *Have I crossed to the Other Side*?

Feeling a presence at my back, I turned and saw my father. He looked younger and peaceful. He moved toward me, holding out his hand. Then he turned as my mother came up behind him. I smiled at their touching reunion. Both of my parents beckoned me to follow them. Before I yielded to their invitation, I gazed back toward Ansel. He held my limp body — his face buried in my neck. He rocked me and sobbed, repeating my name softly, mournfully.

I turned my face from the pain below me to join my parents. A sound halted my movement. It reverberated around me, an utterance as surreal as this place in which I found myself. It was Ansel, crying out in despair.

"A–má–ne! Don't leave me, please."

The three dragons joined their keening to his.

A pang of regret found its way to my heart. *Would I miss his kiss, his warm embrace? Would I even be able to remember*?

The white light was before me. But I couldn't see my parents any longer.

"Mother, Father!" I called out.

"Amáne!"

A warm hand enclosed mine. I was surprised my sense of touch remained. "Father, I can't see you."

"Amáne, it's not your father. It's me, Ansel."

"Ansel? What are you doing here? What about your kingdom, your people?" A wave of anguish flowed through me as I ached for Teravinea.

"You're not with your ancestors. You live, Amáne." His voice broke.

It took me a moment to understand what he had said. I reached out and touched his face. He kissed my hand and an unbelievably glorious heat spread through me.

"Ansel!"

"Yes. I'm here, my love."

At once my whole being was filled with another presence.

"Eshshah!" I called out.

"I'm with you Amáne." The emotion in her *voice* was as near a sob as I'd ever heard. "You should never have done what you did, but I thank you. I am indebted to you for my life."

"No, Eshshah, we are a linked pair. There is no debt."

I tried to open my eyes. Panic filled me.

"I can't see. Why can't I see you, Eshshah? Ansel?"

Ansel soothed me with soft whispers as he stroked my hand. Eshshah hummed to calm me.

Then I heard the Healer's voice, "Your eyes were burned, Amáne. The dragons poured themselves into your healing. We can only hope your sight was not lost. Let me remove the bandages."

My head was gently lifted off the pillow. I caught the scent of Ansel's musky, spicy aroma near me. The Healer's loving hands unwrapped the linens. I felt their tension.

Slowly, I opened my eyes to the most magnificent sight I could ever have imagined. The beautiful eyes of all those I loved most in the world. The golden eyes of my dragon, the brown of the Healer, the blue eyes of Gallen, and the deep green eyes of Ansel.

EPILOGUE

I had, in fact, kept Eshshah alive by a small thread. The three dragons, Sovann, Sitara and Dinesh used that gossamer fiber to call her back.

As for myself, I went to the farthest edge of the Shadows. One more step and I would now be with my mother and father. The dragons' keening along with Ansel's love and strength, had stopped me from that last step to the Other Side. They called me back.

In the three days I was unconscious, work had already been started to repair Castle Teravinea. People are streaming into the city to assist. Stone masons, woodworkers, experts from every field. All traces of Galtero will be purged. The castle will be restored to its glory, as when occupied by Ansel's parents.

The dragon eggs have already been removed from the Hatching Chamber. The chamber is being cleansed from Galtero's caustic effects. Once it is decontaminated, it will be rebuilt. I look forward to dragons hatching and linking at the next ceremony.

Charna now lives in the forest on the other side of the river. I visit him when I can.

The battlefield is still being cleared. Tears mix with the blood that was shed. Funeral pyres still burn. Springtime will bring a special Life Celebration Gathering to honor all those who fell.

Ansel told me a thorough search had not turned up any trace of Galtero. I revealed he had ridden off, with my glaive in his back. I was the last to have seen him alive. I couldn't verify if he lived.

My hair had been singed so badly, Eulalia had to crop it short. Ansel dried my tears and comforted me. He assures me he loves me just as much with short hair as with my long tresses. He smiles as he adds he may even love me more, as now he can always see my face. If I ever need to impersonate a male again, I should be more successful.

Eulalia visited me one day with her hair cropped as short as mine. She said the younger girls have taken a liking to short locks. I was amused she joined them in the new fashion.

It will be at least a fortnight before Eshshah will be allowed to fly with me. Her ribs had been broken. Sovann, along with Dinesh and Sitara give her daily treatments. We are thankful, her wings had not been permanently damaged in that fateful crash. She's expected to make a full recovery.

I am set up in a rather well-furnished pavilion. The Healer is negotiating for an apartment inside the city walls where I'll live with her and Gallen until the castle apartments are ready.

The Healer allows me to move about the camp as long as I take it slowly. I spend a lot of time visiting the wounded. She restricts me from using my gift of healing. I don't protest too vehemently because we now have quite a few dragons who attend to the injured.

The dragons that stayed from the Valley of Dragons chose riders from among our brotherhood. Sitara and Dinesh bonded with the Healer and Gallen. Bonding is not the same as linking. Nothing could replace a linked pair, but for the riders to share with a dragon again, well, it can't be explained.

Dragons and riders now fly over Teravinea.

Fiona's beloved, Kail, has headed home to Dorsal with his brothers.

Eben was found alive on the battlefield. He remains in convalescence, but after several more treatments from his new winged companion, he will continue to enjoy the long life of a dragon rider.

Bern ... he is with his ancestors, but will always occupy a special place in my heart, as will Quinian.

Ansel and I have a royal wedding to plan. We may combine it with his coronation. If I had my way, I would have a private vows ceremony and be done with it. I know I'll have to concede defeat on that subject. No one seems to see it my way. Ansel gives me a stunning smile each time I suggest a less extravagant affair. He says I need to get used to the life of a royal.

I plan on convincing Fiona to move to the City of Teravinea. I don't think it will be difficult. I'll pass the social affairs of the castle into her skillful hands, including the planning of our wedding.

My mother's, Ansel's mother's and Senolis' words still echo in my mind. We have persevered through the flames of loss and misfortune, by which our lives have been formed and enriched.

Who would have thought my dreams and aspirations as a small girl would be woven into such a colorful tapestry — dark as well as bright? I am a dragon rider, linked to the most beautiful dragon ever hatched. I will be marrying the most handsome and caring man, my best friend, the King of Teravinea. I used to think this only happens in children's stories.

THE AMÁNE OF TERAVINEA SERIES:

THE CHOSEN ONE

THE PROPHECY

THE CROWN

BLACK CASTLE

Acknowledgments

Ride over! Or is it? Hmm, we may have to attend a Royal Teravinean wedding. There may finally be a hatching and linking at the next Hatching Ceremony. Did Galtero survive Amáne's last effort to run her glaive through his black heart?

Nevertheless, the fight for the crown has ended — in victory. I have many people to thank for their support along the way. My husband, Lloyd, a Vietnam Vet, offered his input when I ran some of my battle plans by him. My daughters April and Alanna, always supportive. Alanna has given valuable ideas and opinions. Rio, Mila and now Kira (possibly future dragon riders) still inspire. I can't wait until they can read. Son-in-law, Jason, number one dragon fan. My sister, Doreen, always encouraging and spreading the word.

A big thank you goes out to my beta-readers. Scott Saunders, my go-to for weapons and battle advice. My fight scenes passed his scrutiny, except for one of his pet peeves ... I'm not telling. Michael Clark once again offered his opinions and suggestions, which I drank up. Katherine and Melanie Arthur, Allison Ashworth, Clementyne Vega, dancers of Linda Armstrong's School of Highland Dance, passed around my manuscript again and shared their excitement. Forrest Vess spurred me to change up the cover a bit. He patiently endured more of my book banter. Tattoo artist, Pete Walker, from Allegory Tattoo, worked patiently with me to come up with Sovann's awesome linking mark. Thanks to Alea Ferrier for allowing me to use her striking photo of Windsor Castle. My writing was held to a high standard with the input and critiquing I received from my Tuesday night writer's meet-up group, including, but not limited to Bree, Candace, Craig, Devon, Donna.

Thanks to all whose enthusiasm and attachment to my characters make all the hours spent worth it.

Character Names and Their Meanings

AMÁNE - Water - derived from Native American

ANSEL DREKINN - Protector - German; Drekinn - Dragon - Icelandic

BERANI - Brave - Malay

BERN - Brave and Gallant - German. Formerly known as Koen (Brave - French) - Rider of the late Heulwen

BRAONÁN - Sorrow/Tear Drop - Irish/Gaelic. Formerly known as Yaron (to sing or shout - Hebrew) - Rider of the late Volkan

CALDER - Violent Stream - Welsh. Formerly known as Vahe (strong - Armenian) - Rider of the late Bade

CATRIONA - Pure - Old Greek

DARQIN - Angry - Azerbaijani

DORJAN - Dark Man - Hungarian. Formerly known as Ruiter (Rider - Afrikaan) - Rider of the late Unule

DUER - Heroic - Scottish

EBEN - Rock - Hebrew. Formerly known as Haldis (Stone Spirit - Greek) - Rider of the late Salama

KING EMERIC DREKINN - Leader - German. Ansel's father.

ESHSHAH - (Pronounced ESHA) Fire - Hebrew

EULALIA - To Talk Well - Greek

EWAN - Young Warrior - Celtic/Gaelic

LORD FAETOR - Bad/Foul Smell, Stink - Latin

FARVARD - Guardian. Formerly known as Kei (sand - African) - Rider of the late Okeanos

QUEEN FIALA DREKINN - Violet - Czechoslovakian

FIONA - White/Fair - Gaelic

GALLEN- derived from Galen - Healer/Calm - Greek. Formerly known as Kaelem (honest) - Rider of the late Gyan

GALTERO - Ruler of the Army - German

THE HEALER - Formerly known as Nara - Happy - Greek. Rider of the late Torin

HILDRED - Battle and Counsel - Old English

KAESON - Meaning Unknown - English

KAIL - Mighty One - Celtic/Gaelic

KIRA - Dark Lady - Celtic/Gaelic

MILA - Favor, Glory - Slavic

PRATT - Clever Trickster - Celtic/Gaelic

QUINIAN - Very Strong - Scottish. Formerly known as Qurban (martyr sacrificed - African) Rider of the late Alcyone

KING RIKKAR DREKINN - Strong Ruler - Nordic form of Richard. Ansel's Grandfather

RIO - River - Spanish

RYANT - (T added) Young Royalty - Celtic/Gaelic

KING TYNAN - Dark - Gaelic

D. María Trimble lives in Carlsbad, California with her husband. Her days are spent as a graphic artist at a local company. She has been a student of dragonology from a very young age.

Made in the USA
Monee, IL
01 June 2022